So Small A Circle

Mabel Benson DuPriest

Published by DuPriest Books. All rights reserved.

ISBN: 979-8-9889089-2-0

DEDICATION

To the great-grandchildren of John and Christine:

Jim, Ann, Lisa, Laura, Debra,
John, Daniel, Christine, Travis, and Benson

PREFACE

The 1990's saw the end of a generation. Within a few short years, my aunt died, then my mother, then my father. With their deaths, my sisters and my brother and I who lived in three different states were naturally brought together and spent time together in conversation about family memories and events, more time than had been true for years. And we spent time together in our old family home, and at my aunt's house, which had also been a part of our childhood.

Part of our time was spent in clearing out our aunt's house; she had died unexpectedly and had made no provision for her many possessions, lovingly accumulated through the years. Among those possessions was a small blue pasteboard box containing letters which had been sent to her mother, our grandmother Christine: letters from her brother in Sweden, letters from the family she had worked for in Dell Rapids, SD when she first arrived from Sweden, and a few other letters as well. Aunt Emma had also saved other artifacts from her parents: a Confirmation Bible belonging to her mother; a Confirmation New Testament belonging to John, her father. Other letters sent to John from his father in Sweden. A small account book John, as a new immigrant, kept keeping track of his expenses. The promissory note, in payment for the farm which was our home.

Being back at our old home, the farm where we grew up; sharing long talks about the past and our childhoods; reconstructing half-remembered events with those whose recollections supplemented or contradicted mine—these interactions led to the portion of this book which is a child's memoir. Pondering the remnants of the lives of John and Christine, our grandparents, led to the portion of the book which is an imagined recreating of what their lives as immigrants may have been. In this portion some of the characters are based on actual persons who were part of the lives of John and Christine, but the scenes and conversations depicted are imaginary, as are the letters which are presented as having been written by Christine.

TABLE OF CONTENTS

Part I: Endings

LOSS

This is the story of a farm; it is the story of the people who grew up on it, and who grew apart on it. It is the story of how a place draws them home again. Three generations of a family: my family. Two Swedish immigrants at the turn of the 20th century; a farm family in the 1950's; and—at the century's end—adult children of that family brought home again by memories and the land.

* * * * *

> . . . *Memory,*
> *that exquisite blunderer, stumbling*
>
> *like a migrant bird that finds the flyway*
> *it hardly knew it knew except by instinct,*
> *down the long-unentered nave of childhood,*
>
> *late on a mid-winter afternoon, alone*
> *among the snow-hung hollows of the windbreak*
> *on the far side of the orchard, encounters*
>
> *sheltering among the evergreens, a small*
> *stilled bird, its cap of clear yellow*
> *slit by a thread of scarlet—the untouched*
>
> *nucleus of fire, the lost connection*
> *hallowing the wizened effigy, the mother*
> *curtained in Intensive Care: a Candlemas*
> *of moving lights along Route 80, at nightfall,*
> *in falling snow, the stillness and the sorrow*
> *of things moving back to where they came from.*

—from *"A Procession at Candlemas,"* by Amy Clampitt

* * * * *

It was my brother who called to tell me that Aunt Emma had died. September, 1992. Then, one morning in March in 1993, came a call from Marjorie, my sister. Our mother had died in the night. When Edna called to tell me of our father's death, it was no surprise, he had been weakening for several days. That call came just before Christmas in 1995.

To be sure, at least in the case of my parents, their deaths had been preceded by other losses, in themselves a sort of death. Losses of memory, of sight, of the ability to be independent. The loss of living in your own home. Those losses had been accepted as the inevitable consequence of aging, they had been incorporated into our experience, and theirs. But now, with their deaths, came other losses as well. Changes, we knew, would take place—the transfer of property, the distribution of belongings. What was yet for us to learn was the power of these objects. We learned the sadness that comes when objects which gave form to our memories are dispersed, but we also learned how these objects—many of them familiar but now seen afresh, some of the objects newly discovered—had the power to lead us deeper and more intimately into the lives of those we had lost, into the past we shared with them and each other. Objects that gave new insights into the lives of grandparents and parents and at the same time raised questions and prompted imaginings.

* * * * *

It is a cold evening in early November. The day has been cloudy, and now it's as if whatever of the day's light had been in the landscape has been used up, drained away. The pale yellows of the field seem tired, as if they have held up through the summer, all through the harvest, and now it's time to accept the season's being over. The faded sky, darkening into evening, the drab colors of fields and pastures, the bare trees all agree: it is a melancholy time.

The fields where the corn has been picked still hold the clutter of leaves and stalks, forage for somebody's cows when they are turned loose to eat what the corn picker has missed. The wind rises as evening deepens, a prairie wind that twirls and spins the curled, dried-up leaves like Dante's doomed souls at Hell's entrance. Some blow out of the field, some catch on the barb-wire fences, and some collect in dusty heaps in the corners of field. I am startled when a tumbleweed blows across my path, lit up by my headlights and transformed into a spectral whirl.

I drive north from Sioux Falls. I cross Highway 16 where, long ago, there had been a livestock sales barn. Continuing, I slow down, approaching the little town of Ellis, a dozen or so houses scattered on either side of the road, and there on the left, a grain elevator, standing like a sentinel, an elevator visible all the way from our farm in Wall Lake Township, a farm we call the South Place. Beyond Ellis I soon reach Highway 38, where I turn to the west. Among my earliest memories is the construction of this highway. In those days we called it New 38 to distinguish it from Old 38, the gravel road which for half a century had been the main road to Sioux Falls. Old 38 ran east from the little town of Hartford, past our country school, across the bridge and up Skunk Creek hill, where it turned south and then east again and so on to Sioux Falls. New 38, running near our farm, was a real highway, a hard-top road. Now, of course, New 38 is an outdated and neglected state highway, and all the traffic moves along on Interstate 90, a highway that's moved even closer to our farm, shaving several acres from the south edge.

Just past the spot where Highway 38 passes under the Interstate, I turn right on the local road, and in a half mile I reach the lane that leads toward our house. Behind a row of pine trees, a spindly line when I was a child and now a substantial windbreak, I see the house, a dark, rambling shape in the evening's gloom. Windows that on other arrivals would be shining yellow squares of welcome are blank, reminding me of the house's emptiness. I pull up into the barnyard and park the car.

It was always a good feeling, when I traveled home—from graduate school in Kentucky, or from my first job in Virginia, or from Wisconsin where I live now—it always felt good to have finished that long trip, to pull the car up to the gate, get out and come inside. Sometimes my mother would have seen the headlights of my car coming down the driveway, and she would come outside to meet me, wrapped up in an old sweater. She'd be standing by the gate, saying: Here's my sweet Mabel Ann! And we'd go inside to the supper she had gotten ready. Or, if she hadn't heard me, I'd walk in and she'd throw up her hands, and call into the living room: Elmer, look who's here!

Usually the table would be set, the kitchen would be filled with the good smells of supper just ready to be put on the table. Some kind of hot dish, or maybe a meat loaf. Now, the kitchen is cold. I walk over to the electric heating panel and turn up the thermostat. I've brought my supper from McDonalds— a Big Mac, fries, a chocolate shake. As the kitchen slowly warms, I take off my coat and lay it over the back of one of the kitchen chairs. I put the food on a plate and sit down at the kitchen table to eat.

The chilliness and the quiet remind me of times when I would come home from school to find nobody home. That didn't happen very often, but sometimes my mother would have gone to church for a Ladies' Aid meeting, or she might have gone shopping in Hartford. It wasn't as if I were lonely or scared; it was just that things didn't seem normal. There weren't any sounds. There wasn't any movement. It wasn't that I felt neglected, it was simply her not being there that seemed wrong and unsatisfying, that made the house seem so empty. And that's how it seems now.

When I finish supper, it is still early, about 7:00. Walking through the house, I realize how literally empty it has become. The furniture gone from my parents' bedroom, and the davenport from the living room. Their television. The pictures that had hung on the wall—even they are gone. Pictures of us children, and of our children, an aerial photograph of the farm, a crewelwork flower my mother had stitched, and my sister had had framed. None of these removals is a surprise to me, I had taken part in loading up the furniture, of packing the pictures along with clothes and other belongings. The difference is that now I am noticing all these changes in quiet, not in the hustle and bustle of the big move.

My sisters, one from near Fargo, the other from near Grand Forks, my brother from Nebraska, and I had all been together to help. My sisters had previously done the hard work of making the arrangements, the contracts, the interviews, the financial agreements. This decision, to move from the farm to the nursing home, had been my father's. We had tried different options, having a woman to come in regularly to clean and cook, for instance, but their ability to care for themselves, by themselves, deteriorated steadily, and living as they did, in the country, they were unable to take advantage of several programs of meals and visiting nursing care that would have been possible if they lived in Sioux Falls, or even Hartford. At one point we had considered their renting an apartment in one of those two places, or even having them move to where one of us lived. As time passed, however, it came to be that even an apartment in town would be beyond their capacity, and it seemed that to move from the area where they had always lived would be too wrenching a dislocation.

It was a relief when my father made a choice, when he decided that they would move into Sioux Falls, into a nursing home they were familiar with, other relatives having been there, and one where they knew people from their church. They were assigned a fairly large room and were told they could furnish it with things brought from home. We planned and measured spaces and measured furniture and debated, and finally determined what could be moved, what would stay in the farmhouse. After everything was carried into their room and put in place, it did not look like home, but it did look familiar.

The days had been so busy, filled with meetings and renting trucks, and packing, that all our time was occupied. But today, the move was complete. We unpacked their clothes into their chest of drawers, we arranged the pictures, we helped them with the layout of the closet. We went over rules and the schedule. Each of us wondered, Will they fit in? Will people be friendly to them? Will they know what to do? As part of nursing home procedure, I suppose, someone had attached a cheerful picture to their door, awaiting their arrival, saying, "Welcome, Nellie and Elmer Benson!" It reminded me of the name tag that my older son got when he started first grade. Before we left, their friends Ed and Ida—who have lived at the home for several years—came to their room. My mother was getting confused, and a little worried about how she and Elmer would find their way to supper, but Ida just patted her hand and said, Don't worry Nellie, you can walk down there with us.

Marjorie and Edna had left earlier in the day, when the real work of moving was finished, and Curtis left soon after. Their good-by's had been said. After a few hours had passed, it was my turn. So, with Ed and Ida there in the room, and supper on the schedule, I said good-by, and left them there.

Now, at home, I am imagining them, going to bed in their new room, as I am about to go to bed in my old room. I imagine this house, tomorrow, when I leave it—its emptiness and its silence.

It's cold upstairs. I find a space heater in the closet and turn it on. I read for a while, and finally decide to try to sleep. The space heater glows red.

So this is what it's like, I think to myself. Growing up.

* * * * *

As a child I was surrounded by the past, and I seldom if ever thought about it. I had little curiosity about the life of my grandparents—immigrants to this land at the end of the 19th century—and yet, living where we did, the past was palpable. We knew my grandfather had hauled the rocks and set the foundations for the barn that we played in; we knew he had planned the farm-yard buildings and that our house took its shape from his plans. On the lintel of a doorway in the barn were carved two sets of initials: "N. L. B." for my uncle Norton, and "E. C. B." as my father's record. In my aunt's kitchen we

8

saw the dishes and bowls of my grandmother, and in Aunt Emma's parlor, we sat on what had been my grandmother's furniture. But these were not matters for reflection or special consideration. Although—or perhaps because—the past was as much a part of my life as the table our family sat around to eat supper, or the view I saw daily from our kitchen window, I did not greatly concern myself with family history and lore.

Now I realize how little I really know about the past and the people who had been my grandparents, that young couple who long ago made this house the home in which they raised their family: my father, my uncle and aunt. Personal items passed down from them are few: letters saved by my grandmother, a few letters saved by my grandfather, a small record book he kept in his early days in America, Confirmation Bibles brought from Sweden along with one or two other books, a trunk my grandmother used for her belongings when she emigrated, their wedding announcement, their wedding clothes, a few pieces of jewelry. Some photographs. Artifacts that suggest so much to the imagination.

The house is nearly empty, it is silent. It is a house of memories, a night to listen to the past.

Part II: Growth

In the liturgical churches, a cycle called the Church Year is observed, and within this cycle is a period which was referred to in days gone by as Trinity Season. This season begins on Trinity Sunday, a few weeks after Easter, and continues through the late spring, the summer and the fall, right up until the season of Advent at the beginning of December, with its anticipation of Christmas. The Sundays after Trinity are described by an Anglican church historian as "quiet, ordinary Sundays"; and the season, if it can be even called a "season" is the same: quiet, ordinary.

From a child's point of view, this is how "growing up" can seem: a long period of nothing much happening. Quiet days and years, passing by with little drama; one year distinguished from another by ordinary markers: the changes of the seasons, and with them the years' pattern of planting and harvesting; moving up from one grade to another in school; holidays to be anticipated, then celebrated, then remembered.

And yet, the season of Trinity has its own purpose. Its designated liturgical color—green—provides reminder of that purpose: it is the season of growth. And growth, most often, is slow. It is gradual: changes occur, but they are scarcely noticed from one day to the next, until, finally what was a single seed of corn becomes a tall green stalk, laden with its own full-to-bursting ears. So too with this season in a person's life or a family's life. All seems ordinary, unchanging—until the season comes to its end.

* * * * *

Back then, my father likes to say, it was "Root, hog, or die."
The "back then" he's talking about might have been when his parents emigrated from Sweden, not even knowing the English language, with not very much money, and only a few relatives here they could turn to for help. Or "back then" might have been the Depression, when banks closed and dry winds burned the crops or curled up the leaves and seeds dried up and died before

13

they sprouted because no rain fell, and the ground was all cracked and brown. In those days, this phrase tells you, people couldn't be fussy. They'd have to do any work they could get, whether it was hauling rocks or scrubbing someone else's floor. They had to learn to live with things that weren't very pleasant, cold houses, maybe, or dirt floors, or shabby clothes.

And mostly when he says that phrase, we get the idea that whatever you did, you had it do it yourself. No other hog was going to do the rooting for you. Any no other hog was going to feel too bad if you didn't have much luck in your rooting. Life was hard, and people had to be hard. If you needed pampering to survive, you wouldn't make it. You might not have liked that sort of life, but his tone of voice tells us you had to give some respect to those who made it through.

But now the year is 1954, the Republicans are back in the White House and things are different from those old times. "Root, hog or die" surely doesn't apply to us.

As far as I could see—I was eight years old—everything around me was pretty comfortable at present, and I had no reason to think it wouldn't go on being so.

A FAMILY PORTRAIT: 1954

Here's a picture so you can see what we all look like. We're all dressed up, ready to go to church, so we look pretty good. In the summertime, if we get our picture taken, we always stand in front of the spiraea bush by our screen porch, and that's where we are now. It's too late for there to be flowers on the bush, but it's still a nice spot.

That's my mother, standing next to me, looking kind of cross. She was probably worried that we were taking so much time with this picture that we would be late to church. It was her niece, my cousin Lorna Jean, taking the picture, and she liked to get things just right. Lorna Jean and her mother and dad were visiting from Illinois, which is where my mother is from. My mother

15

had taught school for at least ten years, maybe longer, before she married my father and moved out here. Teaching all those years, she learned a lot of poetry, which sometimes makes her say peculiar things. Sometimes, on a cold grey winter's morning she'll look out the east windows of our kitchen toward the pasture hills and say, "The sun that brief December day/ Rose cheerless over hills of grey." That means we're going to have a snowstorm. Sometimes when I'm complaining that my sister isn't being fair, that just because I'm younger than she is doesn't mean I shouldn't be able to play games with her and her friends, or have girl friends over to sleep the night, then my mother might say: "Talents differ; all is well and wisely put;/ If I cannot carry a forest on my back,/ Neither can you crack a nut"—which makes no sense at all.

My father doesn't talk a lot. But then he doesn't really need to because everything pretty much goes his way as far as I can tell. Here he's in Sunday clothes, but during the week my father wears blue "Big Lee" overalls and long-sleeved blue work shirts. In the summer he wears a straw hat, in the winter a cap with ear flaps, a heavy dark denim jacket, and big bright yellow mittens. On Sundays in the wintertime, he wears a suit that's been tailored to fit at Weatherwax Men's Store in Sioux Falls, and a grey Stetson hat. He drives a Packard car, Dodge truck and a John Deere tractor. He likes to listen to the farm reports on the radio, and the Bohemian Band. In the summertime he gets up early and spends all the day long out in the fields. In the winter he spends his time feeding the cattle and thawing out the water tank, so they have something to drink.

When we're all lined up for a picture, wearing our Sunday clothes, my sisters and brother look pretty nice, but they weren't always so nice. Once we were on a trip to the Black Hills and they tickled me so hard I choked on the Lifesaver I was eating and they had to stop the car and shake me upside down by my heels until it popped out and I stopped choking to death. They called me "Miss Priss" and "Lady Legs." I was the baby of the family. That's me in the front.

16

The oldest is Edna Mary, right behind me. Of all us girls, she is my mother's favorite. But I can't hold that against her, she's probably everybody's favorite. I know she spent a lot of time looking after me; when I was really little, she'd always be the one to carry me around. I don't remember, but there are lots of pictures that show her doing that. And if I was bad and got scolded, then she'd get mad on my account. I don't think that's the way it usually works, usually you're glad if your sister is in trouble, because it means you aren't.

Then there is Curtis. As you can see, he is the only boy in the family. That means that no matter what he does, my mother always likes him best; and even though he and my dad get into it now and then, some things are just the way they are because he is a boy. Like the fact that once—this was before I was born—we got a pony, Seabiscuit, and a cart to go with him, and they were my brother's. He got to drive that cart to school and give everybody else a ride. I don't think anybody else got to be the driver, just him. And another thing, he never has to clean his room. He just shuts the door.

Marjorie is next, she's five years older than I am. We all think she's my father's favorite. When she was in grade school, she was a really good baseball player, she could hit home runs over the school yard fence, and there was a glove at school that everyone knew was hers, if she was going to play ball, no one else would ever dare use it. When I started school, Edna Mary and Curtis had already gone on to high school in Hartford, but Marjorie was still there. She was in the sixth grade, along with Marion Artz and Joan Byg and the Kelly boys. Now she's in high school and has boyfriends.

We live in a house painted white, and some places could use a new coat of paint, like the front porch and the screen porch. The screen porch is just off the kitchen, you can see it there in the picture with vines growing all over it. There's a glider on the porch where you can sleep when the summer nights are so hot that you can't sleep good in the upstairs bedrooms. The front porch is across the west end of the house and runs down the south side of the living room too. That porch not only needs paint, but it needs some repair work.

There are railings along the two sides, and quite a few of the spindles that go down from the railing to the floor are gone, some rotted out, some broken. I guess you can see in this picture where there are a couple missing. And there is a row along the roof too, with some missing sections. I guess one reason why it is so broken down is that it's fun to stand on the bottom rail and reach up and grab hold of the top rail and swing yourself out to the grass beneath. The front porch is good for other things, too, like it's a good place to get some chalk and draw out your hop-scotch squares, and sometimes we play house there.

Inside the house, when you first come in, you're in the kitchen, and in the middle of the floor is our kitchen table; it's an oval shape, with space for all six of us. My dad sits at the end by the windows, and then to his left is Curtis, then Edna Mary. Marjorie is at the opposite end from my dad, then my mother, and then me, between my mother and dad. I have to sit there because I was the baby and they thought I needed looking after, but that's where I've stayed until long after that day had passed.

There's a pantry off one end of the kitchen with dishes and pots and pans and our food stored on shelves, with an old pine chest of drawers beside the flour bin. The bottom of that chest is where I used to put my coloring books and crayons, and sometimes the mice liked to come in and chew them up. When I got a little bit older, I learned from watching Edna Mary and Marjorie that they knew where my mother hid the chocolate chips; usually she squashed the bag in between a couple of mixing bowls. Once you knew where they were, you could sneak in when she wasn't looking and help yourself to a handful and she'd never know unless you emptied the bag. Sometimes she'd want to bake cookies, and then she'd come out of the pantry, mad, and say: What's happened to all those chocolate chips? —but nobody ever knew. I like to eat brown sugar too, but I don't because they told me it would give me worms.

The washroom is off the other end of the kitchen. We have an inside pump there for soft water, by that I mean rainwater from our cistern, and on

18

the washstand, there is a pail that holds our drinking water. We have to go outside to the pump by the horse tank to fill up the drinking water pail. When I got big enough to carry the pail, that was my job and it still is. We all drink out of the same dipper, but if you put your mouth right next to the handle, chances are you'll get a pretty clean spot. We also have a sink in the washroom, with a wash pan where we wash our face and hands with Palmolive soap, and we keep the pot under the sink. The toilet is outside, a little building at the edge of the yard, by the trees. It's nasty, dumping that pot, and that's my job too.

Beyond the kitchen is the dining room. We have grey-patterned linoleum on the floor, and a buffet and a dining room table. My mother keeps tablecloths in the bottom drawer of the buffet, but in the top drawer she just puts whatever, and so whenever anything gets lost, like a letter or a check, somebody—like my mother—will say, Well, have you looked in the buffet?—and somebody else—my dad for instance—will start going through that drawer and get madder and madder, and say, I don't know why you can't just leave things be around here. A man just puts something down, and the next thing you know, it's gone. Why can't you just leave things where they are?

We only use the dining room table now and then, if we have company for Sunday dinner, or if it is Thanksgiving or Christmas, or when the corn shellers come. Then we bring it out into the center of the room, put in the extra leaves, and set it for a lot of people. Usually, it stands pushed up against a wall, with an oil cloth over the good tablecloth underneath.

The living room is beyond that, behind the folding wooden doors. We keep those doors shut in the winter—except for holidays—because the living room, like the bedroom above it upstairs, the one we call the west room, is so cold, being three sides to the wind, and one of them north. In the wintertime we just stay in the dining room and bring some sitting chairs in from the living room. But in the rest of the year, we open the doors, and have a room we can take company if they come. We have a brown davenport and an armchair to match, brown plush, with cushions that if you turn them one way, they are

19

brown, and if you turn them another way, they have flowers on them. On the floor is a nice rug with colored patterns on it. When we got electricity, my mother bought a vacuum cleaner for that rug from a traveling salesman. It is called a Rex-Air, and it's a heavy black thing that attaches to a pan of water. When you vacuum, all the dirt from the rug goes into that water. Dumping the pan is another dirty job I have to do. But one reason my mother bought it was that you can use the machine for more than cleaning rugs. When we get sick with a bad cold, she'll put clean water in the pan and put Vicks Vap-O-Rub in the water and turn on the Rex-Air, then we sit there beside it and breathe it in.

There is a piano in the living room, where Marjorie and I have to go practice our piano lessons, whether it's cold or not. Edna Mary and Curtis are through with those, but every Saturday morning Marjorie and I have to go in to Hartford to have our lessons with Mrs. Henrietta Kluck. She wrote a song and it was published in a piece of sheet music. She tells me when I get to be good enough, I can play it. That day is a long way away. Right next to the piano, in front of the window, is a table with a lamp on it, a beautiful maroon and white and gold lamp my mother got free for giving a Stanley party. The west window is nice; the top of it is stained glass, and when the sun shines through in the afternoon, it makes red and gold and green patterns on the floor.

My mom and dad sleep downstairs in a room off the dining room, and when I was little, I slept in a crib at the foot of their bed, but when I got bigger I moved upstairs and now I sleep with my sisters. When it is cold we all sleep together in the south room, but in the summer one of us moves into the west room. Then there is the little room my brother has, and an attic we only go into at Christmas to get the Christmas tree decorations, and that's the house.

But there's more to our farm than the house. We have a big red barn, one side for cows, one side for horses and the bull and any little calves that need a separate spot to be fed by hand if their mother has died. Upstairs there are stacks of hay bales, and holes in the floor where you can throw down hay for the horses or cows. There are lots of things upstairs in the haymow. There is

20

the cream separator that my Grandma used when she sold cream. There is an oats bin that has a chute to downstairs so you can just open up a little door down there and scoop out oats to feed the horses. Great big thick ropes hang down from the ceilings. In the summertime, during haying, they're used to get bales of hay into the haymow, but for the rest of the time, we can use them to swing around from one pile of hay to another. Down at the bottom of the haymow steps is the saddle for our horse Spotty, and all the old harness my dad used back when he still farmed with horses.

We have other farm buildings too. We have a machine shed, and we have another building that is a granary for oats on one side and corncrib on the other, with a space in between where we grind up corn to feed the cows. And we have pig houses and two silos, and groves of cottonwood trees down the hill east of the house, and on around the north side too.

We have a few neighbors we see now and then. Down the road from our farm there is the Van Kekerix family, they live on Joseph E. Johnson's farm. Joseph E. Johnson and his wife Elsie had lived there when my parents were first married and when my brothers and sisters were little but now, they have moved into town. Darrel and Peggy Van Kekerix are just about my age.

Across the road from us is the Melin farm. The people who live there are relatives of ours. That farm was where my grandpa John Benson's brother Lewis Benson had lived. When he got old, Uncle Lewis moved into Hartford, into a house at the edge of town. Now he is dead, and his daughter Esther and her husband Paul Melin and their family live on his farm. My grandpa moved into Hartford too, along with my grandma, back when my parents got married and moved to the farm. But my grandma is dead now, and my grandpa lives there in that big house with my Aunt Emma and Uncle Earl, and Uncle Norton lived there too for a while.

On the other side of the highway and down a long lane you come to where Hjalmar and Augusta Johnson and their son Alvin live. Hjalmar and Augusta were born in Sweden and didn't come to America until they were

21

grown-ups. They still get newspapers in Swedish, they hang Swedish flags on their Christmas tree, and Augusta makes all kinds of Swedish foods: rollepolse, Swedish meatballs, spritz cookies. When you walk into their house up the front entryway stairs and through the white wooden door into Augusta's kitchen, you always smell bread baking. And when you leave, she'll always have something for you to take home, maybe some of her bread, or maybe some eggs. Sometimes she'll give you a big red Delicious apple, that's the kind she always buys.

Here, she'll say, you take them now.

Oh, no, Augusta, we've been taught to say.

Ja, she'll say, you take it. And she'll put it right in one of our hands.

And so we do.

SIOUX FALLS

Other than going to visit relatives or sometimes neighbors, we go to just three places: Sioux Falls, Hartford, and church. If we want to go shopping, or if we're going to do something fun, Sioux Falls is where we'll go. The main thing we go shopping for is groceries, that's nearly every week, but usually we go downtown Sioux Falls too, looking in the stores even if we don't end up buying anything. There is one time of the week that is always our shopping day: Saturday afternoon.

Grocery shopping is my mother's job, and her getting ready for those shopping trips is like planning an expedition. She likes figuring out ways to save money. The first thing she has to do is go through all the ads in the Sioux Falls *Argus-Leader*. The newspaper arrives along with the rest of the mail, usually about eleven o'clock. After our noon meal is over, everyone wants to read the newspaper. Mostly everyone wants to read the funnies, and on Saturday of course it's the colored funnies, but my brother reads the sports, and my father reads the farm market report. When she's planning her grocery shopping, my mother will leave the kitchen table where everybody else is still sitting with some section of the paper held out in front of them and take her coffee cup and go into the dining room where she can sit at the dining room table by herself and concentrate. She has to make her lists. She makes a list of what she needs to get, and then she has to look through all the ads, to see what the sales are. If something is a good price on sale, or if there is a coupon for it, she'll buy it whether she needs it that week or not, as long as it will keep. Then she'll have to figure out which store she'll go to first and which last. She has to do the big shopping at the first place, because that's the place where she'll need a carry out boy. At the other places—as long as she's just bought a bag or two—she can just carry the bags herself, or we can help. That's important because she doesn't like the carry out boy to bring groceries to the car and see it already full of grocery bags, that's embarrassing to her. I guess she thinks it's rude to let the people from one store know you also shop at another. And as far as the last place, that has to be where she buys the ice cream. If she got it early on, at one of the first stores, it would melt while she was shopping in the other ones. So it has to be a place where she will get a good price on ice cream but it can't be the place where she does her big shopping. You can see why she needs to concentrate. Usually we shop at about three different places: Ralph's Fine Foods, the Red Owl, and the West Soo Grocery. Sometimes we go to the Sunshine Store. The Red Owl and West Soo are near each other on the way to Highway 38, the road out of town, but the Sunshine Store and Ralph's Fine Foods are way over on the south side.

If Saturday happens to be a rainy day, and no one can work in the fields, then we'll all go to town. The first thing everybody does, after the dinner dishes are washed and put away and the lists are made, is clean up and put on some good clothes. Then we get into the car and off we go. If we are going shopping downtown, we'll go there first, park the car and divide up so we can all go to go to different places, but we always meet back together in the shoe department of J. C. Penney's where you can sit down and wait.

There are three main department stores in Sioux Falls: Fantle's, Shriver's and J. C. Penney's. Shriver's and J. C. Penney's are both on Phillips Avenue, where most of the stores are, and Fantle's is a block away on Main Avenue. We never buy anything at Fantle's. Laura Benson—she is married to Art Benson, a relative, and is my mother's best friend—she always shops at Fantle's, but we never do. Laura will buy things and take them back, buy them and take them back. We never take anything back. My mother thinks we can't afford to shop at Fantle's, so we almost never even go in.

Sometimes we buy things at Shriver's. We know a lady who works there in the Ladies' Department, and my mother always enjoys speaking to her. She is from a family who went to our church but now she lives in Sioux Falls and goes to Augustana Lutheran church there. She is a widow and has a son to

24

raise. Shriver's is a nice store; they have big glass display windows on the sidewalk that made a kind of porch you walk through to go inside, they have a lunchroom on the top floor, and a mezzanine where they sell shoes.

But almost always we do our shopping in J. C. Penney's. The best thing about Penney's is the escalator. J. C. Penney's had the first escalator in downtown, and in fact, it is the only escalator still. Before there was an escalator, you had to take the elevator with the brass accordion doors, and the elevator woman sitting on the stool saying, Second Floor, Ladies' Wear, please watch your step.

But now that the escalator has come along, there are all kinds of warnings:

Be careful you don't get your fingers caught in the handrail when you get off, be careful you don't let your shoelaces get caught between the steps, be careful you don't let your toes get caught when the steps disappear.

What my mother says is:

Be careful you don't get your head knocked off.

She says this because when we ride we like to lean over the side and stick our heads over the edge to get a moving picture view of the floor below—for instance, if you look out between the first and the second floor, you'll get a nice view of the candy counter—and she can just see us, leaning over, not paying attention and having our heads crack into the up-coming wall. Well, that's never happened, not even close.

Downtown is full of all kinds of stores. There are some like Geyerman's just for ladies to buy clothes in, there are some just for men, like Weatherwax's where my dad buys his good clothes. There are shoe stores and there are dime stores—Woolworth's, Newberry's, Kresge's. There is Sioux Falls Book and Stationery, if you buy something there, they'll put it in a bag that is red and white checked, not just a plain brown bag like everywhere else. There is Williams Piano Company on Main Avenue, where we have to go to buy books for our music lessons—John Thompson's "Teaching Little Fingers to Play," and on up, though so far nobody in our family has got past Grade Three. There are two stores where we always like to stop at and look in the windows: Harold's Photography and Smith's Jewelers. When people get married, lots of times they'll have Harold's Photography take the pictures, and then after a while the pictures will show up on display in the shop windows, so if you know somebody who's gotten married, and especially if you hadn't been invited to the wedding, you can stop at the window and see pictures of the bridal party and all the dresses, pictures of his family and her family, and pictures of them cutting the cake. The window at Smith's Jewelers is interesting for just about the same reason. In that window you can see the china and silver that people who are going to get married have picked out. The plates and silverware are laid out with a little card that says the names of the couple, and it's always fun to decide who picked what you like and who picked something that doesn't look as nice.

We never eat any meals when we're shopping, but when we're downtown for a different reason we might sometimes eat a meal in Sioux Falls, and if we do, there are a couple of places in downtown where we'll go: the Nickel Plate Diner and the Rushmore Cafe. At the Rushmore Cafe they have a big colored picture of Mt. Rushmore hanging on the wall, and a picture of it on the menu too. I always order a hot roast beef sandwich at the Rushmore Cafe. As a matter of fact, my parents told me that if anybody invites me to eat with them—like sometimes after church I go home with a friend and her parents take us out to eat for Sunday dinner—that I should always order a hot roast beef sandwich. First of all, I'd know what it was and I'd eat it, and second it doesn't cost too much money. It would be embarrassing to them if someone took me out to eat and I ordered something that was really expensive. Although we never eat meals out when we're shopping, sometimes we'll stop for a little treat when we're just about ready to go home. Up on Minnesota Avenue is a drug store where we can get Frosty Malts, or sometimes we'll stop at the lunch counter at the dime store for a root beer float.

Something else that is special about downtown are the movie theaters. Of course we don't go to movies on shopping days, but every once in a while, I'll get to go to a movie with a friend, or if there is some special movie my parents want to see we might all go on a Sunday afternoon. Sometimes I go to movies with one of my sisters and her boyfriend when they go on a date. Whenever my sisters go on dates, they go to the movies. A date will go like this: the boy will come into our kitchen, and stand really close to the door, with his hand on the doorknob. My mother will call upstairs for my sister, who'll come down in a hurry and off they'll go. When they get to Sioux Falls, they'll go to a movie theater and get their tickets and go in and start watching whether it's the beginning or the middle. They'll watch it through to the end, and then they'll get to see all the cartoons and previews they've missed. Then they'll watch the movie start up, and watch it up to the point where they came in. Then they'll leave and go to a drive-in and get something to eat. There is one drive-in that all the high school kids from our town who are out on dates go to—Bob's. All the kids from the near-by town—Lyons—go to a drive-in called Lee's. If you went out with a boy from a different town than yours, I don't know where you'd go. Then my sister and her boyfriend will come home and sit in his car in the barnyard until my mother gets up and turns the yard light on and off. That tells them they've been sitting out there long enough.

There are three movie theaters that I've been to, there is the State, the Hollywood, the Egyptian. The State is big and it's beautiful. There is a balcony with a brass rail across the front row so you won't fall down onto the floor beneath, and on the stage there is a red velvet curtain that opens up with a swish, swish sound when it's time for the movie to start. The State is up on the south end of Phillips Avenue, and the Hollywood is down at the north end. The Hollywood is newer than the State. It's all right, but it doesn't have a balcony. The Egyptian is on a side street and doesn't have a balcony either, but it's filled with all kinds of colored tiles and decorations and statues to make it seem just like you're in Ancient Egypt. One Sunday afternoon we stood in line a long time to see *The Ten Commandments* at the Egyptian theater.

Well, after we've done all the shopping we're going to do downtown, and we've all come back together again in the shoe department, we walk back to the parking lot, and then we head off to the grocery stores. Lots of times we'll have had fun, and we'll be happy as can be riding home, though we maybe be pretty tired from walking around. But sometimes, if we'd wanted something and didn't get it, then we'd be complaining, or if we'd wanted something—like shoes for instance, we might have gotten them, but they might be the style we wanted—then we'd be complaining too. When we'd get to the grocery store, we might start complaining about something else. We would always want a treat, like an ice cream cone or a Butter Brickle candy bar, and we'd always hate it that my mother took so long to do her shopping. One time, coming home— I remember it had been a long trip and it was really late in the afternoon, almost night—I was riding in the back seat and all of a sudden I heard my mother talking to us from the front seat, where she was sitting, driving the car. When she started talking I could tell she was mad. But what was a lot worse is that I could hear in her voice that she was crying. She held herself real still, I could see her against the sky that had turned almost black in the evening, and I could see her hands, holding so tight to the steering wheel. It made my stomach hurt to hear the angry words she was saying, and I didn't like to think I was the sort of person she was talking about. For the first time, I realized something: that just like sometimes I feel sad and disappointed, and like nothing I do makes a difference—for the first time I knew that she could feel that same way too. Before then, I didn't know that feeling happened to mothers, but I guess it does.

HARTFORD

My grandpa, who is an old man, lives in Hartford with my Aunt Emma and Uncle Earl. They all live together in a big white house just two blocks from downtown. When my mom and I go into Hartford we go see them. We don't go into Hartford just to visit, though. We go visiting after we go shopping, or do what we have to do in town.

The most important place in downtown Hartford, as far as I'm concerned, is the Mercantile. It's where we buy our groceries. There are two Mercantiles. One is the grocery store, that's the new Mercantile, and the other is the old Mercantile, which is called a dry goods store. They had started out as one store, but then they divided, and the grocery store moved to a building of its own, a newer building a few doors north of the old Mercantile. Back in the old days, when it was all one store, it was the sort of grocery store where you would go in and tell the clerk what you wanted and that person would go and get it for you, but now that it's divided, the grocery store part has shopping carts and aisles where you can walk up and down and pick out your own food, just like in a Sioux Falls super market.

Mr. Campbell—that's how it's spelled, just like I have it, but it is pronounced "Camel"—he owns the Mercantile, and he runs the meat counter in the grocery store. He is a big-sized man with a booming voice, and he wears a little white paper cap, pointed at the front and back like an army hat, and a big white apron, that most of the time has reddish marks on it right across his stomach from when he's been cutting up pieces of meat or grinding it up into hamburger. Unless you are buying meat, you probably won't see too much of Mr. Campbell.

We don't buy meat at the store very often. The main reason for that is that we usually buy a whole quarter of beef and have it cut up and wrapped in white freezer paper. We make sure each piece is labeled with a red crayon-sort of pen, and then we put all the pieces in the locker plant. There are two locker plants, one in Sioux Falls in the old Crescent Creamery, located on the steep Main Street hill on the north side of town; the other is in Hartford and attached to the Co-op Creamery there. The business of a locker plant is to rent lockers in their big walk-in freezers. Not many people we know have freezers, except for the freezer space you might have in your refrigerator, and so for meat and for the sorts of fruits and vegetables you can't put up in glass jars, you take them to the locker plant and then, when you need a chuck roast or some frozen corn or rhubarb, you just go into Hartford, or stop on your way home from Sioux Falls, and pick them up from your bin at the locker plant.

To go into the locker plant in Hartford you walk through a store-front room with a big glass display window with nothing in it. There is nothing in the room, either, except for a desk that no one ever sits at. Then you open a great big wooden door, about ten inches thick, with a heavy metal latch for a door handle. As soon as you open the door, a rush of cold air hits you in the face, and you hurry in so as not to let the cold air get out. Once you're inside the freezer, everything seems like you've come into a different world: you can see your breath, no matter how hot it is outside; it smells funny; and if you talk—and you wouldn't talk much—your voice sounds funny too. If you have a lot of rummaging to do, you wear a coat, even in summer. You have to walk down aisles to find your locker and locate your own bin by its number. After you unlock the compartment, you have to lift and rearrange bags until you find what you've come for: one of the meat packages or maybe a little cardboard package with vegetables or fruit inside. Then you're glad to hurry back outside where things are normal.

Connected to the locker plant is the creamery where my mother sells cream. We have one Jersey cow, milked night and morning by my father. When he brings in the milk pail, we pour the milk though a big metal funnel-shaped strainer with a filter paper to make sure none of the little bits of straw that have fallen in the pail end up floating in the milk we drink. Then we put the milk in

30

a milk pan, cover it up, and put the pan in the refrigerator, where it will sit and get cool until we want to use it at mealtime. Then, each time before we use it, we'll take the skimmer and skim off the cream that has risen to the top. We'll skim it off and put it in the crock, and we'll keep putting it there until we get the crock filled; then it will go into the cream pail, and when the cream pail which is about the size of a gallon is filled, my mother will take it in and sell it to Checker Thomas, who runs the creamery, or maybe she'll trade it for eggs. We drop the cream pail off with him, walk down to the Mercantile to get some groceries, and then when we walk back, there it will be, sitting on his desk, clean inside and out, and inside will be some money or beside it will be some eggs.

Of course we use cream ourselves, in cooking and baking and in coffee and once in a blue moon even making butter. It takes forever, of course, making butter. You can churn and churn away without ever any sign of anything happening. But eventually through the glass you'll see little pale yellowish flecks, and they'll start getting bigger and bigger until you can hardly turn the handle of the churn. Then it's done, and you can put it in a glass mold, a two-pound size, with vegetable shapes in the lid. You pack the butter in tight so that when you turn it out on the butter plate, it will be molded with carrots and cabbages on top and look really nice.

But let's say we haven't used our cream for butter, we've left it at Checker Thomas's creamery, and we've walked down the sidewalk past Lavin's hardware store to do some grocery shopping at the Mercantile. Mr. Campbell would be there behind the meat counter, but the grocery part of the Mercantile is run by two women: Joyce Main and Dorothy Anderson. Joyce Main has white hair and a firm way about her. You never want to fool around when Joyce Main is working; you know she'll always speak her mind about you, even if you are little, and it might not be what you want to hear, and it for sure will not be what your mother wants to hear. The other woman, Dorothy Anderson—we always call her "Dorothy," not "Mrs. Anderson"—she is the littlest woman you can imagine. She is small and thin and has very white skin. Dorothy has reddish-brown hair pulled back under a hair net, bright brown eyes, and a quiet face. Her mouth is broad, and her face is everywhere wrinkles, the wrinkles you would expect, like on her forehead, but also wrinkles on her cheeks, on her upper lip, even wrinkles between wrinkles. She has a sweet and patient smile.

Nearly every time I come into the Mercantile, there is Dorothy behind the counter, wearing a clean cotton house dress and a bib apron. The counter Dorothy stands behind isn't like the check-out counters in a Sioux Falls grocery store, it's a U-shaped counter, and you can put your groceries down on any part of it, and Dorothy will ring them up. Actually, she won't ring them up, she writes them down. She has a little carbon paper pad, and she lists every item you've bought, slowly and carefully. Dorothy has beautiful penmanship. For each order, she'll first write the date on the top line, then "Elmer Benson" and then she'll write the name and price of each item, carefully shaping each letter of every word.

The reason she has to write everything down is that we never pay when we buy anything, we just say, Charge it. And they never send us a bill. Every once in a while, my mother or father will come in with a check book, and Dorothy or Mr. Campbell will take that little carbon paper pad and add up everything we've bought and we write them a check.

But the Mercantile isn't the only place in town where you can buy groceries. We could shop at the Home Market which is run by Lefty Gehler, on the other side of the street, by the service station at the north end of Main Street. That is where my Aunt Emma shops.

Neither the Mercantile nor Lefty's is the oldest or original store, though; that had been Engelcke's store. Mr. Engelcke used to live in a brown and yellow house across the alley from where my grandma and grandpa lived, and everybody shopped at his store until he closed down the business and retired to that brown and yellow house. It always made my mother happy to be able to say that during the '30's when there was no cash money to be had, she asked Mr. Engelcke about charging and he said, Elmer Benson can have credit here as long as he needs it.

Even when he was a little boy, that credit business was an idea my brother understood pretty well. There's a story about him that people liked to tell; it happened when he was only about five or six. He was staying the day in Hartford with our grandpa and grandma, and Curtis was being such a bad boy this particular day that Grandma had to scold him. He thought to himself that he would buy her a present to get back on her good side. So, he left the house and walked the block and a half to downtown and went to Engelcke's store. He walked in, walked up to the counter, and said, I want to buy a broom.

So Mr. Englecke gave him the broom, and said to this little boy who could barely see over the counter, And how do you want to pay for it?

My brother said, Charge it to John Benson.

And dragging the broom behind him, out he walked, big as you please, not knowing that there in the store, behind the stove along with some other old men, sat his grandpa—who, I guess, thought Curtis was pretty funny, and must not have minded paying for a new broom.

The old Mercantile is just a few doors down the street from the grocery story Mercantile. It is a great big store with a high ceiling of pressed metal painted white. It has ceiling fans to cool you off in the summer, and in the middle of the store, an oil burner you can stand around in the winter, and warm up your cold hands. It has all sorts of things that come to mind when you think of an old store. It has an old cash register, brassy and decorated, where the numbers show up on what looks like little paper cards when the clerk rings things up. It has a big ball of string that the clerk uses to wrap up the brown paper packages, and of course there is a huge roll of brown paper with a cutter for the clerk to tear off big wide sheets. I say clerk, but who I mean is Ethel Pippett. She runs the Mercantile.

Here is where you can buy all kinds of dry goods, like school supplies and even jeans and shirts. But the best thing about the old Mercantile is the ice cream freezer. It's right by the cash register, maybe they put it there so you could get your ice cream on the way out of the store. If my mom says I can get a cone, then Ethel Pippett lifts the lids of the freezer so I can see all the different flavors of ice cream she has, each in a round cardboard tub. If I don't want a cone, I could get a popsicle, or an Eskimo pie. If it is a special day, I might get a Drumstick that costs a dime while the other ice cream bars are only a nickel. But if I decide on a cone, Ethel Pippett says, One scoop or two? I say, One. Then she takes the ice cream scoop from the crock where it's been standing in water and shakes the drops of water off before she digs deeps into the ice cream tub. She pats and packs the ice cream into the cone and hands it over. I start licking right away so it won't drip all over my hand.

Ethel Pippett is always dressed in nice-looking clothes, and has grey hair waved close to her head. I've always liked her because when it's my birthday, July 13th, she'll give me a free ice cream cone, one scoop of butter brickle, sometimes maple nut. She remembers it's my birthday because I was born just one week after her grandson, Bob Doss. He lives far away in Missouri, and so she gives me a cone and talks about him. I don't know him, but I can't help but like somebody who gets me free cones year after year, just for being born the same time he was.

Ethel Pippett's husband, Mort Pippett, used to run the service station on the corner. The service station is where men come to sit and talk, just like they do at the grain elevators. I like the gas pumps. One is white glass on top and the other is red. Maybe they're supposed to look like crowns, but they always make me think of ice cream cones.

Mort Pippett delivered the gas and fuel oil to our farm. On our farm we have our own underground gas tank for cars and a great big oil drum on a wagon for tractors, so that when our cars need gas or our tractors need fuel, we'll have it right there. When Mort Pippett made a delivery, he'd always bring a candy bar along for the kids. One day—and this is another thing that was before my time—my brother really wanted a candy bar, so he went to the

34

telephone and called the operator and asked for Mort Pippett's gas station. When somebody answered my brother said, You're supposed to deliver five gallons of gas to Elmer Benson's today.

I guess five gallons seemed like a lot to him. Mort Pippett must have thought that was an odd order, but he decided to come out anyway. When he got to our place, he said to my father, Did you order gas? My father said, No. He asked my mother, she said, No.

Finally, they figured it out, but whether my brother got his candy bar or a spanking I do not know.

Other businesses in Hartford are Engmann's Drug Store, Lavin's Hardware Store, a cafe or two, the Community Bank, and a post office in a great big stone building on the corner where, on the second floor above the post office, my Uncle Norton has his law office. Then there is a beauty shop, a barber's shop, a cobbler's shop, and a little red brick building where the doctor's office is. When I was a baby the town doctor was named Dr. Leraan; he delivered me and my sister Marjorie, too. But he moved to Sioux Falls, and eventually we got a new doctor in town, Dr. Petres, a refugee from Hungary. When my grandpa got sick, Dr. Petres was the one who looked after him, and they got to be good friends. Dr. Petres comes to see him every evening. Then there is the American Legion Hall, where we go to see cartoons on Saturday afternoons, and where some people go to wedding dances on Saturday nights. There are three bars. There is the bar in the basement of the American Legion Hall called the Dugout. There is a place called Liquors On and Off Sale. Then there is the Pool Hall, down at the south end of Main Street where high school boys like to hang out. I've never known any girls to go into the Pool Hall, but they like to drive past in their cars and make a U-turn and go past it again to see what boys are in there. My father goes in the Pool Hall to buy Copenhagen snuff. There are also the Odd Fellow's Hall and a Masonic Meeting place, and off Main Street another creamery, a blacksmith shop, two grain elevators, and at the edge of town, a lumber yard. And that's pretty much it.

When we come into Hartford for some business or shopping, we'll usually go visiting too. When I was really little, we used to go visit Ruth Paulson; she was another relative whose father had been Lewis Benson, my grandpa's brother. When her father died, she moved into his big house at the west side of Hartford. The reason we went to visit her was that she was really sick. She had cancer. My mom would go in to talk to her, and I would stay in the kitchen and drink a glass of milk and be real, real quiet. Then when she died, her husband, Oscar Paulson, sold the house to Mr. Campbell and moved away, and we haven't gone back there anymore. That's too bad because it's a beautiful house, with a nice drive leading up to it and trees on both sides that make an arch over your head.

Just down the road from that place is where Art and Laura Benson live. Art is Uncle Lewis's son too, and Laura, his wife, is the person my mom likes best to visit. They'll sit at the table and drink coffee and have a cookie, and then Laura will give me some grape juice or Seven-Up and my mom will tell me to go somewhere to play, then they'll talk in real low voices. I don't care if I can't hear, usually I don't even know who they're talking about. My mom always says Laura is just like a sister to her, and that's nice, because all my mother's real sisters live far away in Illinois, where she came from. And Laura says the same about my mother, even though she has her own real sisters nearby. Sometimes, on Sunday evenings we'll all come to visit, my dad and my sisters and brother, and those times are the best, because they have a TV—they are just about the only people I know who do have one—and we get to watch it. Laura usually fixes scalloped potatoes and ham, and then after supper we watch Ed Sullivan on the Toast of the Town, and sometimes even stay for Loretta Young.

Most of the time though, we'll stop and visit Aunt Emma and Uncle Earl, and Grandpa. My grandma died when I was just two years old, so I don't remember anything about visiting her. They have a great big house, a kitchen and a bathroom, a side sitting room where Grandpa sits in his rocker and looks out the window at Maybelle Fetter's house and reads the newspaper, and a dining room, and two front rooms. In one of the front rooms is a sofa and a rocker to match that have lions' heads on the arms, and in the other front room is a sofa and easy chair that look just like the ones in our house. Upstairs are lots of bedrooms, and right at the head of the stairs, a room that has books all up and down one wall from the floor to the ceiling. My Aunt Emma used to be a teacher before she got married, and all those books are hers. When I got old enough to read, I went up there and looked through the rows, and sometimes I borrowed books from her. It was more interesting to stay in that room, looking through all her books, than to sit at the kitchen table and listen to people talking.

I don't go upstairs though until we've had something to eat. When we get to Aunt Emma's house we come in the back door into her kitchen and take a seat at her kitchen table which is right by the window. Sometimes we go in first to see Grandpa. But pretty soon Aunt Emma puts on the coffee pot and puts cups and saucers on the table for my mom and the other grown-ups and a glass of milk for me and plate of something good to eat. Cookies or bars or maybe some bread she's made. My Aunt Emma is a very good cook.

FALL

When I think of fall, I think about school, and about going back to school after summer vacation. Back when I was only four or five, when fall came, it meant that my sisters and brother would go back to school, and I'd be left at home alone with only my mom. We'd do this and that during the day, but it was never as much fun as when they were all in the house too. My mom and I would listen to "Back Stage Wife" and "Stella Dallas" on the radio, and sometimes she'd say, Let's take a nap. And I'd say, Okay. It was always nice, to lie down together on her big bed, all cozy and warm. But when I woke up, I'd be mad because I'd be there all by myself. What made me mad was that she'd tricked me, she'd just pretend she wanted to take a nap, and then when I fell asleep, she'd get up. When I woke up, I'd sit there on the bed for a while and be mad, but then I'd hear everybody back home again, in the kitchen having something to eat after school, so I'd come out of the bedroom, and get a cookie too.

One warm fall morning—I must have been four or five—I went along with Curtis to school, riding on the crossbar of his old brown and white bike. It started out with my just riding along to the end of the lane, but then I said, What about down to the plum brushes? then, How about to Van Kekerix's lane? then I figured I might as well ride along to the bridge. When I'd gone that far I was closer to school than home, so I rode along the whole way. When we got to school, he went inside, and I was supposed to walk home, but I stayed there and played around by myself. Then I got tired and bored, and I guess I forgot about walking home. Instead, I wanted to come in the schoolhouse and sit down and cool off, and I thought it would be fun to see what was going on inside. So, I knocked on the door of the school. I heard the teacher coming down the hall, and I saw her through the window in the door, but when she looked out the window, I guess I was so short she didn't see me, because she never opened the door, she just walked back into the classroom. So I climbed up on the porch railing and sat there for a while, swinging my legs back and forth, just letting time go by.

Pretty soon up the road comes Guy Artz, our hired man, driving our truck in a great big hurry.

Where have you been? he says to me as soon as he jumped out of the cab. Does your mother know where you are?

No, she doesn't know, I said, but Curtis does.

But that fact didn't seem to make a difference to him.

Well, you get in this truck right away. She's been worried sick and sent me to look for you. You're going home right now.

When I got home, I was in trouble. She didn't care that Curtis knew all along where I was and that I was just fine sitting there at the schoolhouse. She thought I'd walked down to the creek and fallen in and drowned, or maybe I'd gotten into the pig pen and they'd eaten me up. So that was my last visit to school, that is, before I started myself.

Every fall before school started, we'd go to town and buy school supplies. Except when I started first grade. That year, a week or so before school began, the mailman drove down our lane instead of just leaving the mail in our box. When he drove down the lane like that, it meant someone was getting a package. This time I was the one. It was addressed to me: Miss Mabel Ann Benson. I had never had a package before, so I was excited, and everybody else was too. When I opened it up, inside were all my school supplies, sent to me by my Uncle Earl. My Uncle Earl was out in the western part of the state, working on a construction job, and he had made up a package of all the things I would need the first day of school and then mailed them to me. There was a big tablet with a red cover and an Indian's picture on it, there was a little Rainbow pad, with all different colors of paper. There was a jar of Carter's Paste, a scissors with round ends, six yellow pencils—all sharpened—a ruler, an eraser, and a pencil that was red at one end and blue on the other. The best

39

thing was my box of crayons: two rows! —twice as big a box as my mom was planning to get me. I took those things, and laid them out on my bed, side by side, so I could see everything at once, and the night before school started, I did the same, laying them out on the floor beside my bed, so I would be sure not to miss anything in the morning.

A new year of school meant a new pair of shoes, and usually new clothes too, to wear on the first day. When I started school, I wore a dress with a sash that tied in the back. That was a bother, because I couldn't reach back to tie it myself, and if it came undone, I'd have to get somebody else to do it for me or let the sashes hang. When it got colder, we'd wear jeans under our dresses to keep our legs warm.

When I started school, I was the only one in the first grade. That's because we went to a country school, Johnson District #54, where all eight grades would be taught together in one place, in one room. It was the same school my dad, and my Aunt Emma and Uncle Norton had gone to when they were children; that is, it was in the same place, but their school had burned down and then this one was built. Their school had a different name, too, it was called Wilder School, and our school was named Johnson School, because the land had come from the farm of Mr. Joseph E. Johnson who owned the land across the road from us where now the Van Kekerixes lived. The school yard was one acre big, and the schoolhouse sat right in the front of the school yard, a white wooden building with a porch across the front. The front door faced south, and all the windows in the building were on the east side, no windows at all on the north or west.

Not only was I the only one in the first grade, but there weren't any children in the second grade or in the third grade, either. The next closest to me were the girls in the fourth grade, Peggy Van Kekerix, Doris Byg, Bonnie Brown, and Bonnie Artz. I guess it's because there weren't any other little children is why I got so much attention.

40

Mrs. Ollerich was our teacher, and she was really nice to me. She taught me to read by showing me flash cards and showing me how to sound words out. Then she would take the flash cards and put them on a big posterboard with slots for the flash cards to fit in. She'd put the cards in order so that the words would make a sentence, and I'd get the idea of how you wouldn't just read one word, but you'd put a few words together and then you'd have a sentence that said something. Before long I could read about Alice and Jerry in Friendly Village, and I would do all this sitting in her lap, with one arm around her neck and one hand pointing at the words in the book. Until one day I had to stop pointing and just read.

I got the feeling she didn't like my sister Marjorie as much as she liked me, and the next year, when I was in second grade and there were three little first-graders, then she wasn't quite as nice to them as she had been to me either. But I had no complaints.

In our school, unless your class—like reading or arithmetic—was called up to the teacher's desk, and you had to go over the problems you were supposed to have done and check your answers right or wrong, or you had to read aloud through the story you were supposed to have read silently to yourself and get all the new words right—except for those times we called Class Time, you could do what you wanted, as long as you worked at your desk and didn't make too much noise. That's why I liked school. If you felt like drawing a picture and coloring it, you could. If you wanted to go look at the books in our school library, you could. If you wanted to do a project, like cut a jack-o-lantern out of construction paper, you'd have to ask if you could go get things out of the supply cupboard, but then you help yourself and make whatever you wanted. Nobody told you what to do when it wasn't class time.

There were lots of new things to pay attention to at school. For instance, going to the toilet. If you wanted to go to the toilet you'd check and see if the sign was turned to green or red. If it was green, it meant you could go, if it was red, you had to wait. There was one toilet for the girls and one for the boys, and one sign for each too. One thing I learned right away was how to tell time better than just saying where the long hand was and where was the short hand. We had a yellow clock hanging on the wall, right under the picture of George Washington. We'd start school at 9:00 a.m. At 10:30 a.m. we'd have morning recess for fifteen minutes. At 12:00 noon we would have dinner time and noon recess for an hour. At 2:30 p.m. we'd have afternoon recess, and at 4:00 p.m. school was over. Another thing I learned was that I couldn't just talk anytime I wanted. I'd have to hold up my hand, then if the teacher saw me, I could ask her something or ask to talk to somebody else.

When school started, we'd all take our seats in our desks and quiet down. Then Mrs. Ollerich would tell us to stand up, and we'd put our hands over our hearts and say the Pledge of Allegiance. Right after the pledge—at least when I first started school—we'd pray for the soldiers in Korea. Then we'd sit down for opening exercises. That would take fifteen minutes. Sometimes we'd sing, or we might play a little game like Dog and Bone. If it was chilly in the schoolhouse Mrs. Ollerich would wind up the record player and put on a march like "Stars and Stripes Forever" and we'd walk up and down like soldiers in the aisles between the desks.

We would have opening exercises after our noon hour too, but then Mrs. Ollerich would always read to us. She read us a whole book called *The Black* about an Arabian stallion that becomes a racehorse, and another about a collie called *Jinx of Jayson Valley* that had a very sad ending. Another sad book was *Girl of the Limberlost*, but at least it ended happy. After playing outside for an hour it was nice to sit down at your desk in the cool schoolhouse and put your head down on your arms and hear a story.

We did all kinds of things during recess and noon hour. The big kids, like Marjorie and her classmates would play baseball. I didn't usually do that unless they decided that the whole school was going to play, but there was a little bat that I could use if I wanted to. Sometimes we'd play Andy-I-Over, where we'd choose up sides, and have two teams on either side of the schoolhouse and throw the ball over the roof. When you threw the ball, you'd have to shout "Andy-I-Over" and then wait to see if somebody caught it. If they did, then everybody on that side would run around the two ends of the schoolhouse and try to tag as many people on our side as they could. We played other games too, like "All Around" and "Captain May I," and sometimes we played on the merry-go-round down at the far end of the school yard.

After school we had duties. Duties were jobs we did to clean up the school. There were jobs for big kids like sweeping the floor of the schoolroom or washing the blackboards, and there were jobs for little kids, like pushing desks out of the way for the sweepers, or pounding the erasers. Some jobs were worse than others. Washing the blackboards was bad because it took so long and if you weren't careful, they would be all streaky and you'd have to wash them again, and by then everybody you were walking home with would have left. For little kids, pounding the erasers was the worst job because you'd get that yellow dust all over your hands and everything and anyway, they never got clean, even when you pounded them on the schoolhouse wall.

In the fall, walking home from school was fun because usually the weather would be nice and sunny, and we'd take a different route than we took other times. Instead of walking home on the road, we'd walk through our neighbor's pasture—which was an old gravel pit—cross the creek where the rocks made steppingstones, and walk on through our own pasture, up the hill and on down the pasture lane and home. Fall was the only time we could do that, because in the winter there would be too much snow to get through, and in the spring, it would be all muddy and slushy. But in the fall, the trees would be bright yellow, and the sky would be so blue, and there would be all kinds of things to see and catch if you could. The gravel pit was an old one, all the sides of the holes they'd dug long ago were covered with grass, and there were different things there than you'd find in a regular pasture. For instance, there were piles of stones you could climb over, and in those piles there were some purplish flat stones that made a chalky mark, so you could write messages using

43

one stone to write on another. Skunk Creek went through the gravel pit too, just like it did the pasture on our farm, and sometimes we would stand at a wide spot and practice skipping stones on the water. Sometimes we'd see a turtle, or a snake on the way home. When I was in second grade, we were walking through the pasture, and we found some kittens. I don't know where they came from, we didn't see a mother cat, but I caught a little yellow one and took it home, and she became my cat Blondie.

Then, when we'd get home after school, in the fall, then we'd have to change our clothes and get busy. My first job was to take lunch out in the field to my dad or whoever was working with him. My mom would pack up a sandwich and a thermos of coffee and a piece of cake in a lunch pail and I'd walk down the lane to the field. When he saw me coming, he'd pull up to the end of the row, turn off the tractor, climb down and sit down in the shade of its wheel to eat what I'd brought. Then he'd stand up and stretch, and put his gloves back on, and say, Thank you, and get back to work. One of the big jobs my dad had to do in the fall was silo-filling. He'd drive the corn chopper up and down the corn rows, filling the wagons up with silage. My brother, and the hired man, or some other men who might be helping would drive the wagons back and forth—full wagons from the field to the silo, and empty wagons back to the field. My dad and other men would have put pipes up to the very top of the silo, and then there was a machine that pushed all that silage up the pipes, and they would put in wagonful after wagonful into the silo until it was all filled up. There's nothing that smells the same as silage. Whenever you smelled that smell, you knew it was fall.

Sometimes, after I took lunch out to the field, Marjorie and I would have to carry baskets of ground corn down to the cattle shed to feed the steers. Then I'd bring in a pail of drinking water for the night, and then I'd take my basket out to the pig yard to pick up cobs that we burned in the trash burner that heated up our kitchen. If there was any time left, we'd play, but before long it was getting dark, because nights come on early in the fall. Then you'd hear the tractor coming in, and sometimes see its headlights and you'd know it would soon be time for supper. You could see the lights through the kitchen windows, and see our mom inside, getting supper ready. It might be getting cold, you could see your breath, and it was good to come in the house where it was warm. When my dad and brother came in, they'd wash their face and hands. One of my sisters would set the table and another would get us each a glass of milk. My mother would dish up. I'd pull the chairs up around the table, and then we'd all sit down to supper.

WINTER

Winter lasts a long time. It's lucky there's so much going on. For one thing winter is exciting because we have blizzards. They are not exactly fun when they're going on, but they're exciting, and then they give you something to talk about afterward. Blizzards don't happen as much as they used to, people say. I guess that's right; there's only one that sticks out in my mind.

It happened when I was five. The blizzard started while school was in session. It started to snow, the wind came up, and things just got worse and worse. School had to be called off in the middle of the day, but then the problem was, how everyone was going to get home. First the teacher—who happened to be Esther Melin who lived across the road from us—called everybody's houses to tell them to come and get their kids. We lived a half mile from the school, that was one of the shorter distances, and my dad was able to drive through the drifts in his truck, even though the snow was piling up fast. But when the teacher had called the Van Kekerix house to tell them to come and get Peggy, no one was home. Her parents were over at her Uncle Marinus's farm, helping out with something, and they couldn't get out of that farmyard to get to their own house, let alone pick up Peggy. So my dad brought her home too. And the Bygs—Vinette, and Joanie, and Doris—they lived nearly two miles away, and the road to their house went up Skunk Creek Hill, which no one could travel through in weather like this. So they went home with the teacher.

I found all this out when my sisters and brother came home from school, ahead of their usual time, with Peggy along with them. The wind howled around the corners of our house, the snow was falling so thick you couldn't see to the barn, but we were safe and warm inside. All that night, snow kept falling and the wind kept blowing, and in the morning, we saw we were really snowed in. There was snow piled in hard white drifts around our house and up the lane. It looked soft to the eye, but it was packed in hard, so hard you could stand on the top of the drifts and walk over them. The drifts were way too hard for a car to get through. We were snowed in until the snowplow made its way to our house, and that would be a while.

Up there at the Melin house, the Byg girls decided they would walk down to our house, where they probably thought things were a little livelier. It wasn't a long distance, and they bundled up good. The sun was shining, but it was a bitterly cold day; the wind, when you were out in the open, took your breath away, and made that space behind your eyes ache.

We didn't know anything about their plan and were just sitting around the kitchen table when suddenly Joanie Byg arrived at our door, pounding on it, sobbing and crying. She had been walking to our house with Doris, her eight-year-old sister, but Doris kept falling down, and Joanie thought she was dying, freezing, lost in the snow. My brother put on his coat and boots, hat and mittens and walked down the lane, and in a few minutes he and Doris were back. She was covered with snow and was laughing; she didn't know she'd nearly died. Now, with the Byg girls and with Peggy, and all of us, we had a houseful, and we had a lot of fun running through the house, yelling and jumping on the furniture. When I discovered I had a loose tooth, they all chased me around the house, each one wanting to be the person to get to pull it out.

Eventually the excitement of Doris's adventure and my loose tooth died down, and we all started getting tired of being cooped up with each other. This was the third day of being snowed in. Especially Peggy was getting tired of it all. She was getting homesick and lonely. We could tell because she stood behind the folding door that went into the living room and wouldn't talk or come out. Finally, someone got the idea of asking her what she liked to eat. Chocolate pudding, she said. So my mother made Jell-O chocolate pudding and then said, Come and eat dinner, we're going to have chocolate pudding for dessert. It was lucky she had that on hand, because by this time we had eaten our way through a lot of food, a lot of hot dogs, a lot of macaroni and cheese, a lot of boiled potatoes. Peggy did come out from behind the door and sat down to eat with the rest of us, and no sooner did we finish that good dessert than who should we see but Peggy's father, Harry Van Kekerix, standing at the door, ready to take her home. He'd walked down our long lane to come get her. And after she left, it was the Bygs who returned home, and then soon after that everybody was plowed out.

The snowplow always comes at night. I'll be lying there, asleep in my bed. In my room I have two windows, side by side, that look out to the south, right down into our barnyard; and in the middle of my sleeping, lights—orange and white—will come flashing on and off into my room, shining through my windows so I can see the lights on the walls and on the mirror. I'll hear my dog Buddy bark bark barking as loud as he can, then I'll hear the sound of a machine's engine, and then those sounds that only come from the snowplow. There are the chank and chink sounds from the chains that hang down from the plow, and the scraping and whining sound of the blades on icy packed snow, and then there are the scrunch and crash noises of big chunks of hard snow that the snowplow breaks up and throws aside. Hearing those sounds wakes me up, and by the time I am wide awake, I know it is the snowplow, and by the time it gets to the barnyard, I'll be up kneeling by the window, looking out. It comes into the yard, makes a little turn to the left, then backs up, turns around and gets ready to head up the lane and out again. While it's in the yard, my father usually comes out and says something to the man in the cab. He'll shout something back, but he won't climb down, and they won't talk for long; there are still many places to go, and all night to work. The sounds and the light fade away as he drives back up the lane and away. And then I know that tomorrow we'll be out again, and everything will be back to ordinary.

Of course, you never know when a blizzard is going to happen, maybe you won't even get one during the whole season, but you always know that there is Christmas to look forward to in the middle of winter, and all the things that go with it. One of the most important things about Christmas every year is the Christmas program. There are two, one at school and one at church.

When I was in first grade, I could hardly wait for the Christmas program. Neither could our teacher, she had us starting to get ready by the middle of October. There is always a lot to do. We have to decorate the school room with green and red paper chains, we have to make paper snowflakes to tape on all the windows. And we have to sell raffle tickets. But the biggest job is getting ready for the program.

The program was always pretty much the same. We'd start with a song, like "Jolly Old St. Nicholas" or "Up on the Housetop," and throughout the program there would be other songs we'd all sing together, and there would always be a song at the end, to round the program off. Some years when I was in school, the teacher would play the songs on the piano and we'd all sing with her until we learned it, but Mrs. Ollerich said she wasn't a singer, and maybe she didn't play the piano either, so instead of her trying to teach us the songs, she said, I am going to have Bing Crosby teach you to sing.

And so she would wind up our record player, which was a big wooden box with doors you could open in the front for the sound to come out, put the needle on the record, and we would gather around to hear Bing Crosby sing "I'm Dreaming of a White Christmas." Then we'd sing it along with him until we knew the words.

The other parts of the program, other than songs, were the recitations and plays, and they took a long time to get ready too. Everyone had to memorize a recitation, a piece they'd have to say all by themselves alone on the stage. Then there would be some plays for everyone to have a part in, some for the little children and some for the bigger ones, so we'd have to memorize those parts, and when we got our lines memorized, then we'd have to practice with actions, and learn where we had to walk and stand, and when to go off the stage, and when to come back on.

We had a real stage at our school, a wooden platform that raised us at least a foot off the ground. It was in three sections and during the year it was stored in the school basement. You knew the program was pretty near when Cecil Byg, and Leroy Andreson, and my dad—those three were the school board—would come to school and carry the platform sections up the stairs and set them up over by the north wall. Then we'd have to squeeze the desks together in the rest of the room, and we knew there wouldn't be much schoolwork done now, it was too close to the program time. The stage platforms were centered so that there was backstage space on the either side, where we could go when we weren't doing a song or a piece or on stage in a play. We pushed the piano into one of the backstage spaces, too, so Velma Brown—she was Bonnie Brown's mother and the organist at the Methodist Church—could sit there and play for us when we sang our songs. After the stage was put up, we hung the curtains from the wire that was strung from one wall to the other. The curtains were dark blue, with sheets pinned on the inside so that the audience couldn't see through. We all had to take turns as curtain pullers.

The day of the program we'd push all our desks out of the schoolroom into the boys and girls cloakrooms, and carry up benches from the basement and somebody's dad would bring in a load of folding chairs from the Legion Hall in Hartford, and we'd set them up in rows for the audience to sit in.

The program is held at night, so that everyone's parents and family can come, and because it is such an important event, the teacher dismisses school at noon so we can all go home and rest. You'd have to take a bath, which for us meant taking the wash pan full of hot water and your soap and towel upstairs where you'd stand in front of the heat register to keep warm while you washed yourself part by part until you were clean all over. Then you'd lay out your Christmas dress to see if it needed ironing and you'd check your church shoes to see if they needed to be polished. Each winter I would get a new dress for Christmas; I would wear it at the school program and the church program, and

I would wear it on Christmas Eve which was dinner at my grandpa's house in Hartford and Christmas Eve service at Benton Lutheran Church, and then it would be my church dress for the rest of the winter. That year, when I was in first grade, my dress was a jumper and white blouse with a Peter Pan collar. My jumper was dark blue corduroy with suspenders over my shoulders and a band across the front and back; and stitched on the band in front there were little dancing Swiss-looking boys and girls in red and yellow. After we'd gotten dressed, we'd bundle up in our coats and boots and snow pants and head for the schoolhouse.

There's a lot of hustle and bustle when we arrive, but then we gather back stage and when the teacher can tell everybody is there, she quiets us down and then lines us up on the stage; somebody opens the curtain, and the program begins. Once it began, you'd look out into that room you saw every day, and it looked like a place you'd never seen before. We never were at school at night, so to look out and see the lights on, and darkness behind all the windows, that was really different. And the schoolhouse would be full of people. I'd see people I didn't even know. All the benches and chairs would be filled, and in the back and down the hall, people standing up. I'd look out, while I was singing as loud as I could, to see where my mom and dad were sitting, and to see if they were looking at me. They were.

After the program is the time for fun. We'd all be relieved to have made it through without forgetting our lines or falling off the stage. One year, when we had a Thanksgiving program, not a Christmas program, one girl—Doris Byg—did fall off the stage. But that wasn't the worst. We were all dressed up like Indians wearing pants and shirts made out of gunny sacks, and we were supposed to be doing an Indian dance. While she was dancing around the stage just like the rest of us, her pants fell down. But after the program, if you had done something bad you could forget it, and if you got through without any problem, you could just be relieved it was over and be glad to hear your parents

51

tell you what a good job you'd done. So we were in the mood to have a good time.

First there's the drawing for the raffle, and it's always exciting to see if somebody you sold a ticket to has won. Then we usually have a cake walk. All of our mothers would have donated cakes for the prizes. We do the cake walk up on stage, after we've cleared it out a little bit, and set chairs in back-to-back rows, one less than the number of people who had bought tickets. When we have that all ready, Velma Brown plays the piano, and we circle round and round, pushing each other out of the way to get a chair when the music stops. If you're left standing, you're out, and another chair gets taken away, and around we go again until finally there is just one person left, and that would be the winner who gets a cake. We'd go on and on all through the evening until all the cakes were gone.

Sometime during the evening, we gather around the Christmas tree set up in the school room and exchange gifts. Weeks before the program we'd all have drawn a name of some other person, and got him or her a gift, and then we'd all have a little something for the teacher, some perfume, like "Evening in Paris" or a box of hankies or maybe stationery. She'd have presents for us too. And then of course there were the gifts we'd made for our parents. What I had done to make a present was to press my hand in something the teacher called Plaster of Paris. After a while it got hard, and I painted my hand white and all the space around it blue and put a string on the back so my parents could hang it up.

After all this is done, we always have something to eat down in the school basement. At the foot of basement stairs is long, oilcloth covered table, set up just for tonight. We line up and walk down the length of the table and mothers dish things up on our plates. Early on the day of the program, some mothers would have come to school to begin cooking barbeque on the old, wood-burning cookstove. All the time we were at school we'd smell it cooking. Then some of the mothers would come to the program a little bit early, and get the coffee pots started and the cocoa, so they'd be ready right after the program. They made the coffee and cocoa in great big speckled pots. Those pots of coffee and cocoa sat there on the hot cookstove along with the big pans of barbeque, and all during the program that good warm smell came right upstairs making you hungry for something to eat. We'd stand in line to pick up our sandwich and some potato chips and Jell-O and pickle and maybe a piece of cake, and cup of cocoa, and then we'd try to find a place to sit down and eat before we spilled it.

Finally, we get back into our coats and boots, holding tight to all our presents, and we go out into the star-filled night so cold it could crack. With our breaths we can make feather plumes, or pretend we were smoking cigarettes; then we snuggle together in the cold car, and drive down the gravel road home.

Once the programs were over, we could get serious thinking about Christmas and Santa Claus. Santa Claus came on Christmas morning when I was little, but Christmas Eve was a big celebration too. Then—at least when I was little, it changed later—we'd go into Hartford and have Christmas Eve with Aunt Emma and Uncle Earl and Grandpa and Uncle Norton. Aunt Emma would fix all the foods that Swedes—and that's what my family is—like to eat at holidays, like lutefisk. All the grown-ups liked lutefisk except my mother; she didn't like it all that much, but she would eat it. My brother liked it, and I never could tell about my sisters. I didn't like it, but I had to take a little bit. I'd cover it with gravy and mashed potatoes and hope that when I took a mouthful, I wouldn't be able to tell what I was eating. That's what I would hope, but there was no use pretending that you didn't know what was in your mouth when you felt that slippery fish in there while you were chewing. I'd eat it first to get it out of the way and enjoy the rest of the meal.

Everything else was good. There was a lot of mashed potatoes, and the gravy was creamy and sweet tasting. Sometimes there were Swedish meatballs, which almost made up for having to eat the lutefisk. There were good vegetables my aunt had put up during the summer, like green beans, or corn. She'd serve us Swedish tea ring with our dinner, and her watermelon and beet pickles and her homemade apple jelly. For dessert we might have mince pie, with whipped cream or maybe we'd have a cake, a Silver White Cake, which Aunt Emma made from my grandma's recipe and there'd always be a plate of spritz cookies too.

There were ten of us around the table, and the table looked really nice with its white cloth and all the dishes you'd only use on holidays. There were little glass dishes and little forks that you wouldn't see every day. Most of them had been my grandma's and Aunt Emma liked to use them. There were always lots of dishes to wash after a meal like that. My sisters and I would help carry things from the dining room back into the kitchen and my mother would help Aunt Emma with the dishes. The men would sit in the front room and rest.

One thing I didn't like about Christmas Eve was trying to stay awake for church. I was supposed to take a nap after supper because we wouldn't leave for church until nearly midnight. They would tell me to go lie down on the couch in Grandpa's sitting room; it was red plush and had one regular arm and one arm that be put down, so it was plenty long enough. But I knew that if I fell asleep it would be worse when I woke up and would have to crawl out of that warm cozy spot and get into a cold car, so I tried to stay off the couch, or at least stay awake. But before I knew it, somebody would be shaking me, and saying, Time to go to church.

That was a cold ride. And it was a long ride. It's nearly ten miles from Aunt Emma's house in Hartford to our church. There are closer Lutheran churches, but this is the one our family has always gone to. When we got there, it was strange, like it was strange at the school program, being there at night when you're used to being there during the day. It made you realize that Christmas Eve is different from any other time, and when you came out from church, then it was Christmas morning. Everyone would say, Merry Christmas, and then we'd go home to bed.

On Christmas morning my mother had to get up early and get the turkey in the oven. That always made her nervous, I guess because it was so big. I'd hear her, and start smelling things, and then before long we'd all wake up and go downstairs and see what Santa Claus had brought. The year I was six I got a doll with a plaster head and a blue dress who cried "Mama" when you turned her upside down. I named her Betty Ann. And I got another sort of doll too, with stuffed arms and legs—they looked like she was in a red snowsuit—and a blue checked silky front and a one little blonde curl of real hair on her forehead. My brother got a basketball, and my sister Edna Mary got a camera with a flash attachment so she took a lot of pictures. Marjorie got a jackknife and some games.

After we opened our presents, it was nearly time for Christmas dinner in our own house, and we'd have turkey and dressing and all the same sorts of potatoes and vegetables and pickles and dessert and so on just like on Christmas Eve, only not so many fancy dishes and silverware. Then we'd have a lazy day, after dishes were done, and after Christmas we'd still have school holiday through New Years, to play outside and sleep late.

This is what Christmas was like when I was little, and still believed in Santa Claus. One year I was looking through my mother's dresser, just for fun, to see what was there, and I saw a box of comic books. I thought that was funny, I never knew my mother read comic books, but then I forgot about it, until Christmas morning when there was that same box of comic books, and it said on it: to Mabel Ann from Santa Claus. And I realized that Santa Claus's handwriting and my mother's were just the same. After that, we had our presents on Christmas Eve, after our Christmas Eve dinner and before we went to church, which made a lot more sense, and made things easier for my mother on Christmas morning too. By that time, we'd stopped going into Hartford to have Christmas all together. By then my dad and Grandpa and Uncle Norton had had their falling out, and we had Christmas at our house, with maybe Aunt Emma and Uncle Earl coming out. One thing is true, things change as you get older.

Spring

My father always says that his favorite season is spring. I guess that's because he's a farmer and he's excited about getting out there and planting things. I don't feel the same way because there is so much mud in spring, and even though winter is supposed to be over you can still get tricked when there is a storm that comes late. By spring, even though I like school, it seems as if it's been going on awfully long. I guess that why they plan so many different trips and events, because we're all getting pretty bored with the same old thing. At our school at the end of winter, when it is just barely getting to be spring, we take our trip to the circus, and then later we have Tour Day, and County Chorus; and by then it is almost summer, and nearly time for school to be out.

Every year the Shrine Circus comes to Sioux Falls, and every year all of us in our school get free tickets from the Masons in Hartford. The circus is held in the gymnasium that's part of the Sioux Falls Coliseum. If you were there to see a basketball game, you'd see the basketball court, but when the circus comes to town, they cover the floor with tarps and set up three big rings. We sit on bleachers up the sides, sometimes really high up, and hang on tight to the money we've brought along to buy cotton candy, so it doesn't fall out of our pockets onto the floor below.

First there's a sort of parade, with all the performers coming in and walking around the entire floor so we can get a good look before the performance begins. There are elephants, each one hanging on with his trunk to tail of the elephant in front of him, and riding the elephants are beautiful ladies with feathers attached to their heads that sway back and forth just like the elephant do. And there are trapeze artists who walk together in a group, all wearing the same color costumes, smiling and waving at us as they walk around. And of course there are all kinds of clowns doing cartwheels and riding in silly machines. Then they get busy with their acts. You might have the cage with the lions and tigers in front you, with that lion tamer walking around so fast and quick and snapping his whip. The lions stretch their heads over to one side and growl and show all their teeth; they don't look very tame when they do that, they look pretty fierce. When the lion tamer cracks his whip and makes them jump from platform to platform, or roll over on their backs, they do what they're supposed to, but they don't look like they enjoy it. They look like they'd rather swat him with one of their great big paws. But the scariest act is the trapeze artists. Every time one of them swings from one person to another, or from one trapeze bar to another, you hope they won't crash down to their death right in front of your eyes. My friend Celia Byg—when I was in the second grade, she was in the first—her grandmother, Mrs. Miller, had once been at a circus where the trapeze artist really did fall and was killed, and Mrs. Miller hadn't wanted to go to the circus again from that day to this, and when Celia told me that story, I could see why.

When you see all those circus performers, you can't help but wonder what their life is like, doing their exciting work and going from place to place. I've seen *The Greatest Show on Earth* and if this circus is anything like that, I know that there is probably a lot going on behind the scenes. Like that glamorous lady elephant trainer, in her purple-colored, glittering costume, with the feathers in her hair—you wonder if maybe she is in love with acrobat who can walk on his hands, and if the lady trapeze artist is jealous.

Since it is a Shrine Circus, there are men walking up and down the aisles, selling things, wearing those funny little maroon hats with tassels and a shiny design. Once I saw Cecil Byg—he's Celia's dad—walking up and down selling programs. When we are back at school, after the circus, we get the names of all the Masons in Hartford who had given us the tickets, and each of us has to write one of them a letter and thank him for our free ticket and tell him what a good time we had and tell him which of the acts we liked the best. One year I sent my thank-you letter to my Uncle Norton.

Tour Day is fun in a different way from the circus. Tour Day is when we spend the whole day going to different places in Sioux Falls and take a tour at each place we go to.

A place we go to nearly every year is John Morrell and Co., a meat packing plant. John Morrell is a very big business, and lots of people in Sioux Falls and Hartford too work there. It's a different life, working in a factory and getting a paycheck every two weeks no matter what, a lot different than being a farmer and working hard and maybe getting a good crop and maybe not. This is what my mom and dad say, anyway. They say working in a factory gives you different ideas. Whenever a Democrat gets elected, which isn't very often, my dad always blames the labor union workers at John Morrell and says they didn't know what they were doing.

Anyway, it was exciting to tour John Morrell because we'd always wonder if we looked through the wrong door if we'd see them actually killing the cows or pigs. Some girls would say, If we see that I'll faint; some boys would like to show off, and they'd say that they'd like to see it, that they'd seen animals killed before, that there was nothing to it, and maybe when they grew up they'd work at Morrell's and kill steers themselves. There was another thing to think about too. It always smelled bad there. Would it smell so bad that we would faint or throw up? Nobody ever did; in fact when the man who was giving us the tour gave everybody a raw wiener, each one of us ate it right up.

We go to lots of other interesting places on our school trips. Once we went to Terrace Park Dairy, where they bottle milk, but where they also make Nordica Brand Cottage Cheese and ice cream. One year we went to Old Home Bakery, where we saw a machine that could squeeze out thousands of squirts of bread dough, bread-loaf size, each into its own pan. When we went to the Sioux Falls *Argus Leader*, we saw teletype machines bringing in news from all over the world, right while we were standing there watching.

One of the most interesting places we go on Tour Day is the Pettigrew Museum. Once there was a man called Mr. Pettigrew, and when he died he gave his house to the city of Sioux Falls for a museum and along with it a lot of things that he had collected during his life, especially all sorts of things that had to do with Indians.

I remember going there for Tour Day when I was in the first grade. When all the cars that had been driving us around to our tours had parked, and we all climbed out, we gathered on the street corner in front of the museum. There on the corner right in front of the house was a great big stone, almost a boulder, set into the ground and surrounded by an iron picket fence. Someone said, That's Plymouth Rock—and being only six, I believed it. Now I know better.

We went in, and almost right away we saw the most interesting thing in the house: a real Indian teepee. It sat right in the center of the main room, and you could go under the flap doorway and look at the things inside, and then you could climb the steps up to the balcony that went in a circle all around the teepee and take a good look at the outside. It was really tall, higher than the ceiling of the main floor.

There were things inside the teepee that might have been there if real Indians lived in it, beds, and bowls, and piles of fur, and a fake fire in the middle. But the thing that caught everybody's attention, and something that wouldn't have been there, was a skeleton. That was scary. There he sat with that hollow-eyed, grinning skull grin. We stood there with nothing to say. Until one boy, from another group that was part of the same tour as our school, said, I bet that skeleton dreams tonight.

I believed that too, like I believed I'd just seen Plymouth Rock.

When Tour Day is over, we've all have had some treats: a wiener, as I said before, or—what was a lot better—some ice cream at Terrace Park Dairy, or a doughnut from the Old Home Bread factory. And we all come home with our hands full of packets from every place we've been, with pictures and brochures and so on. We carry all those papers home, and save them carefully, until we realize we're not ever going to look them again, and anyway, we'll be getting another whole stack next spring, when we take some more tours.

By the time County Chorus comes along it is usually warm enough so that you won't need a coat, and it's sometimes warm enough so that you can wear your Easter dress. If it's too cold for that, you wear whatever Sunday dress you have, because you always want to look nice on that day.

County Chorus takes place on Saturday, and when I was in the first grade it was held at the YMCA, down on Main Avenue in Sioux Falls, later it was moved to the South Soo School over on the far side of town. County Chorus is when all the rural schools like ours in Minnehaha County get together for a big musical event.

How it works is that certain songs are chosen for each grade level, then, nearly all year long, we'd practice these songs in our own school. It was almost as much work as the Christmas program. Even though the songs were assigned by grade level, in our school each of us would pretty much learn all the songs because there weren't enough people in any one grade to sing by themselves. Especially that was true for me. But the idea is that when we all join together at the County Chorus, we'll divide up into age groups, practice our particular songs all morning, and then have a concert of all the songs in the afternoon.

At that first County Chorus, I had to go all by myself with all the other first graders from the other schools in the county, and everybody else from my school went to their own groups, including Marjorie who went to where the sixth graders were. First, though, she took me to the room I had to be in, and when she left, she told me she would come and get me when it was time for noon lunch. I stayed with my group and practiced, and then when it was over, I stood by the door, waiting for her to come. I waited and I waited, and got more and more scared, thinking she'd forgotten me, and knowing that I didn't know how to find my way around in that huge building to go look for her. Finally she came along, not even thinking she was late, and then when I saw

61

her, I got over being so scared. We went to a special room to eat lunch, and had chocolate milk along with our food, which didn't happen every day, and I decided this wasn't so bad after all. Later on, in other years, I wasn't so scared about everything and could take care of myself better. Then I really liked County Chorus and didn't worry at all about being lost.

One thing that happens every spring—even on the same day every spring—I haven't been able to do because I'm not old enough; it's just for high school kids like Edna Mary and Curtis. That is Egg Singing. That's kind of a funny name, but that is just exactly what it is.

On April 30, and that is a date I can remember because it is my brother's birthday, on that night young people gather at our church; they get in cars, and all night long they go to the houses of all the people who are members of the congregation, and they sing a long song with lots of verses. The song is in Swedish, and it is about saying that May is welcome, that's the second line in every verse, only in Swedish. The last line in every verse says Summer is so lovely for us young ones. The song starts with a verse that says Good Evening, here we are coming into your yard, and then the next verses go on to talk about how nice spring is, with little birds singing, and with hens laying nice big eggs for pancakes or omelets. Then after about five verses, the song asks for money or eggs. It ends up with their saying Thank you, thank you— "Tack och tack" in Swedish—and Good-by until next year. Then they get back into their cars and drive off to another farm. That's only if they got some eggs or money; if no one comes to the door, they'll keep singing until somebody does come and give them something.

Nobody really minds being wakened up in the middle of the night by the Egg Singers, though, because most of the people they come to, like my dad for instance, did the same thing when they were young, and I guess some people, like our neighbor Augusta Johnson, had gone Egg Singing in Sweden back in the days when she was a young girl there, and so everybody is expecting it. What I like is waking up, and hearing people laughing and rustling around down by our door, then as I get more awake, I start hearing the song. By that time my parents will have turned on the yard light, and be up too. Then I hop out of bed, and look out the window, and see if I can spot Edna Mary or Curtis, or if I can recognize anybody else.

After they finish, they drive away, and I go back to sleep, but I know Edna Mary and Curtis won't be home until it's daylight. After they've finished the Egg Singing, they all go back to church and eat breakfast—I guess they eat eggs—and count their money.

And the next day is the first of May.

SUMMER

On the first Sunday after the last day of school, we have the school picnic, and when that happens, you knew that summer has finally arrived.

During the last week of school, everything winds down. All the school trips are over, and you've come to the end of all your schoolbooks—you've finished all the stories in your reading book and done all the problems in your arithmetic workbook. Then we have the last set of six weeks tests and pass all our books back into the teacher for next year's class to use. Then we give the schoolhouse a really good cleaning, putting everything back into place for the next fall, and we empty out our desks. On the last day of school, you have a lot to carry home—all the school supplies you hadn't used up, all your old papers and art projects. We all say, See you Sunday, at the picnic. And even people who have been mad at each other wave back and forth as we go in different directions down the road.

Everybody comes to the school picnic. Of course, the teacher and the students come, and all the parents, and the brothers and sisters, but also the grandmas and grandpas. Even neighbors whose children might have already graduated from Johnson School want to come, just for the fun.

There is always lots of food—three, four, picnic tables full. When we are called to come and eat, here is what we'd see: pan after pan of fried chicken, in navy blue and white speckled enamel roasters, enough fried chicken so that everybody who wants to can have a drum stick; then there are meat loaves, some with a catsup barbecue sauce on the top; pans of barbeque and buns for sandwiches; and plates of sandwiches already made up—bologna and ham and egg salad. Hot dishes too—tuna hot dish, hamburger and macaroni and tomato hot dish. And there are big bowls of potato salads and big pans of pork and beans, plates of carrot sticks and celery sticks, and bowls of cut up cantaloupe or watermelon. A plate or two of deviled eggs. Then there are big plastic bowls of fruit salad made with marshmallows and whipping cream, and salads made with little shell or ring macaroni, and all kinds of Jello salads, red and green and orange. And then there is a section of the table with only desserts: all kinds of different pies and cakes—rhubarb pie, raisin pie, lots of cherry pies, custard pie, of course lemon meringue pie, banana cream and chocolate cream pies. And cakes: chocolate cakes with glossy brown frosting and walnuts scattered over the top; sometimes a spice cake with a brown sugar frosting, or a German chocolate cake with a coconut and nut frosting. Ice cream comes packed in brown cardboard containers with dry ice to keep it frozen, each square wrapped in a little piece of paper and as hard as a rock.

When we have all run in from the swings and slides and found our baskets and gotten our own plates and silverware, we are ready to eat. Then Leroy Andreson—he is President of the School Board—asks somebody like Roy Brown to pray. We all bow our heads and shut our eyes, and he prays out loud, or else we sing, Be present at our table, Lord, be here and everywhere adored. Thy mercies bless and grant that we may strengthened for Thy service be. Amen. Roy Brown has a good voice, he's a tenor in the Methodist church choir. Then we line up on either side of the picnic tables covered with food and work our way down, loading up our plates as we walk.

After we eat and eat until we are full, we run to play some more on the swings and slides. Then it is time for the most important part of the day: getting our report card. Just before it's time to go home we all gather around the teacher, and she passes them out. On one side there are the columns where all year long our six-weeks grades have been filled in, and now we have the last column filled in with our last set of grades. But it is the other side we all look at first, because there is a line on the other side that says, I do/ do not recommend that this student be passed on to Grade_____. That's what tells us if we've passed. When we see that next year we will be in a new grade, it is time to go home. Our mom gets our basket, and we tell the teacher good-by and say to our friends, Good-by, see you in the fall. And we go home to start enjoying our vacation.

After the school picnic is over, it's nice to think we don't have to get up early on Monday morning for school, and that there are three whole months ahead of us for having fun.

Summer was the time for playing. Oh, we had some work we had to do, chores and things, and my mother was always telling us to clean up our room, and then too when my sisters and brothers got older, they had to do more farm work, and then one year Edna Mary got a job in Sioux Falls, and she was gone all week long. But for me, when I was little, mostly all I had to do was play, and what made it even better is that back then, I had people to play with too.

I think the worst thing that ever happened when we were playing happened to my sister Marjorie. We were playing with Marian Artz and Bonnie Artz who were daughters of our hired man. We were down the hill by the steer shed and swinging on ropes that hung down from the silo, which was something we did all the time. The steer yard fence was wooden, and it ran from the pig house over to the silo, and then there was a feed bunk that stuck out from the side of the silo. What we'd do is this: you'd would pull one of

66

the ropes from the silo up over your shoulder, climb up on the fence and stand there balancing on the top rail, then you'd take hold of the rope, and, with all your might, push off from the fence. As you swung out from the fence, you'd wrap your feet and legs around the rope, and if all went well you'd swing out and land in the feed bunk. If you didn't push off hard enough you might not get to the feed bunk, and you'd just be there dangling. Then the rest of us would have to try to grab the rope and pull you in or you'd fall off and land in the steer yard and that was full of manure. But if you pushed off really hard, and sailed through the air far enough, it felt great, flying through the air like a trapeze artist in the circus.

One day Marjorie got the idea that if it was fun, flying in the air from the fence to the feed bunk, a longer ride would be even better. So she said, What if I climb up on the pig house roof and jump from there? That seemed like a good idea to everybody. For one thing, when you pushed off from the fence, you sometimes not only didn't make it to the feed bunk, sometimes you hit the silo if you didn't swing out far enough. If you swung off the pig house roof it would be a straight shoot to the feed bunk, no danger of hitting the silo. Another thing, if you ran down the roof, you'd get a really good start, much better than just pushing off from the fence, and think of how fast you'd go.

So we all said, Great, give it a try it. And so she did. She took the rope over her shoulder, climbed the fence by the edge of the pig house, climbed up on to the pig house roof. She climbed up the slanted roof nearly to the ridge, then she gathered the rope up to her chest and wrapped her arms around it, and she braced herself to push off in a running jump. And she jumped.

What none of us had thought of was how very long the rope would be. She flew off the roof with better speed than we'd ever seen, and more force too. Then she landed. Not in the feed bunk, like we'd thought, but face down in the steer yard. We were all so shocked, we just sat on the fence and looked at her, spread-eagled in the dirt. One thing was true, it looked like it had been a good ride, up until it ended. When she could breathe again, she got up. We climbed down off the fence, and decided to try something else.

When we wanted to think up something to play, we didn't just sit around and argue, we had a system. Whoever thought of it first would shout: Let's suggest! and then right away shout, Last! What this meant was we all had to come up with some idea that we'd suggest to play, and give everybody else our suggestions, first to last. So as soon as someone yelled, Last, right away someone else would say, Second to last, then, somebody would say, Third to last. Then, finally, of course, someone would have to be First. What was bad about being first is that you didn't have much time to think up a good suggestion, and almost never would anyone else agree to what you wanted to do, and what was good about being last is that it was a pretty sure thing that we'd do what was the last suggestion. It seems to me that it was almost always Marjorie or Marian Artz who was Last, and almost never Bonnie Artz or me. Marian was Marjorie's age, and Bonnie was three years older than me.

Lots of times in the summer, what somebody suggested was that we work on our plays. We worked on quite a few plays, but we only performed two, and both of those were on the same night, "The Courtship of Miles Standish" and "Goldilocks." We spent a lot of time rehearsing "The Life of Jesus" but we never got a chance to perform it, which was a shame.

One reason it would have been such a good play to put on is that we not only could have all played some interesting parts, but we could have made a lot of the scenes very life-like by using Seabiscuit, our pony. He would have been a good addition to the Nativity scene, and it would have been perfect to have him for the Flight into Egypt and of course for Palm Sunday there is Jesus riding on an ass, and a Shetland pony would be fine for that. We could have even done a parable, like the story of the Good Samaritan who found that man by the side of the road, when he came along, he was riding on a donkey.

Well, we all got excited about these good ideas, but then we started to have arguments. First of all, we had arguments about dividing up the parts. We couldn't all be Jesus. But then we got the idea that after all, we could. What we would do for our play would be to show him at different times in his life, that way having him be different shapes and sizes and even looking different would make sense. I was going to be Jesus in the Temple, Confounding the Elders. There was a picture of Jesus doing that in our Sunday School auditorium, and so I knew just how he looked, standing there, with his arm over a big book, which I suppose must have been the Bible, with one of his fingers pointing to something on the page.

I liked my part, but not everybody was so happy. What caused the problem that brought everything to an end was how we were going to do the story of Jesus Curing the Blind Man. Marjorie seemed to be pretty much running things, that is, about who was going to play what part. So, in this story—and this is the story where Jesus leans over, spits in the dirt, makes a mud pack, and puts it on the Blind Man's eyes—I don't know who Jesus was going to be but Marjorie said Bonnie Artz should be the blind man.

So she said, I won't, we're in the barn, and I don't want that dirty mud in my eyes, and Marjorie said, If you want to be in the play, you'd got to. And each said that same thing to each other over and over again until finally we got sick and tired of hearing them argue and decided to let forget the whole thing.

We had better results with our other plays, we actually put them both on, in front of a real audience. We performed in our granary which was empty because we hadn't combined the oats yet. It was nice and cool to practice in there out of the sun. It had a wooden floor, where we could bring in chairs for the audience, and we could even hang up a curtain by nailing up a string that ran from one wall to the other.

Marjorie had read this poem about Miles Standish and John Alden and Priscilla in school and decided to turn it into a play. It was the summer before I entered the first grade, I was five going on six, and I couldn't read yet. But we all had a part. I was Priscilla, Marjorie was John Alden, Marian was Miles Standish, Bonnie was the White Bull that Priscilla rode into town on her

69

wedding day and she was also going to be the narrator to fill in all the parts you need to know and don't get just through the conversation. It wasn't exciting, being the narrator, I guess Bonnie almost never got the good parts, but it certainly was an important role because without it nobody would know what was going on. When she complained that's what we told her, and besides, she didn't have to memorize any lines like the rest of us did. She complained about being the White Bull too, but we decided she didn't have to do that during the rehearsal, only the night of the play, and I wasn't so big that she couldn't carry me at least a little ways, walking on her hands and knees.

Bonnie didn't have to memorize her lines because she was just going to read

them. But I didn't know what to do. I couldn't read, how was I going to memorize my lines? My sister would say them over and over, and I would try to say them back. The only line I really learned was, "Why don't you speak for yourself, John?" Another line, this one I never could figure out, was when Priscilla is saying, "The hedgerows are green in England now." Well, I had never seen a hedgerow or knew what one was, let alone knowing why anyone would care if it was green. And when Marjorie read me that line to memorize, she would say, "The hed-ga-rows." I'll bet she didn't know what a hedgerow was either. It's hard to memorize something if it doesn't make any sense, and I got fed up.

Finally one day I was so mad and fed up I just shouted at her, I can't learn it, and I won't! The next thing I knew I was flat on my back, smashed down in the gravely barnyard, with Marjorie sitting on my stomach holding a hammer over my head, saying loudly, You *are* going to learn those lines. I thought she was going to kill me, but she didn't, she let me up, which was a mistake on her part, because right away I ran straight inside the house and told my mother on her, I said that Marjorie was going to kill me. My mother said, No, I don't think so, why don't you just sit down in here awhile and eat some graham crackers. So I sat down and had graham crackers and milk, and thought, They can practice all they want in that hot granary, I'm through.

But later on, I guess I got the main parts in my mind, anyway Marjorie let up on me, and everything went along fine. The other play we were going to put on made up to both Bonnie Artz and me for our problems with "The Courtship of Miles Standish." Bonnie had pretty blonde curls so naturally it made sense for her to be Goldilocks, and I was happy to be Baby Bear, because I knew I wouldn't have any trouble with those lines.

Finally the time came along for our performance, in front of our mom and dad and Edna Mary and Curtis and the Artzes. We were all ready, and after the chores had been done, and the dishes were done, everybody came to the granary to sit down and see our plays. Then the trouble started. It had gotten so dark by then that Bonnie the narrator couldn't see to read her lines. Of course, we'd never thought about that since we'd only practiced in the daytime. There was no electricity in the granary to turn on a light to see by, and I guess we didn't think to go get a flashlight. So Bonnie had to go to the granary door and lean out as far as possible to catch the little daylight that was left to try and read her part. But then, of course, she was so far away from the audience, and leaning in the opposite direction, so nobody could hear her, including us, but we all did the best we could, and the audience clapped when it was over. By the time we got to "Goldilocks" it was dark as night in the granary, but luckily everybody knew the story, and another good thing, it was short.

There were all kinds of other things we'd play too, sometimes together, sometimes I'd play by myself. I'd pretend I was an Indian, and build teepees and make bows and arrows, and sometimes I'd play with my dog and pretend I was a dog too, or even a horse, if I'd been reading about horses. Sometimes I played with dolls, we used to take them apart and see how the cryer worked. Once I had a doll I really liked, an Indian doll my dad brought me from the Black Hills. I was playing with it out in the steer yard, and when I got called for supper I went in and forgot about my doll until the next morning and then it was nowhere to be seen. I guess the cows ate it. Sometimes we'd go down in the pasture and go swimming in the creek, sometimes we'd get to go into Hartford and go swimming in the pool.

At nighttime we'd be tired after all that playing. We'd have to wash off our dirty feet before we got into bed. We'd lie there, Marjorie and I, and sometimes we'd have one last thing to play: Let's Pretend. When one of us would say that, we knew what to do. We had a story that we'd made up, each one of us was a character. We were two girls, Vassie and Harriet. They were grownup girls, who dressed up in nice clothes and went out on dates. I was Vassie and Marjorie was Harriet. I was adopted into Harriet's family, not a real member, but that was all right, because my boyfriend was her brother Jim. What we'd do when we played Let's Pretend, is that each of us would tell the other one what had happened that day in the life of Vassie or the life of Harriet. Each of them had exciting adventures, but I guess not exciting enough, because before the second story got told, we'd be asleep.

Of course, not everything that happens in the summer is nice, I learned that last year.

For one thing, Edna Mary went away to work at a job for a family in Sioux Falls, and then we weren't all together anymore. She'd only come home on the weekends. But the other thing is what happened to my father.

Nobody told me what was going on, the first thing I knew my dad was in the hospital, and everyone acted like they were worried sick. We would spend all day in the hospital waiting room, on those plastic sofas, and then go in to visit him for a little bit. Luckily my sister Edna Mary bought me three books, one was two books in one, on one side it said, "Just Like Daddy," and then when you turned it over and upside down it said, "Just Like Mommy." On the Daddy side you read about a little dark haired boy sawing wood and things like that, and on the Mommy side there was a little girl with blonde hair sweeping the floor, and smiling, as if anybody with any sense liked to sweep a floor. I'd read the Daddy side over and over again. The second book was called "Bambi's Children" and told about how hard it is to be a deer, with people always trying to shoot you. The third book was the best, it was called "The Little Mailman of Bayberry Lane," and it was the story of a little chipmunk, the mailman, who has a surprise party for Mrs. Goose so she can make some new friends. All the time we sat in the hospital, I'd read those books over and over again, and when I was reading them, they made me feel good because they were such nice stories, especially the story about Bayberry Lane, where everyone was so kind, and Mrs. Goose was such a good cook, she was always making walnut cakes and lemon tarts. I didn't pay too much attention to what was going on in the waiting room, it was just my job to be quiet and keep still, and that I could do when I kept reading my books.

Then after a while we brought my dad home, with a patch over his eye. He had had to have an operation to have his eye taken out, and now he had to wear a glass eye. I thought that would be horrible, to have a doctor put an eye in and take it out. But I guess my dad got used to it, he never complained.

Something else was going on that summer too, I'd hear my mother and father talking in loud voices, and then not talking at all. But sometimes my dad would talk to himself in a loud voice in the barn, and my mom would sit on the front steps and not say anything, but I knew she didn't like what was going on, whatever it was. What I could figure out was that my dad was mad at my Uncle Norton and Grandpa; that they had done something that he thought was wrong, and he thought he was right to be mad at them. I think my mother just thought he didn't have to be as mad as he was, or didn't have to stay mad. So she was mad because he was.

All this going on was another reason I was glad I could read. My dad used to say, I'll be glad when you can read, and I won't have to read everything to you—even though he would read to me every time I asked, the comic strips and even whole books like *Black Beauty*. But now I could read by myself, and I read what books I could find in my house, and my own three books which I kept reading again and again. When I had a good book to read, I'd just go upstairs and lie down on my bed and read and stay out of it all.

Part III: Beginnings

For many of us, as we grow older, there comes a time when the questions we never asked as children come up in our minds, questions that puzzle and intrigue us. Then, when we find family photos in old pasteboard boxes in attics and storerooms, we are teased by the images of these persons, teased into imagining the thoughts, the selves, the secrets behind their faces.

There's a photograph, hanging in my house, that links for me the past and present. I never recall having seen it when I was a child; my brother found it when we were going through my aunt's boxes after her death. It is dated on the back, 1909. When I look at that photograph, I see the house where I grew up, the porch where I played, the tree that stood outside my bedroom window. The persons pictured in the photograph are all dead, some a half century dead. It is the past, gone forever in the persons whose images we see; and it is the present, the place that—though changed—still remains.

A FAMILY PORTRAIT: 1909

Here is the whole family—John, Christine, and their children—posed on the front porch of their newly completed home. It is a substantial, commodious house, sturdy, yes, but also decorated, portraying not only survival, but success and prosperity, or at least the intention to succeed and be prosperous. Look at the decorations in the pediments above windows and porch, look at the turned railings that descend from the eaves that surround the porch; notice the gingerbread wooden carvings that embellish the porch pillars. Although the photograph does not show this, the large west window is topped by a panel of stained glass: loops of gold, and droplets of crimson; and embedded in the glass pane of the porch door, rectangles of blue, of moss green, of orange.

Up and down the steps of the porch, see where the containers of flowering plants have been placed, and, around the house, small new trees planted. It is the fragility of the trees we notice, and the attitude of hopefulness they convey: hope of withstanding the long hours of withering summer heat and the years of implacable prairie winters. One is so newly planted the tag still dangles from its branch. Behind the house, to the north, the cottonwoods reach up, trees that will continue to tower around the house for decades, a century of rustling their musical silvery leaves in the winds' subdued moods, of lashing their branches across the sky during storms, of wafting through the blue summer sky the fluffs of cotton that sometimes look like flakes of snow, they are so silent and thick-falling.

Look at the couple who built the house. How proud they must be!

Let us first look at Christine. She seems to be half-sitting on the porch railing, with her back against the supporting pillar. Decorously, tastefully dressed: dark skirt, white shirtwaist with puffy sleeves and its blousy front decorated with what seems to be innumerable little tucks. Tucks pressed smooth with a flat iron, ironed with special care for this portrait. The image reminds me of my aunt—Christine's daughter—recalling her mother's pride in her skills.

Mr. Carpenter, he used to say, It is Christine I want to iron my shirts; no one can iron a man's nice shirt as well as Christine.

How small her waist is! Cinched with a black belt, it draws the eye, which then traces the curve of her hip as she rests her weight on the railing; or, moving upward, traces the curve of her matronly breasts, discreetly draped by the folds of the white shirtwaist. The shirtwaist rises to her throat, where a band of black—a ribbon? a detachable collar? —completes the tasteful ensemble.

She is not standing erect, but even so her image gives a impression of height, and though she is slim, her shoulders are broad and strong-looking. Her hair—always described as auburn—looks dark in the photograph. Although she has parted her hair in the center and pulled it back with some severity, there is still a softness, and indistinctness to its outlines. One wisp has escaped its bounds and angles across her forehead.

79

Her expression is intriguing because it tells us so little. Her eyes look out, directly at the camera. They are straightforward, but grave. Her cheekbones and her jaw are broad, her nose is straight. She is not smiling. Her mouth is full-lipped, and closed. It conveys restraint, rectitude. It is hard to imagine that mouth quickly smiling, or impishly bending itself to gossip or flirtation or time-wasting nonsense. In a curious gesture, she has brought her hand up to her face. Is it shyness that brings her hand to her cheek, her knuckles grazing it gently? Or was she brushing back another errant thread of hair, invisible to us, but something she could feel as the summer's breeze played across her face, something she could feel and wanted, decorously, to restrain? The gesture seems self-effacing, uncertain. Although she projects an aura of strength and solemnity, the gesture hints at a tentative quality, a quality that contradicts her appearance and serves to complicate our initial impression.

Once I asked my oldest sister about the Grandmother I never knew, who seemed to be held in great esteem. Was she a remarkable person?

Yes, I suppose she was, Edna says. But I always remember her as looking kind of stern. She wasn't the sort of Grandma who was fun for little children. I don't remember her ever playing with us.

Look at her hand more closely. We see only the back of the hand and her bent fingers. How big that hand is. It seems incongruous to see such a large hand on a lady dressed with refinement, on a body shaped otherwise to slimness and grace. Was it thickened by the years of labor in other person's households, and her own, now just beginning, or do her hands show the generations of peasants and land workers who stand behind her?

My grandmother's hands were, perhaps, something she was sensitive about. I remember my mother saying: I would be working and hot and helping Grandma cook for threshers, and then when Emma came in the kitchen and started to do something, Grandma would say: Oh Emma, your hands, your hands! And I used to think: Well, what about *my* hands?

80

It is her left hand that is visible, but the photograph is too indistinct for us to see if she is wearing her wedding rings: two golden bands, one slightly wider than the other. Two bands, that through the years grow thin and delicate, rings that are passed on to daughter, to granddaughter, rings that are too precious finally to wear every day as she had done. The gold of the bands worn by Christine's own scrubbing, sweeping, kneading.

Behind Christine is John. John Benson. Perhaps the photographer from Hartford said, *Strike a pose, John. Don't look so stiff!* For if Christine looks reserved, John has a jaunty appearance: hand cocked on hip, hip slightly thrust out, one hand resting in a proprietary way on the porch railing. Yet this pose is more mysterious to me than Christine's reticence. I never saw this dapper character in my grandfather. But perhaps the visual pictures we carry in our memories are our own constructions: maybe the stiff, stern old man I picture in my mind's eye is the grandfather I have created, and not the John Benson he himself saw in the mirror, or wanted to show to the camera's eye.

An anecdote my sister repeated to me doesn't fit the grandpa I remember. She told me about an episode she'd heard from our cousin, Gene Benson. He said that once when he was a little boy, he was riding home from church in Uncle Lewis' car and Uncle Lewis and Grandpa raced all the way home.

You mean in their cars? I asked. Driving home from church on those gravel roads? Grandpa did that?

That's what Gene said. He was just a little boy when it happened. He said he was sitting in the back seat, scared to death. Can you imagine those two old men doing that?

Like Christine he is dressed very well: dark suit, waistcoat, white shirt, tie and a wing-tip collar. His hat shadows his face, and his chin is turned down, his features are indistinct. It is a dark face, a craggy face. Christine's face is open to our view, John's is not. We cannot see into his eyes; they provide no clue as to what he might be thinking. John stands behind the family group. He has bought the land, he has built the house, he has created the family. He stands there as the paterfamilias.

The three children are the focal point of the photograph. Their central position declares visually that these three are the reason for all the effort, the plans, the house: Elmer, in his little dark suit, Norton, in his. And in the center of all, primly propped is Emma.

Norton is the eldest, he is on the right. He is ten years old. Of all the characters in this scene, it is only Norton who can be seen to be really smiling. There are the shy beginnings of a smile on his sister's face, but Norton's smile opens his mouth, lifts the shape of his face. He too, like his mother looks directly at the camera, but with an expression of interest, perhaps even enjoyment. In what must have been an awkward gesture, he extends his left arm across his body, placing his hand on Emma's arm. I can imagine Christine saying: *Norton, hold your little sister's hand. There, that's right. Now just hold it there!*

He's not holding her hand, though. It appears more as if he is holding on to her arm as if she were going to run away. As he reaches across, we see that the sleeves of his suit coat are too short. We see as he grasps Emma's arm the same big hands of his mother.

Like his mother and father, he is dressed very well. Dark jacket and pants, dark stockings and leather shoes, and a broad brimmed black hat—just like a man's. His white shirt with its stiff collar is set off by a bow tie of some indistinct, light color. Like other images we see from this same time, Norton presents the appearance of a little boy in a man's clothing. A little boy, a man's work.

He seems to be enjoying this experience: a break in the monotony of work and chores, a chance to dress up, a visitor from town. He is the eldest son.

Now we look at Emma. Emma Josephine Benson. She is only four, the youngest of the three. She is indeed a darling, a picture-book child, a mother's pride and joy. Look at her clothes, made by hand, by Christine. The dress itself of some light color but white sleeves and collar emerge as contrast. The top of the dress, blousy, like her mother's, is likewise decorated with some type of needlework, and the hem of the short skirt, stiffly starched, and standing away from her body in carefully arranged folds, is edged with a broad band of lace, allowing a glimpse here and there of a stiff white petticoat   A white ribbon bow pulls her hair back from her broad forehead. Black stockings and little leather shoes, soft, with a row of tiny buttons, complete her outfit. And look at her hair, hanging in golden curls, one curl grazing her cheek and falling over her shoulder, the hair on the other side of her face falling down her back. Hair that has been washed for this portrait, then curled, then carefully combed out, parted with precision, and arranged into ringlets.

Unlike her brothers who are seated on either side of her, Emma stands. Her arms at her sides, her legs together, her little feet turned out at a forty-five-degree angle. She is an image of docility. Like her father, she has her chin held down, but unlike him her face does not appear shadowed, only shy. Her mouth begins to curve, tentatively, into a smile. She peers at us, from under her brows. She allows Norton to hold her arms, and her fingers fall in a curve like a doll's hand. Emma, placed between the two boys, she in white, they in dark clothing.

At last we come to Elmer. Elmer is eight, and of the five his expression is most alive. His mouth is not smiling but is bent into a quizzical expression, his eyes look out intently, sharply. His face seems to question: how long is this going to go on? And his hands, they are not neatly posed like Norton's but allowed to find their own position. He is leaning his elbows on his knees, his hands bend into each other loosely, naturally. Again, the same big hands of his mother's. Look at his left hand, whole and mobile, but before too long this boy's hand, caught in the machinery of a corn picker, is broken and stiffened and scarred. After that, John reverts to harvesting corn by hand, slow but safer for his boys.

Elmer is dressed like Norton, black suit, hat, black shoes and stockings, a white shirt. His bowtie is dark. Elmer does not sit erectly, like Norton. He leans forward, shoulders hunched. Unbuttoned, his coat falls open as he leans. He looks like a farm boy, dressed special for the occasion. He looks as if he would rather be doing something other than posing in his best clothes.

Why are they gathered together on this day, for this portrait? Whose idea was it? A summer's day given over to picture making rather than work would not be a casual decision. Arranging for a photographer to come the three miles out from Hartford to the farm would have involved expense, an expense—for this frugal couple—that is surely non-essential. For whom have they gone to this trouble and this expense?

Perhaps for themselves. To celebrate the completion of the house. To have a permanent record, a sort of trophy, that says: *Look, here is the proof that we have done what have intended.* Or for perhaps the picture is made for the relatives at home in Sweden: for John to send to Pernilla and Bengt, his parents, or to send to Sven, the grandfather who raised him, and stands as father in John's memory, a photograph sent to show that he too—like his brothers and his uncles—has prospered in America. *Look at my* house, the picture says, *a big, white American house. And here is my family, my two healthy sons and my pretty little daughter, and see my wife Christine, a woman any man could be proud of.* And a picture for Christine to send to her mother Johanna: *here is the house we dreamed I would have, someday in America, a big sturdy house for my children, and house that's ours, John's and mine.*

The photographer takes the picture. The photographs, matted in dark taupe arrive in the mail.

John, I can't see your face. The man should have told you to step forward.

Humph. You can tell it's me, can't you? That's enough for me.

Emma, come see your picture!

When the boys see the portrait, they jeer at each other's appearance.

Look at that silly grin.

Well, at least I'm not playing with my hands like an idiot.

Secretly, each thinks he looks just fine. Silently, each thinks Emma looks like a princess, and each is proud of his stately mama, his bold-looking papa.

It is 1909, or thereabouts, as Emma one day writes on the back of the portrait. Years from the date it was taken, sixty years, and far away from its location on the Dakota prairie, while I am traveling in Sweden, I am shown this photograph by an elderly woman named Hildur. Hildur, is Christine's niece, daughter of Christine's brother Anders. She speaks to me in Swedish:

Here is a photograph that my papa had. We think it is of his sister Christine, in America.

Yes, it is, I say. That's my father, Elmer, sitting there in front. That's our house, the house we all grew up in. My mother and father still live there.

She had a fine family, Hildur says. And it looks like a nice, big house.

85

Christine

LEAVING HOME

Christine: Like many women, the story of her life is structured by the houses in which she lived, the places she called home, and the places she made a home. The house I think of most is the farmhouse where she is pictured in the portrait. But the first house where, in my imagination, I see Christine, is a house far away from the South Dakota prairies, a house in Värmland, Sweden.

* * * * *

Christine left Sweden in 1887, never to return. She left in Värmland a mother and a brother, neither of whom ever traveled to America. At age 19 she emigrated and never saw her family again. Such separations were not unusual in those times, but Christine was different from many other immigrants in that, as a young woman, she came to America on her own, without family members.

The house from which she may have emigrated is located on the shores of Lake Vänern, a large lake in central Sweden. I remember my aunt mentioning how when her mother was a girl, she loved to ice skate. *They skated on Lake Värnern,* my aunt said. *There was a section of land nearby where she lived that jutted into the lake; they called it "the Big Nose."*

When I travelled to Sweden at age 24, I was brought to this place by Gottfried Bergius, Christine's nephew, born two decades after her departure for America. He believed this house may have been where Johanna Bergius, Christine's mother, worked and perhaps Christine with her.

Before coming to this house, we had walked through the graveyard of a near-by church.

We think this is where Johanna is buried, he says.

I gazed at an unmarked grave beside a stone wall.

We were little children when she died, he continued. Our father was already dead, and Mother was so poor then.

I had heard tales of those hard times: *Mother had sent her brother money to be used for her mother*, Emma tells me. *Her brother wrote back saying he had used the money to buy Charlotta, his wife, a sewing machine. With so many children, she had need of one. He wrote that Christina should not worry, that her mother would always have a home with them. But Mother didn't like that, and after that she never liked Charlotta very much.*

But her brother, Anders Gustaf, also died at an early age, leaving a widow with young children, as had his father before him, leaving his mother to the charity of a daughter-in-law, herself hard-pressed.

Very little has come down to her children and grandchildren from Christine's life in Sweden. We have record of her Confirmation: inside a leather-bound Bible is written: "To Kristina Bergius: Björsbyn, given to her on her first communion, 30 July 1882." A Swedish translation of an excerpt from *Pilgrim's Progress*, presumably a gift from her mother, since "Johana Anderson, Björsbyn, Långserud" is written on the flyleaf. And we have a large, wooden, gray-painted trunk with her name and her address in America painted in a fading, but still-readable script.

But having seen what may have been her house on Lake Vänern, I can imagine the young Christine, and her life on its shores.

* * * * *

It stands like a manor house, at the end of a long, graveled drive, on a broad expanse of green that slopes gradually down to the shores of Lake Vänern. On either side of the large clearing in which the house is located stand tall evergreen trees, and among them white slanted bars of the delicate birches. Behind the house glistens the water of the lake. Standing quietly, you can hear the sound of placid water, lapping the pebbled beach. Sky, forest, lake. The green grass. The sun is warm, but it is a welcome warmth, and the breeze just flutters the blue and yellow flag hanging from the pole placed in the grassy plot at the front of the house.

The house is yellow, yellow as custard, yellow as butter. Numerous outbuildings confirm the impression that this is the household of an established, prosperous family. Not an estate, perhaps, but certainly the home of gentry.

It is 1887. Christina is 19.

Johanna Bergius lives in this place as the hired woman. She has been here since the death of Knut, her husband. Knut Bergius, dead of the lung disease, leaving Johanna alone with two children, her older child, Anders, who was 14, and Christina, her daughter, only 8. Johann is grateful to the Gustafssons, the family who lives in the house, the family for whom she has worked. They allowed her to bring the two children with her, to share her whitewashed rooms under the sloping roof.

When the family first came to live at the Gustafsson's house, Christina played sometimes with the Gustafsson children. They skated together on the frozen lake, they played under the trees with dolls, they all went with the two mothers to gather lingonberries in the woods. Almost as soon as Johanna began working for them, Anders could help with the farm work, and Christina also did the small tasks Johanna was able to pass on to her. Under Johanna's careful eye, Christina wiped the good teacups. She learned how to whip eggs until they were light and airy, and the whites until they were stiff enough to hold the sugar; she learned how to sew: first, how to sew a straight seam with tiny precise stitches, and then how to make simple dresses for her dolls. She learned embroidery, white on white, and cut work that could be used for table linens or pillowcases.

But now they have grown. Anders has been gone for a few years now, working in the lumber trade. He is tall and strong, big-boned like his father. Christine is big too, strong and healthy. She has been doing a woman's work alongside her mother since she was twelve. And it is hard work: up before dawn, winter and summer, to get the fire going, to get the water heated for

91

breakfast, for washing or bathing. Making the breakfast, serving it, doing the dishes. Scrubbing the stone flags of the kitchen. Baking. Mending. Washing the clothes. In the harvest, helping cut and shock the grain. Feeding the farm animals, picking the eggs, milking the cows.

Johanna has always worked hard, but when she and Knut married, and he had his blacksmith trade, her hard work was in her own home, she was working for her own family, for her children. Now she works for them still, but she belongs to the Gustafssons. Kind as they have been, she feels the bitterness that comes from having nothing that is yours. No place you can call your own, no work that is your own. When she and Knut were young, this was not the life they dreamed of for themselves, or for their children.

Now Christna is working just like Johanna. Her red hair, held back by a kerchief, escapes in wavy lines and stocks to her sweaty forehead. She is baking the limpa bread, kneading it on the long wooden rable. She pauses, wipes her forehead with the back of her hand. Stopping a moment from her own kitchen work, Johanna looks at her. A few years ago, Christina was confirmed in the church in Långserud. Christina wore white, she had a flower given her by the Pastor. With the others she stood around the curving altar rail, painted white and gold, and confessed her faith, and received Holy Communion. This meant she weas grown-up.

Johanna still sees that scene in her mind's eye, she holds it as a memory. But what of Christina's life now? Johanna knows things she does not want to talk about with Christina, things that happen to working girls. The eldest son of the Gustafssons, he is home now from the university at Lund. She does not want him to look at Christina, to watch her. And she does not want Christina's life to be as her own has been. Johanna has known the joy of work, when it is working in your own kitchen. How can Christina ever know that, how can she ever be more than a hired girl, either for the Gustafssons or someone else? Or worse yet, be like the girls who have babies with no husband, who go away, to Karlstad, or Stockholm, and no one knows about them again. God forbid.

All around them young people are going to America. Many times people leave in groups, brothers and sisters together, young couples with their babies. These people are starting new lives but starting them together. Johanna talks to Anders. But Anders is strong and healthy, he is making a living. Why would he leave Sweden, where would he go?

There are the Olsons, he says, who have gone to America, Dakota is where they are. Their life is hard, harder than mine, I think. Besides, he says, I have met a girl. Her name is Charlotta. I don't want to leave her, and I don't think she wants to go to America.

Johanna keeps watching Christina. Her daughter is shy, but she has courage. She has learned all the ways of the house, and all the ways of a farm too. She can do fine ironing, she can make a perfect krum kakor. She can pluck geese and make downy pillows.

On a certain day in 1886, Johanna receives a letter. A month or two ago, she had asked Mrs. Gustafsson to help her write a letter and address it to a former neighbor who now lives in American with her husband. Selma and her three sisters—Augusta, Lisa, and Emli—had all grown up in the little village of Björsbyn where Johanna had lived while Knut was still alive. Augusta and Lisa were still in Sweden, but Emli went to Chicago, and Selma left for America when Ole Olson came to Björsbyn looking for a wife. Selma's mother had recently died, leaving her daughter a small inheritance. As the village shared its news back and forth, Johanna had learned of the inheritance, and also had learned that her old acquaintance sounded burdened down with children and housework. So Johanna had written to Selma Olson, Dell Rapids, Minnehaha County, Dakota, U. S. A., and now Selma has written her back.

Mrs. Gustafsson brought the letter home from the post office, she gave it to Johanna; they sat down at the kitchen table and read it together.

Dear friend Johanna, I have received your letter from Värmland. I think of you often, and I send my dearest greetings to all old friends. Not so long ago I got a letter from Sisser Lisa telling me she was healthy, I suppose you see her when you have a chance to go the Elofsbyn. Please greet Fru Gustafsson and thank her for that she went to see my mother when she was so ill. Now she is with God. I read in your letter about your daughter Christina what we talked about when I left with Ole that could maybe happen. We have been here on our new farm in Dakota now over a year, and it is a better place than Nebraska. We now have three children Wicktor, Ann, Agnes so I am busy and soon another to arrive. Thank God for good health bus somedays there is more to do than I can manage with the little ones and then the housework too. Ole has 160 acres of land here and we have had a good year. He says to tell you that we will send you money for her journey if she wants to come and work for us. Would she agree to work for four years? Maybe there will be other people coming from the neighborhood to America for her to travel with. I would be glad to have her here to have someone from my old home to talk to. It sometimes gets lonely here for a woman, it is easier maybe for a man who goes to other farmers. Now I must tell you it is cold here in Dakota, tell Christina to bring warm clothing if she comes. Now I must close, and I send greetings from Ole, and all my good wishes, Selma Olson.

Have you talked to Christina yet? Mrs. Gustafsson asks.

No, no. I wanted to know first. I was afraid to say anything unless it could be.

But if she does not want to go?

I don't know. She is young and she goes alone. But now she could go, now she has a family to go to. She won't be all by herself there. I can't go, I am too old.

Well, Johanna, go find her. I think she is outside picking eggs. Tell her about the letter. Of course it has to be up to her. She can stay here for a while, if she doesn't want to leave for America, but you know we can't keep her on much longer. It is hard times now, and she'll have to find another place before too long.

Christina reads the letter. She folds it, and returns it to the envelope. She looks at the stamp, and the postmark. How far it has come. Many people from their old village of Björsbyn and other neighboring villages have gone to America. Friends of hers have family in America, and she has seen their letters, but this is the first she or her mother has received.

Mama, she wants to say, I would be afraid to go. I think I remember Selma's husband. Didn't he have a loud voice, and didn't he drink?

She looks at her mother. Johanna is looking so strange. She looks like she is smiling and about to cry both at the same time. Christina remembers when Anders came home one day from town, and told her and her mother that someone had hired him to work with a lumbering crew up north, that he had to get his things together and leave with the other men. He was only fifteen. Johann had said, I'll go get your extra shirts and socks—and she busied herself in a corner of the little room they shared. Anders had gone down to the kitchen to drink a cup of coffee before leaving, and see the dogs one last time. Johanna was folding the shirt, with her back turned to Christina, but Christina knew from the little sounds she heard that Johanna was crying. When she turned around, Christina noticed the look on her face, her mouth holding tightly to a smile, her eyes wet. She sees this look again.

Mama, what if I go? What about you?

Oh, I'll be all right with Gustafssons for a few more hears. Then I can move in with Anders if he marries Charlotta. Maybe I'll take a boat to American and come to you.

I won't stay forever, Mama. A lot of people go to America and save their money and then come back. When you are old, we can live together, you and I.

Johanna puts her arm around Christina. They are sitting on a bench beneath a tree. Christina leans against her mother, and reaches around to touch Johanna's cheek.

I think I should go, she says.

95

Johanna talks to Mr. and Mrs. Gustafsson. They go into Karlstad and talk to the men from the steamship company. On the big lake, Lake Vänern, steamships sometimes journey through the canals, to and from Göteborg, on the coast. When the money arrives from the Olsons, they arrange for Christina's ticket. The steamship will leave Karlstad and will make a stop right at the jetty by their house. Christina will take that ship, go Göteborg, then board another steamer to Liverpool. She will change there for a steamer to New York. It is a long journey for a young woman going alone, but the steamship company has arranged for a group of emigrants to travel together to Dakota. They will be guided on their way by a man returning to America with his new wife. He will have his passage paid for acting as translator and guide to this band of newcomers. Among the group, too, will be a cousin of Mrs. Gustafsson who is going to Chicago.

Now Christina and her mother pack her things. Christina has a big wooden trunk, painted gray. On the top, incised into the wood, her name. On the side, painted in black letters: Christine Berger, Minnehaha Co., Dakota, U.S.A.

Why did you write "Christine Berger"? Christina asks the man who painted the address on her trunk.

Oh, those Americans, "Bergius" is too hard for them. You'll have a new name in America, missy. Everybody does.

Christine Berger. Who will she be? Christina thinks.

Now it is time to pack the trunk. Remembering what Selma said in her letter, Johanna makes sure all the warm shawls are included: any little frays in the wool are mended, they are washed, folded, and packed carefully. All the stockings are darned, and the underwear bleached. Aprons are there, but also one nice shirtwaist. Christina packs the Bible she had been given when she was confirmed. She packs the *Pilgrim's Progress* Johanna had read as a girl. As a parting gift, Mrs. Gustafsson gives Christina a small book of hymns with

Christina's name inscribed, also the date, and "from your Friend, Elise Gustafsson."

Be a good girl, she says. Don't forget to go to church, and remember your mama and all of us in your prayers.

I will, says Christina.

April 23, 1887.

On the morning she is to leave, the whole family comes to see her off: the Gustafssons, husband and wife, the son from Lund, and his four sisters. The farm workers carry her trunk down to the little rock jetty. A boat will be sent in from the steamship to carry Christina and her trunk way. Johanna has folded some bread and cheese and sliced rollepulse in a shite napkin. Two brown boiled eggs are also tucked inside. They are for Christina to eat on the trip to Göteborg..

Now, Christina, is your money tucked in where we put it?

Yes, mama.

And your ticket, give that to the man as soon as you get on board ship. You have your other tickets safe?

Yes, Mama.

No one knows what else to say. The silence is uncomfortable, but does not last long. The ship appears, gliding silently, a huge white shape on the blue lake. As it approaches the jetty, its horn cracks the silence: a shrieking whistle that echoes back from the evergreens. Smoke billows from the smokestack, a dinghy with two men inside is quickly launched, and they row to the jetty.

Suddenly the scene of stillness bustles. Those who seemed not to know what to say now all talk at once:

Good-by Christina! —Be sure to write and tell us about America! —God bless you, Christina—You'll be back soon with a fine handsome husband! —Don't lose your ticket! —Don't talk to strange men! —Don't lose your money! —Keep well! —Don't forget to write! —Don't forget us!

Only a brief embrace from Johanna, then Christina, the trunk beside her, is seated in the dinghy, the men row the boat away.

Johanna and all the others are waving, Johanna with one hand holding her dark shawl so that it obscures her face, the other hand waving her white handkerchief. Soon, as the dinghy gets closer to the steamship, the others turn away. Johanna stands, waving. Christina is far enough away now, Johanna can drop the shawl and weep openly.

Christina sits in the dinghy, her back to the ship she is approaching. With one hand, she grasps the wooden seat beside her, with the other she returns her mother's waves. Soon they have reached the ship. The men are polite, they help her up the ladder. Christina moves to the end of the ship, from where she can see her mother, still standing. She sees the white fluttering of mother's handkerchief. She just hears the faint call:

Good-by Christina, good-by. God Bless you!

As the ship leaves, Christina stands at the rail and watches until the scene vanishes from sight. Soon her mother's voice cannot be heard, her features cannot be seen. Soon she is only an indistinct figure of a person on the shore. Christina watches until the house, the yellow house, itself becomes small, until it is only a spot of color between the trees, and then it lost to sight.

Finally Johanna turns from the shore. Inside the house she hears chatting and laughter. She smells the coffee, and sees sthrought the open window, the white curtains fluttering out past the windowsill. She walks up the path, and back inside.

* * * * *

Christine never did return to Sweden, but she kept contact with her family and her oldl home. Christina's daughter, Emma, kept the letters her mother received. Among them are two from Anders Bergius, her brother. The first, written nearly seven years after her departure, reveals that Christine, so far away, had not forgotten her family nor their welfare.

Emilsdal, December 30, 1894

Beloved Sister!

We all wish you a Happy New Year and we all, each one of us together, also want to pray that the Lord may grant us to live also the year that now is so near its beginning that He even then may so graciously protect and keep us from harm, danger and all evil, and we have good reason to also together thank Him for his fatherly care of us during the now ending year.

We have now here been through the greatest festival of the year, Christmas, quietly, just with a visit to Church for the Christmas Day early service. It was richly lit as usual and this year also decorated with green around the altar and the pulpit, which was left after an event that is celebrated here from about two weeks before, namely the 300 year remembrance of Gustaf II Adolf.

We also have a great reason to very heartily thank you for your welcome letter our mother received eight days ago. And for the big Christmas present that was enclosed. How could we reward you for all your sacrifices for us, who never have anything to give you back, but it might interest you to know for what purposes your gift has been used and then I will first mention that Harald [Anders' son] *was given pants and a sweater from Farmor* [literally, his "father's mother," that is, his grandmother. In this case, Christine's and Anders' mother Johanna] *and Charlott* [Anders' wife] *was given a woolen shawl and that Farmor will get a length of cloth for a woolen dress. I should also mention that Harald is growing and is very good. He is now walking by himself and he will soon have his first birthday to celebrate January 2.*

Farmor also is sound and healthy. She greets you especially for your great love and thoughtfulness of her and she prays that God may bless you and reward you.

I don't have any news to tell you except that Lina in Norlgarn has a son with Carl who lives on the cape, but they are not married, which probably has to do with an illness that Carl has suffered for a long time and still is suffering. Lina's two brothers, August and Frans have returned from America. And I can mention a dreadful incident that happened here in lower Kalsater a while ago, namely that the company manager Ulman murdered himself

99

and the most gruesome part is that he fired three gunshots into his head before he died so that the whole face was shot off and he still lived for two hours after he fired the last bullet.

Our relatives are all well and I send you greetings from them. Emma in Björsbyn is gone. She is working on a small place under Stömna [a local manor, or estate].

And at last you are most heartily greeted from your Mother, brother and sister-in-law and little Harald, Sincerely, your brother A. G. Bergius.

A second letter alludes to a plan that was never realized, a poignant reminder of the longing Christine must have had to see once more her old home and her family, and their desire to see her.

Emilsdal the 13/10/ 1895

Beloved Sister,

After a long delay I want to send you a few lines again to answer the letter our mother received a while ago. We are very glad to hear that you are healthy and we are also all healthy until now.

You mention that you are planning to make a trip to the old Sweden in the fall. We think that it would be very nice if that would become reality. I think that you also would find that it would be nice to at least one more time see the old country of your childhood. I know that you think that you don't have a home to go to and that may be true but I hope that you have not yet forgotten our conditions here, but you know what the home of a worker looks like, so I think that you could bring yourself to make us a little visit. Of course it is expensive to travel such a long way just to visit but it is not at all as expensive as when you went.

Yes, now this summer is past and fall has arrived. In this area it has been a golden year. There has been a rich harvest of all kinds. We had terribly rainy weather during the time when the rye was to be harvested so that it did not turn out so very well and some oats and potatoes that were on land that lay in a south direction got destroyed but here where we live there was plenty of food in other places.

Mother tells you what she does during the days now since the work outside is over. She looks after the children and takes care of the cow and then she is wondering if she couldn't come to be nurse-maid for you soon. She thinks it would be nice to exchange places and at last she greets you very much and wishes you welcome home and we all do the same. It would be so nice to celebrate Christmas once more together on this earth, wouldn't it.

your brother

A. G. Bergius

Welcome

THE PRAIRIE HOUSE

Christine came to America, her passage paid by an acquaintance of her mother's with the agreement that she work for the family on their farm near Dell Rapids, South Dakota, until the price of the fare was paid back. My aunt Emma told me this, but she did not have many details: *Mama never talked much about when she was in Dell Rapids. In fact, I'm not even sure of their names. I got the feeling those years must have been hard times for her, and she didn't much like remembering them.* She worked for this family according to the agreement, but she did not stay beyond the specified time.

Among the letters Christine saved are these from two little girls, probably children from the family for whom she worked. As they describe their life, they provide a picture of the life Christine would have shared in the prairie house to which she came in 1887.

On the 25th of January, 1895, Agnes writes:

Deer Christina I am going to write a little letter to you and if I dont spell all the words all write why next time I will do better I am going to thank you for the letter you send to me I heard that you hade a good thime through christmas we dident have any christmas three and we was sitting in the house all the tine and it have bean so cold but now it is warmer so we are going to school andnot mis one day and we have a horse and bugy and drive to school and we are 66 children in our school and i wish you would come and see us some time and i will be 11 years the 16 march and i which we was so clouse to eachother so we could go and see us and we would have a good time and I hope you will come over to us in the summertime and stay a while and it would be fun for we havent see you for a long time and gusta will write a nother time to you for she can't write very good yet you ask me what it was whit Oskar and Adolf and Oskar is so big and fat like a mountan and Adolf is very big to and he want to hang around mama all the time and I am study engelska withe most and I dont get no more to tell

Agnes Olson

pleas will you write some more time to me.

102

And on the 17th of May, 1896, her sister Augusta writes:

Deer Christina. I will try for the first time to write a little letter to you. Now it is spring and all is green and nice. I wish you would come and stay all the summer and if you would come. we would have lot's fun we would have a picnic out in the trees. and now we have been to the norwegian school and now it is two weeks that it is not school and this week we is going to do the house cleaning and than we are so busy. and I think you have forget me when I wrote to you. It is long ago so that you might have forget it. and my little brother can stand by the chairs along now. and agnes is the chicken's mama this year. mama has got to much to do so that she cant race chicken this year. please answer soon this is all I can till you this time.

Augusta Olson

When Christine received the letters, she was in a different house. She was in Sioux Falls, working at her new job. But she read them through, folded them carefully back into the envelopes, and put them away with her things, to remain safely through the years with other pieces of her life, two voices from her days at the prairie house.

* * * * *

It is May 24, 1887. Christine's journey has nearly ended.

She is seated beside Ole Olson, on the wooden seat of a spring wagon. Its metal-bound wheels lurch and jolt on the road, as they negotiate the iron-hard ruts into which the clay has dried. They are traveling from Sioux Falls, the closest destination of the railroad to her journey's end: the Olson's farm. Leaving Sioux Falls, they had traveled first on roads that were smooth and covered with gravel, but those roads turned into dirt roads, and now, the travelers have turned off into two dirt tracks through the prairie grass. This is the lane that leads to the Olson house. In the distance, Christine can see the farmhouse. She will soon be at this place which will be called home.

They travel silently.

Earlier this morning, when Christine stepped down from the train, she saw Ole there waiting for her. He stepped forward and shook her hand.

Ja, you must be Christina? Hello, hello. You are all right? The trip was alright? We will go on to the farm now.

Christine nodded. She told him her trunk was also on the train, and he asked a man in the station where it had been unloaded. Christine could see it, up against the brick wall of the station.

There it is, she called out to him, and pointed toward it.

Ole and another man picked it up and carried it to the back of the wagon; they heaved it up on the back and secured it with a rope. It rides there now, lurching as they do, as the wagon bumps its way toward the house. Christine glances back at it often. It is just a wooden box, but to Christine it feels like a friend, the one thing that has traveled this journey with her, the one thing from home.

They had left the station behind them several hours ago. As they had made their way through the noisy streets of Sioux Falls, Christine looked about her. Everything she looked at was unfamiliar; the impression was confusion, with no building or street distinguishing itself from any of the others. Ole, eager to begin the journey home, turned the wagon west, through the town, and then, on its outskirts, north.

As they drove, they traveled over wide sweeping hills, covered with grass that moved always, as the wind riffled it. Here and there were trees, trees growing up by the sides of creeks, trees leaning towards each other, as if in conversation, as if glad for companionship in this lonely land. But the hillsides and broad valleys were bare of trees, only the grass, long and silvery, in continuous undulation. As they passed along, she saw some fields plowed, ready

104

for crops. The black earth lay turned over in thick curving lines left by the plow's furrowing, glistening in its deep richness. But the fields were only part of the landscape. Much of the land was open: pastureland, or prairie not yet brought under cultivation. Christine had known not to expect forests and lakes, but still, how strange it seemed to let her eyes move from horizon to horizon with nothing to break the sweep, with nothing to rest on, to focus on. That was something she could not have imagined. It seemed unsettling to her, as if all directions were the same, and there was nothing to give meaning to a scene. And yet, at the same time, it felt good. Yes, she began to understand how new everything was in America, and to feel the newness. The landscape here, the spaces here—they had not been divided up into the small, defined plots she was used to. And she liked how the wind could blow over it all, and not be stopped, how the wind felt on her face, how it shifted her skirts and fluttered her hair. How, riding along a high plain, the land stretched itself out before her gaze, miles either direction, until it yielded to a hazy horizon.

Occasionally they would pass by a farm. Some looked as if they were already well established, with a house built, and a red barn, a windmill and a windbreak of trees planted. Others were more sparse, just a small frame house, hardly more than a shack, exposed to the weathers and the sun.

What will his house be like? Christine wondered. She did not want to ask.

Ole would point out the farms of other Swedes he knew.

There's J. C. Johnson's place. There's Hjalmar Swenson's. That's a good farm he's got there. He got here when land was still cheap.

At one point they saw in the distance a church, painted white. It was not on a hill but stood on a rise that elevated it above the surrounding area, so that its spire could be seen miles away.

As they rode past, Ole said, That's the Swedish church. Near our place there's too many Norwegians. No Swedish church there, only a Norwegian church. And some Dutch starting to come now, too. When we go to church we go to the Norwegian church.

Now as the day lengthens, they reach the Olson house. Christina sees it at the end of the lane, not looking as prosperous as some, but not as lonely as some others. It is a white frame house, one story, with a half story above. It had been painted white, and is still white, but some strips of gray wood show through. The three sides of the farmyard include the house; a rectangular barn, painted red; and a corn crib. Between the corn crib and barn is a well with a hand pump and a tank for the horses. In front of the house, planks have been laid for a walkway to the door. On either side of the walk Christina notices patches of grass: a few strips of green between patches of gravely dirt. Near a corner of the house, chickens scratch and stare and flutter. Behind the farmyard, running parallel to the house is a line of trees, trees that had been planted when the land had been homesteaded as a claim several years before.

Ole drives the wagon up near the door. As he pulls her trunk to the end of the wagon, Christine climbs down, then stands still. She hesitates before walking up to the front door. She does not know what to do. Should she knock? Should she wait for someone to come out? She had traveled thousands of miles in discomfort, oftentimes in embarrassment, sometimes in fear. She had enjoyed, to some degree, the adventure of her travel, the new sights, the big cities, the vastness and drama of the ocean, the various landscapes and persons. But throughout the weeks of travel, she had focused her imagination simply on achieving this moment of arrival at the destination, this place, a farm near Dell Rapids, the family to whom she was coming.

Now, here she is. She had thought only about getting here. What would occur when she finally arrived—that was not a scene she had imagined. She stands awkwardly, peering toward the house, her hands held together in front of her, uncertainly. The sun, as it is lowering, causes her to squint.

In moments, and just as Ole is calling, Hello! —the door opens. Children tumble out, then, embarrassed by their eagerness, stand still, half-turned toward her, half looking away. They clear away from the doorway enough to leave space for their mother to emerge from the shadowed house. Selma Olson comes out to greet her new girl, Christine Berger, a newcomer just arrived from Sweden.

In her arms is a baby, the fourth child of Selma and Ole, a little girl. Perhaps it was the effort taken to dress her that has caused Selma to be slow coming to the door, for the child is clothed in a clean, many-buttoned infant dress and wrapped in a white blanket, evidence of attention that has not been extended to the other children—one tall boy and two little girls, one just a toddler. Or, indeed to Selma herself. Selma's fair hair, pulled back into a braided bun, has pieces straggling loose; the front of her apron shows signs of the day's work.

Selma, holding the baby in the crook of her left arm, extends her right arm to shake hands with Christine.

Hello, she says. Welcome to our house. Come in. We can have coffee before supper. And she leads the way inside.

Christine follows her. Ole tells the boy to help him lower the trunk to the ground, and to help carry it into the house. The two little girls follow their mother and Christine into the house and cluster together near the door.

The house is dark inside, and warm for a day in May. The room they enter is the kitchen, and it occupies the part of the house that is only one story. Beyond the kitchen is a sitting room, and off of that is the bedroom of Ole and Selma and the baby. From the sitting room a steep stairway leads to the single upstairs room, a room shared by the other three children. This is the room where Christine will stay.

The kitchen is dark because shades had been pulled during the day to keep out the glare of the afternoon sun. Now Selma opens the shades, and indicates a chair where Christine can sit down, a chair, one of four, pulled up to a wooden table in the center of the room. With the shades open, the room appears more cheerful. Two windows look out to the west and there is a

107

cookstove between them; the walls have been papered. In the corner sits a big metal tub, with a washboard propped inside. A pantry adjoins the kitchen, and through its open door Christine can see shelves where bowls and plates are stacked, and standing under the shelf a big flour tin. It is to the pantry that Ole now carries the parcels he had brought from Sioux Falls. Then, without another word, he goes out to lead the horses to the barn, and to do his evening chores. The boy, without a word, follows him.

The coffee pot is on the stove, a blue enamelware pot. Selma goes into the pantry and comes out with two cups, and a little bowl of sugar. She speaks to the little girl watching silently by the front door: Go down to the cellar and bring up a little cream.

Var så god! she says, and hands Christine a cup of coffee.

Tack, says Christine, Tack så mycket, Mrs. Olson.

No, no Christina, Selma says, and places a hand on Christine's arm. We were old friends in Sweden. I'm not so fine yet, you know, for you to call me Mrs. Olson. I'm just Selma still.

Christine smiles. Selma goes on to say:

Well, Christina, I'd have hardly known you. You've changed a lot since I saw you last. Well, I've changed too. You probably wouldn't have known me either.

And Selma smiles, a quick rueful smile by which Christine understands that she knows herself to be unkempt, and she knows Christine has noticed. Selma resumes,

Now you have to tell me the news. Were you able to go to Mama's funeral? What is it like now for Lisa and Augusta? They write, but sometimes it's hard to tell in a letter.

Christine tells Selma all she can of her sisters, of the changes in the village they had both at one time known as home. Who had died, who had married, who had come to America. Who, it was rumored, would be returning from

108

America. Christine tells Selma she has brought a letter from Lisa and will give it to her as soon as she unpacks.

For a moment each woman stirs her coffee, and keeps her eyes fixed on its milky swirls. Then Selma raises her face, and speaks to Christine.

I hope you will like it here. The children aren't too much trouble. But things are so different here, so many things to do that we did not have to do at home! You'll see. I hope it won't be too much a surprise. I haven't had a girl before. In Sweden I would have never had a girl, but Ole said it was all right, there was too much for me to do with the babies. And mostly, I don't have nobody to talk to. You know a man don't talk like a woman likes to talk, and my man don't like me to talk to him. At least he says I talk a lot when I could be quiet. And then when he is in the fields it's just me and the babies. I hope you don't mind me talking to you. I wish I had a cake for you, that would be nice, your first day, but today, it was so hot, even though it's just May still, I didn't want to start the cook stove. If it was not so hot I could have made you a nice cake. We do have lots of eggs, and milk, and I didn't mind using the sugar and flour because I knew Ole was bringing more. I think I will have more coffee. Can I pour some for you?

* * * * *

Dell Rapids, Dakota, U.S. A.

August 17, 1887

Dear Mama, I write you today and send you my dearest greetings. I want you to know that I am safe here with the Olsons. It has taken me a long time to write. I hope you have not had worries for me. I think Mrs. Gustafsson's cousin was going to write to tell her I was with them, and got to Chicago all right with them. Now I am here and can tell you about my life here.

Christina puts down her pencil. How will she find the words to write? What will make her mother read this letter and smile, and think, Ja, she's fine. It's good she went. It will be a chance for her. What should she say?

You would be surprised to see Selma Olson now. She has changed a lot since she left for America. She was glad I saw her Sister Lisa before I left and could bring her a letter and news. She has four little children. She did have two others but they died of diphtheria. She has one boy Wicktor and three little girls Anna, Agnes and Augusta who is just a baby. Agnes now is 3 and Anna is 5. I think it will go fine working for Selma. She likes how I cook, and the children like the cakes I make for them. Ole has 160 acres here so you see he has almost as much land as the Gustafssons. Just like what people say everything is bigger here. But he has to do it almost all himself. It is hard for him with so much to do. The boy is too small to help too much. I think I will help when it is time to harvest the grain.

Christine does not write about all she thinks. She looks around her, at the couple she lives with, at their house, at the life they have together. She watches, she considers, but she says nothing. There is no one to whom she can say it.

But she notices things. How Selma sweeps the house, but leaves dust in the corners. How she kneads bread on the wooden table but does not scrub it clean first. She notices that Selma's mending is done with loose, careless stitches that unravel more quickly than they are put in. But she also sees how there are always children, children who cry, or who are ill or who tug on skirts, needing to be picked up. She sees how Selma's face, by day's end, is often drawn with exhaustion, and she hears how Selma's voice is often sharp with exasperation. She notices too how Ole works, and eats and sleeps, and keeps his laughter to share with other farmers who occasionally stop by, or whom they meet on the infrequent times they all go into town.

I think it is a hard life for Selma. She tries to keep a good house but it is hard with the wind it is always blowing in the dust there is more dust here than at home I think and always there

110

is the wind. And then it is lot to do with the children. I think of our kitchen in the Gustafssons house and wish we could be as clean and nice. But she is not lazy, she works hard and when the children are older it will be easier for her. She says I am a good help.

One thing she will not tell her mother about is Saturday nights.

The day she arrived was a Wednesday; on Saturday evening, Ole came in from the hay field earlier than he had on the other nights, and washed his hands and face well. After supper, with no more or no less conversation than usual, he got up, took his hat, harnessed the horse to the wagon and drove down the lane. Christine looked at Selma with a question on her face.

Oh Ole, said Selma. He likes to go to town on a Saturday night. It's hard for him, working all week. He likes to go to town to have some fun.

She said this as she was stacking the plates from supper, not really looking at Christine.

What is the town like? asked Christine.

Oh, we'll go there sometime. Not on Saturday night. We'll see it when we go to church. If we don't go this Sunday, we'll go next Sunday, then you'll see the town.

When Christine was going to bed, Ole still was not home. She fell asleep, but was wakened suddenly. Outside the window, the night was very dark, but breaking the late-night silence were the sounds of stumbling and muttering from downstairs. She could tell someone had lit the kerosene lamp. She heard Selma's voice, tense, but quiet. She could barely make out the words.

Be quiet now, Ole. You'll wake the children. Did you get the horse put away?

But hearing Ole was not difficult.

Goddamn kids. Can't they put the horse away? They just eat and sleep and can't help a man when he needs it.

Hush. I'll go outside and put the horse in the barn. You sit still.

Christine heard the door shut as Selma went outside. She heard Ole muttering. When Selma returned, his voice was louder, more angry,

I thought I told you to leave that horse alone! That's a job for a man, putting a horse away. I don't want nobody saying Ole Olson lets his wife do a man's job. But no, you just go ahead like you don't hear me, just like I'm nobody. Is that what I am to you, nobody?

Sssh, Ole, please. Remember Christina, what will she think?

I don't care what she thinks! She can think what she wants. She's no better than us, she's not as good. Who paid for that passage anyway? I did. She's your girl. She's my girl, I paid her way. She can think what she wants. She don't need to think she has fancy ways that make her better than us.

Christine had heard too much, did not want to hear any more. But the voice went on, and Selma's responses continued: cajoling, fearful, but insistent.

Quiet, Ole; please Ole; Ole, the children; let me make you some coffee, Ole.

At the end of one such comment, Christine heard the sound of a slap, she heard Selma's sharp intake of breath, a short gasp, maybe a sob. She heard Selma walking away from the kitchen and shutting the bedroom door. Then, again, Ole's voice: loud, as, still sitting in the kitchen, he made sure his words found his wife through the closed door:

It's all that talking that makes me mad! Shut up, woman. It's you who make me want to hit you.

Then the light was gone. She heard his footsteps, slow and heavy and as he walked to the bedroom. There was the sound of the bedroom door opening, then shutting again. She heard the "clump, clump" of Ole's shoes as he kicked them off. From the bedroom, words rose through the thin boards of the ceiling: Selma's voice was clear.

No Ole, not tonight.

Ole said nothing.

It was a hot night, but Christine pulled the quilt up around her head, covering her ears, finding the silence that would separate her from the sounds and the passions of the house.

No, this is not something Christine will write to Johanna.

* * * * *

Dell Rapids, Dakota, U. S. A.

January 10, 1888

Dear Mama, Now I will write you and send you my dearest greetings. Also Jul greetings, God Jul, och gott Nett År! Now I will tell you about Jul in America. I thought of you so much and when I was baking I thought of you and our old home and I prayed that you are happy and healthy. I hope all is well with you and say hello to the Gustafssons too. And when you see Anders give him my dearest greetings. This year is not too much snow, but cold. But when it was time for the Julotta service, Ole put the wagon on a sleigh, they call that a bob-sled and so we go to church. We go to the Norwegian church, but it is much the same, I can understand it all just about. When we left the house the little ones were asleep but they were covered up with blankets and a fur blanket too. The fur blanket was a buffalo skin. I sat in the back with the children and we were warm. We had a good dinner. We had lutefisk that Ole bought in Sioux Falls, and Selma and I made the meatballs. Then we had potatoes and we had rice pudding and spritz kakor. I had made little dolls for Augusta and Agnes they took the dolls to church but I made them keep the dolls in the wagon. It was good to hear the old hymns, Jeg ar så glad, we sang it in Norwegian. Oh here in Dakota it is hard to have a Christmas tree because there are not trees like we have in Sweden. To get a tree you have to buy it and Ole first said no too much money and then he said yes because all the children wanted a tree. He saw their sad faces and so he said yes and then they were so glad. Wicktor went to town with him to Dell Rapids and they brought home a little pine tree in the wagon. At home we would think it was small. We had some candles, and the children and I cut stars out of paper for the tree. It made a good smell in the house it made me think of

113

my old home. Tell Mrs. Gustafsson thank you for helping you to read my letters. I am hoping you are all well, and I pray for God to bless you all in the New Year.

* * * * *

Dell Rapids, South Dakota, U. S. A.
June 20, 1888

Dear Mama, I hope you are well when you read this. I wish you would thank Mrs. Gustafsson for writing for you, and telling me the news of the old home. Here we are fine. But I must tell you there is a new baby now, little Adolf, and he was born at the end of April, just at spring time.

As the summer turned into fall, Christine had noticed Selma being even more tired than usual. Instead of rising from the table after a meal, she would sit still, arms folded in front her on the table, resting her weight on them. When carrying water from the pump, she would often stop, and press her hands to her back as if it ached. When the floor needed mopping, she would not notice it. Silently, Christine did more than before. She did not wait to be told to do a job, but scrubbed what needed scrubbing, swept and tidied and baked. At mealtimes, when the food was passed around the table, she saw Selma silently push the bowl aside; one day in late August, when the two of them were going out together to the barn to pick eggs, Selma put down her bucket and ran behind the barn. She was out of Christine's sight, but as Christine listened to the coughing and choking sounds of Selma vomiting, she saw the other woman in her mind's eye: bent over, bracing herself with one arm pushed up against the wall of the barn.

Selma said nothing to Christine, as her waist thickened, and her pregnancy became obvious, and Christine said nothing to Selma. But to herself, Christine thought:

114

What a fool. Poor thing. Already too many babies, and two more she lost, and now another baby coming. Why let a man do what he wants and it's you who has to be sick and tired. Nothing will ever be better here. Too many babies and she'll be worn out with no more in her life than if she had stayed home. There it was work, work, work like a horse, and here for her it's the same. No difference for a woman. Unless you can make it better. That Ole, he ought to be better too. When he drinks he doesn't think and then now here's another baby. Well, it is hard for them. Agnes so little and Augusta still a baby too. And now Selma feeling so sick. Maybe things will be better when the baby's here.

Selma felt bad at first, but then in the winter not too bad. Then in spring she got real big and hard for her to work at all. Then I was glad I was here to help. She had to mostly be in bed, and there was all the cooking to do, and cleaning the house for spring. She was too tired to tell me what to do so I just did what we used to do at home, and she was glad. She wanted the house clean for the baby. Then there was some baby clothes to make. She had some but some were old or we couldn't get them clean.

By March, Selma slept at night in the double bed, alone. Ole slept on a pallet on the floor. During the day, Selma stayed in bed, just getting up for Christine to help her to the privy, or if it was too cold or icy to go outside, to the chamber pot.

Thanks Christina. You're like a sister now.

Ja, we've got to take care of you now. Here, now you go back to bed. I'll sit here with you while, I've got darning to do I can do right here.

Is Gusta still asleep?

She's still quiet. I think she's asleep. You want her in bed with you?

No, let her be in her crib. If anything happens to me, Christine, you write to my sister Emli in Chicago. Gusta's too little to be here with no mama.

115

She makes no noise, but Christine, with eyes on her darning, knows Selma is silently weeping.

Ja, Christine says, now you're going to be fine. Soon when the baby comes, you'll feel good again.

When time came for the baby, I was hanging out wash but Selma called and I ran in. I could see it was time. I ran out to the barn where Ole was and said to get the lady who comes to women when their time has come. He left right away. Pretty soon Selma was scared he wasn't back but then he came with the lady Mrs. Klein a German lady, and then after awhile the baby was born. I helped Mrs. Klein when she told me what to do and took the baby when she took care of Selma. Now Selma feels better again, but is still tired. All the other little ones want to see the baby, and he is very strong. His name is Adolf. I say like the Old King, and they laugh.

Let me hold Adolf! says Agnes. Christina, it's my turn now!

First go wash your hands, says Christine. Babies have to be clean. Now, sit still here in this chair and I'll let you hold him in your lap.

Christine holds the baby up in the air, above her head. He smiles down at her, his little mouth lifting like a bird's tiny opened beak. His arms outstretched, his fingers curved in tiny semi-circles. She nestles him once, quickly, before placing him in Agnes's lap. She helps Agnes adjust her arms to keep him safely cradled.

Ja, she says, such a sweet baby. And you too Agnes, you're a sweet little mama.

Now I will say good-bye for now and I hope you are well. Send my dearest greetings to all old friends.

* * * * *

Dell Rapids, Dakota, U. S. A.
April 30, 1889

Dear Mama, I had not heard from you for so long and then came the letter from Mrs. Gustafsson. I hope now you are better and I pray for your good health. How long it is since I have seen you and the old home. Now I am starting to make new friends but old friends are not forgotten. Especially Mama. Selma too sends her greetings and prayers for health again. We are now having some days that are nice here, not so cold and no more snow. This year we have a very bad winter with much snow and so very cold. The snow started in October and then it just snowed and snowed till spring. People say they have never seen such a bad winter here. At Jul there was snow over the windows of the house so we had no church. We stayed inside, and it was hard for anyone to be happy. Then we wished we had a tree but no one could go to town. Ole had to tie a rope to the house and the barn so he would not get lost in the snow when it was so hard coming down. Then after all the snow it was so cold. Some people we know had their cows to freeze and die, and some people we heard about were in town and went to go home and then it snowed hard and they got lost and they froze too. But we are safe and thanks be to God we are well. Winter here is like in Sweden, it is dark early in the evening but maybe not so soon dark as in Sweden. But the children can't go to school because it is so cold. Wicktor the oldest boy and Anna are learning English. They have some books here and when they read I listen too. Ole can talk English good, but Selma not so good. I am learning it pretty good. And now I say good bye and keep on with prayers for you to be in good health in the new year.

* * * * *

Dell Rapids, South Dakota
June 21, 1890

Dear Mama, Now today is Midsommer, and I think of you and all old friends. I wish I would see the dances and have the fun we used to have on Midsommer. Some people here get

117

together for a picnic too and have fun. Today the sun shines, and we have nice days. Here the summer gets so hot, not like at home, but now it is still just warm and so nice. Here there is a bird we do not have at home, he is called meadow lark and sings such a beautiful song. He likes to sit up in the grass and then fly up to surprize you. When the children and I sometimes go to the river we see him as we walk along and then they like to run to chase and try to catch him. And we see the red-winged blackbird too, and he sits on a little weed sometimes and sings so loud. We do not have the same flowers we see in Sweden, and in Värmland, but here too are nice flowers that grow wild in early summer. You would like to see them I think. Sometimes we go out with a tablecloth and bread and meat and make a little picnic for fun. Then we are all glad it is warm and not winter. That is what the children like to do, and I like to do it too. Now I have been here three years. It seems like a long time since I was home. Now we go to church almost every Sunday, and I see girls who work on other farms. Some girls work for families in town. I think they have a lot of fun. One girl, Anna is her name is going to work here in Dell Rapids and then she is going to work in Sioux Falls. Sioux Falls is a city not so far away from here. There are quite a few Swedes who live there. They get together and have a good time. There are not so many Swedes here where I live more Norwegians than Swedes. Anna talks about working out West. She says there are a lot of places that are fun for a girl in the west of America and she wants to see the mountains. I think that would be a long trip, but I think it would be fun to be in Sioux Falls. There is a Lutheran church there that is Swedish. Now I will close with my dearest greetings and I wish for you every good thing and send greetings to Anders and Charlotta and all old friends.

* * * * *

The letters written by Christine—indeed, her experiences—can only be imagined, but among the letters she received and kept are several from a woman writing from Dell Rapids. She signs herself only as "Selma," but references within the letters indicate she must have been the mother of Agnes and Augusta; she must have been the woman for whom Christine worked.

These letters, the first group, written in the winter of 1895 and early spring of 1896 and sent to Christine who by this time is living in Sioux Falls, depict a life of stress and hardship, a life marked by too many children and too many worries about them and about the family's income. An isolated life. A life Christine may very well have determined to avoid.

Dell Rapids the 19 Nov 95

Dear Sister Christina.

I want to write a few lines to you now. I can not quite remember if it is your turn or mine to write first. If it was my turn, please excuse me.

And first I want to thank you so much for what you did for me when I was in SiF[Sioux Falls]. . . .

And since then I have had enough of work. First I had threshers. And then we had to have a well drilled for we were without water and it is so deep that we have to buy a windmill so it will cost almost a hundred and fifty dollars. So Ole went to the bank and borrowed 100 dollars so we are more hard up for money than we have been for a long time. So Ole asked me to ask you if you are in a hurry for the money we borrowed. He would be thankful if you could wait a while. You know that you will get as large an interest as from anybody else. If you can't tell us, for you know that if you need them he probably can scrape together that much. Perhaps he will come to Sioux F. during the fall and then he will probably talk to you about it himself.

I am now alone with the little ones during the day for the four oldest now go to school, so I have it quite nice during the day, but it works out well in a way, when we are well. Thank God for the precious gift of health. And Otto is big and good. We are now alone in the kitchen for the others have gone to bed.

I can even greet you from Sweden. I recently got a letter from sister Lisa and she says that they are all well both in Elofsbyn and at home. And she tells me that Sister Augusta has been home this summer and visited and she says that yesterday she got a letter from her with the sad news that one of her children had fallen into a water trough and drowned. And it was then two years ago the boy fell into the river and died. Can you imagine a worse

119

grief. And may God be a good friend and comforter to her. And may God help all of us who have little ones. And you can not believe how terrible I think it was but I can not even comfort her so this world is a valley of sorrow especially for some people. I complain often. May God forgive me. And may God help me.

And you must excuse my sloppy lines. And a thousand dear greetings from us all, signed by your sincere friend Selma.

I ask you kindly for a few lines of answer. And at last a thousand thanks for what you did for me when I was with you. Live well.

Dell Rapids, the 14 Feb, 96

Dear Friend Christina

You must forgive me that I have not answered your dear letter but my time is so well occupied every moment that it looks like there is no time for anything. When I got your letter all the children were in bed ill except Wicktor was up but he was also ill and I have been feeble also. I don't know what it was. They were ill for one week. It looked like it was the grippe but praise be to God now they are all well. But Otto is cross because he is teething. He already has two. Otherwise he is big and fat.

But we have had it so hard this winter because we have no water. You know that I told you that we got a new well, made last fall but even that one has given out so we have bought every drop of water the whole winter. So we have nothing for all the money it cost us. So yesterday we got two people who are going to make us another well, but today it was too cold to work. So we are going to big expenses and perhaps we will not even get any water. So I have a house full. We are now 11 in the house and the children now go to school. Anna is home today and is helping me. Agnes is rather sickly all the time, so she can not really help me. I don't think that she will get old if she doesn't get healthier.

Christmas is now long gone and it is not worth to speak about. We were all healthy during Christmas and the children got small things but otherwise it was as usual.

I have not been outside the house since early last fall when I went to church. But most of the time I am ill on Sundays because I scrub on Saturdays and it seems like I don't tolerate it.

We have had such nice weather the whole time so it is hard to never get out. There are many times I am ready to faint, but one must recover, but you ask if we have sold our farm yet, but that day will probably never come, I think, don't you think. You have it pretty good with only two people in the household. It could get lonesome at times but you can always have some company. I wish I had a whole day to talk to you for I have a lot to say. But I have to go and make supper now. I have recently sewn the children a gingham dress each but times are so hard that you soon cannot get anything for you cannot get credit. We have borrowed money a couple of times. You don't mention the money we borrowed from you, so you are not going to send the sheriff, are you, but it may soon be better times than now.

And now I have to stop for today.

Please don't wait so long to write to me. And I can greet you from Emli. I got a letter a while ago. She has good days she said because she just reads novels. And I hope that you will come here to see us this summer. You will get so much good food and I will go to Dell to meet you. And now at last a most sincere dear greeting from us. Ole did not go to Sioux Falls last fall as he had planned.

You will have to excuse me that I write with pencil, but the children have the pen at school and if I don't write in the evening it will not happen.

Your sincere friend Selma. All the children greet you.

In this letter Selma has described concerns and difficulties, but in the next letter, written a month later, she sounds truly in despair.

Dell Rapids, the 20th March, 96

Dear Christina,

I will now try to write a few lines to answer your dear letter that I received so long ago. You will have to excuse my delay but I will tell you that the children have been so ill that it has been a heavy time. Adolf was ill first so we got a doctor. We thought it was

121

diphtheria but it was not. And ever since one or two have been ill during a three weeks time.
Otto was ill for two weeks, when he cried night and day so some nights I was not in bed, but
now thanks be to God they are all rather well. Otto is not so well because he is teething. He
has three now.

So now I am so behind in all my work so I don't know when I will catch up. And
I work every moment, but the worst is that it never shows afterward. So many times I think
that Life is a burden and that Death would be a blessing. I just don't know how it is with
me because there are times when I am ready to die. May God give you that you never have a
feeling of moments like that. And I don't know why I am so melancholy. If I could live such
that I would be happy on the other side of the grave then it does not matter how it is here
because it is only a short time that soon will be gone. O God help me here and after this life.

And I have had so many people all the time for we have had well diggers here again,
and now we have finally got water. So the other week we got the wind mill moved. And then
there was so much bother, for some days it was too windy and some days it was too cold so it
took almost one week before it was done because we had to have one from Del. And he did
not come until he thought the weather good enough. And then the others came back and forth
because they were many. So I have had to do all I could this winter. It has been the most
difficult winter I have seen but the weather has been good.

And now I have to tell you my news. You did hear that Ole has been in a lawsuit
with Huntomer at last but they have not got the papers yet from pir [Pierre, S. D., the
capital of the state] *so they do not know how much the damages are. Carli Huntomer*
came here himself and told this and now Ole and he are such good friends that he has been
here and helped with the windmill. What do you say about that? I think they are like hens,
the longer they fight they become friends.

And I have recently had a letter from Sister Lisa. They are all healthy, but she
says that times are bad.

So I have to stop with a dear greeting form us all. Your friend Selma.

Burn my letter when you have read it because it is not for anybody else but you. I
am today alone at home with the four youngest children because the others are not back in

school again, but it is soon over which is a good thing. And I hope that you will write me a few lines when you are able to.

All the children greet you and we hope that when spring arrives and gives us encouragement and all turns green and lovely that you will come and visit us. Won't you? Then we will all be happy and have no sour faces.

I have not been out yet more than once to church this winter. I see you are out often. Emli is in Chicago still. She does not mention Sweden. I have not had a letter for a while because I am so slow to answer, but Wicktor got one not so long ago. She will never come to Sweden, that I believe.

The last letter is written in spring, when all is "green and lovely," but, although we do not hear the same despair, we see that the encouragement of the new season has not been completely sufficient for Selma.

Dell Rapids, May 17, 96

Dear Christina.

A hearty thanks for your dear letter that I received one week ago. I makes me glad to hear that you are healthy and well. We have not been quite well. We have had colds or what ever it is, but I suppose it will get better when the weather gets more steady.

I see that you have had a lot to do. And so do I constantly. And then you never see anything after my work. And then I am very ill at times. . . .

It is now spring and everything is so beautiful, but it does not make much of an impression on me. I don't know why, but I always have so much to do that I don't have any time to spare but I must continue a few more years and then I will have better help. If one did not have to work so hard, perhaps one would be more glad. And this week I will finish house cleaning but as you know when I finish in one end then it is as nasty in the other end.

And now I have to stop. I hope to talk to you face to face,

> *signed by your sincere*
> *Sister Selma*

Write and tell us when you come so we will meet you in Dell.

* * * * *

Surely, Christine must have wondered, was Selma's anxiety and hard work any improvement over the anxiety and hard work of the old country left behind? If Johanna's and her own dreams were to be fulfilled, there must be in the new life in America more pleasures and security than she had experienced so far.

THE CARPENTER HOUSE

The 1892 City Directory of Sioux Falls includes this listing: Berger, Christine. Domestic for C. Carpenter.

Sioux Falls, incorporated as a village in 1875, was by the 1890's a small but thriving city. A promotional publication issued by a local dry-goods store, "The Bee Hive Advertiser," gives this description: *In 1882 we were a city of 2,164, whilst in 1892 we are a veritable modern Babylon with 15,000 all told. Whilst in 1882 a paltry few wooden structures comprised our city, today we have the largest number of handsome structures---perfect specimens of man's art—of any city of our size in the world.*

While the writers of this article intend, no doubt, to suggest the grandeur and size of Sioux Falls by allusion to Babylon, other qualities are also suggested by that comparison—pleasure-seeking, for instance, or sensuality; and these too are appropriate. In its early years, Sioux Falls was notorious as the destination for persons seeking a quick divorce. Dakota Territory (and later the state of South Dakota) required a waiting period for a divorce to become final that was half the length of time required in the rest of the country, a provision which attracted many Easterners who wanted to end marriages as quickly as possible and had the wherewithal to pay for this convenience. Since Sioux Falls is located near the eastern boundary of the state, it was the city that profited most from the lucrative divorce trade. Eastern travelers would come to Sioux Falls, take up residence in the Cataract Hotel—one of the city's most "handsome structures,"—or other, less grand lodgings, and, while waiting for their divorces to become final, would through their living expenses, contribute to the incomes of owners of hotels, rooming houses, eating places, and, of course, lawyers. This influx of money from the East allowed Sioux Falls to weather the hard times of 1891, even building new businesses and homes during what was a time of struggle for other locations.

A description of one of those new homes: "Mr. C. C. Carpenter, a banker . . . built an elegant mansion of chocolate brick and slate at 9th Street and Duluth Avenue at a cost of more than $10,000"—attests to the prosperity enjoyed by at least some of the citizens. Mr. Carpenter, however, did not rely on the divorce trade for his fortune. A banker who came to Sioux Falls from Albion, New York along with his wife, Frances, he arrived with a fortune, or at least a modest fortune, already established. He and Mrs. Carpenter settled in Sioux Falls in 1885, and they and their capital, were, apparently, made most welcome. By 1889 they had built their big new house on the corner of Duluth Avenue and Ninth Street.

And, by 1892, Christine had relocated to this "modern Babylon." Indeed, as the hired girl for Mr. and Mrs. Charles C. Carpenter, she was employed at the very center of the social and financial elite of the city, residing—albeit in the maid's room—in the "elegant mansion," a mansion located in a neighborhood designated as Sioux Falls' own "Nob Hill," where homes could be found of a number of the other financial and political leaders of the city: the Pettigrews, the Boyces, the Tuthills. Homes that were a far cry from a prairie farmhouse.

And even though she would have continued to have a heavy load of work, the tasks would have been of a very different type: serving at table, laundering fine clothes, opening the door to callers who represented the social elite of the city. Expectations and standards would have been high; perhaps it was here at the Carpenter house where she developed those housekeeping skills which years later so impressed her daughter-in-law: *One thing Grandma always used to say about sweeping a floor: There are no round corners in my house!*

Among the possessions that had belonged to Christine is a photograph album, a very handsome, plush covered album, its covers now faded to rosy peach. From my earliest recollection, the album was a fixture in the front room in my aunt Emma's house, the house where my grandmother lived until her death, observed there in its prominent location on the lamp table in front of the window, observed but never examined. For years I thought it was a Bible. Once, as a child, I undid the silver clasp and glanced at what was within, but seeing it to be a collection of photographs of dead people I didn't know, I lost interest. Now, opening the album, I find an envelope, empty, yellowed with age, and written on the front: "For Christine With the good wishes of Mrs. McKennen and Mr. Gale."—the sister and brother of Mrs. Carpenter. And, looking through the photographs—of herself, of John Benson, of other Benson relatives—I notice photographs identified as being pictures of Mrs. Carpenter, and of her son and daughter-in-law—Mr. Gale Carpenter, and Mrs. Gale Carpenter.

Also among her treasured possessions, a gold pin that had been given to her by Mrs. Carpenter, a pin she is seen to be wearing in the photos taken of her on her fiftieth wedding anniversary.

And among her letters, there was this note:

Sioux Falls, S. D. May 16, 1895

Miss Christine Berger

    Dell Rapids

Dear Madam

    Gale Carpenter received a telegram from his folks in New York saying his father was seriously ill, not expected to live, and for him to come.

    He left on this morning's train for their old home. He asked me to write you to come here by the first train so as to get the house in shape for them when they return.

    He left the key with me at the Central Drug Store.

    Have also written Mr. Olson, with whom he said you were stopping.

                    Respectfully

                      Ed. W. Dow

* * * * *

It is the end of the day, Tuesday, May 21. Christine, at last, is alone, up in her room. She sits in the rocking chair placed by the window. Rocking quietly, she sits in stillness, hands in her lap. Her gaze is drawn to the elm tree, whose branches finger her window; in the circle of brightness spread by the streetlamp she notices, idly, the buds which in a few days will uncurl into the tender green of spring. She sees the carriage house beyond the tree, notices that there is a light shining through its window.

Alfred, she thinks. He's still awake too.

Outside, the night is very dark. Beyond the door that separates her room from the family quarters, all is silent. Asleep, she hopes.

Now maybe she can sleep, Christine thinks. In her own bed, and now everything's over. But maybe it's not so easy to sleep there alone. And Mr. Gale, he's tired for sure. Traveling to New York, and then right back again with the body and his mama. It's hard to believe he's gone, and him not looking so sick when they left. It was a shock. It must have been a shock to her, his getting so sick like that. But seeing all those people here today, that must have helped her. Thank goodness, everything was nice for all them. Even with her only getting here just before, we had a nice house for today. We didn't have to look slip-shod in front of all those people. That's something anyway.

Christine loosens her stays, her skirt, and her shirtwaist, and, too tired to fully undress, blows out her lamp, and lies down on her bed. She'll have to put her clothes away tomorrow, they all need laundering anyway, rank with the sweat of the day, spotted with a few marks betraying kitchen and serving chores.

But sleep does not come at once. Though her body seems to be dissolving into the thin mattress on which she lies, losing itself in the pleasure of pressing her back and shoulder blades against it, of stretching out her legs and letting her feet return from their aches and numbness, her mind is still active with jumbled images and feelings: pictures of the day unreeling themselves before her inward eye—the vastness of the crowd: how the whole yard was filled outside, and inside the crowd in the hall and the music room; the dignity of the visitors and solemnity of the service; the coffin there in the living room with its dead body like a waxy sculpture, the pillow of roses and— what were they—carnations? And then too her feelings—various, complex, unreflected-upon—tumble against each other, feelings of sadness and the empathy of sorrow rising into her throat, to be sure; but she also feels pleased with herself, satisfaction with having accomplished a difficult task well; and, weaving through all: curiosity—the ordinary curiosity she has always felt about her employers now having been intensified, as the demands arising from the rituals of death have pulled her into an unaccustomed intimacy. Then too there is the sense of having been whirled along, these last few days, by tumultuous events. And now the surprise of quietness. Now, at the end of the day that has seen the funeral of her employer, Mr. C. C. Carpenter.

129

"He is Dead" declared the headline of the news story on May 17. And today: "Dust to Dust: Last Sad Rites Over the Body of Charles C. Carpenter— An Immense Throng at the Funeral."

It's not been so long, really, that she's been at the Carpenters. Even so, now it seems that she almost feels at home here. But it wasn't that way at first. How anxious she had been, how worried about being able to meet the expectations of this American family who lived in such a grand house!

* * * *

Dell Rapids, South Dakota
August 15, 1891

Dear Mama,

 I send you my dearest greetings with the hope that you are well, and Anders too is fine. I am in good health this summer and I did not catch the fever the Olson children had here. They are good now too and we are glad to have had good crops this year on the farm.

 Now I have been here with the Olsons four years, and I don't think they can keep me on for hire. And also I would like to move too. I have a good chance now to see about a new job, one in Sioux Falls. There is a man in Dell Rapids, he is from Värmland, his name is Gust Uline. He has been a friend to the Olsons and helped Ole with loans from his bank. He has been nice to me too a girl from Värmland, and sometimes we talk about the old times at home. He knows of Långserud, and the church there but not our little village of Björsbyn. I asked him if he knows the Gustafssons and he thought so but was not sure. He is a banker here, and rich, and he is also going to Sioux Falls for other banking business too.

 Now he tells me news about a job. He has a friend there in Sioux Falls, a banker too. His name is Mr. Carpenter and he has a wife and son. They now have a big house in Sioux Falls, Mr. Uline says it is very fine, one of the finest in the city. They had a girl working for them but she was not good at doing the work they wanted. He said they want a hired girl who can work hard, and I can do that. I said to Mr. Uline about my language, it

130

is not the best English. He says if I work good, they won't mind about my language, and that I can learn more there too with everybody speaking English, no Swedish. He said he told them he knew I was a good worker and a good girl and they said I should come and then Mrs. Carpenter will talk to me and see if I will do. It is a big change for me, but a good chance too and in Sioux Falls are other young people like me, and a Swedish church too. Mr. Uline says not far from the Carpenters and so now maybe I can go to church more and so I will go to Sioux Falls one day soon when Mr. Uline says it is time for me to meet her. I will go by train.

If I go there then I will write you and tell you my new address.

* * * * *

Hello Helen?

Frances Carpenter, not even five feet tall, had to stand on her tiptoes to talk into the telephone. Newly installed, it was more of a challenge than a convenience, she thought. Nevertheless, she was determined to learn its ways. Talking to her sister was good practice.

Yes, Helen, can you hear me? —I can hear you, but not too well. Well, I am calling because your note came today about the literary club meeting this afternoon. —What? Yes, I thought too it should have gotten here yesterday. Anyway, I would have come, even just hearing about it now. –Yes, I know Josephine expects us to be there, rain or shine, but today I can't be there. You can tell her it's her husband's fault! As it turns out, that girl he heard about – Yes, the girl Daniel Glidden heard about from Gust Uline. —Oh you do too know him, from Dell Rapids, on the penitentiary board, that's how Daniel knows him. A banker too, Charley knows him from the bank, and thinks a lot of him, I guess. –Yes, she is coming by train today so I can meet her, and I can't let her come for nothing. –Yes, I hope so too. Heaven knows that other girl was a headache, more interested in having a good time than paying attention to her job. Thank God nothing happened to her while she was here. That would be the last straw. I've heard good things about these Swedish girls from the country, so let's hope she'll be one of them. —All right. —What? —What? I can't hear you. —Oh, no don't sign me up to be hostess next month, let's wait and see if this girl works out. She'll probably need a bit of coaching. —Well, I'll talk to her, and if she looks good, she can spend the night and get started, cooking tonight and tomorrow morning, so we can see how she does, and if it's all right, she'll go back to Dell Rapids for her things and come back as soon as she can wind up her other place. —No, by train. Train from Dell Rapids. I think I'll send Alfred down to meet her, maybe I should go too. —Yes, I suppose so, but taking a little trouble now is worth it if she stays for a while at least and does the job right. Well, I'll go now, give Josephine my regrets. What were we supposed to be reading, anyway? Do you know anyone who's actually read it? —Oh, of course, Caroline. She would be the one. No doubt. —Yes, you too. Good-by.

Frances does decide to drive down to the station; it would be too bad if Alfred couldn't spot the right person, and the girl is probably nervous enough without worries about being left at station, or finding the right way up the hill to Duluth Avenue. In fact, she decides, looking at herself in the mirror in the hall, she might just tell Alfred to stop at home, and pick up the girl herself. Get a first-time view outside the house, see how she looks when she's not aware of being watched, that might be a good thing.

So, at 1:30 p.m., Frances Carpenter is waiting at the Chicago, Milwaukee, and St. Paul station as the train from Dell Rapids pulls up to the platform. From this train, originating in St. Paul with Sioux Falls as an intermediary stop en route to Chicago, an interesting assortment of persons disembark. Frances waves at a friend of Charley's. She sees the usual business travelers, she notices a handsome couple being met by a lady and gentlemen she knows slightly, neighbors from a house a few blocks away on Prairie Avenue. She's curious about their appearance, too little luggage for a long stay. On the other hand, maybe it is all being shipped separately, and they are coming to settle. She'll have to ask Ella Pettigrew, she always hears the news first. Now she puts her mind back to her business: where is this girl?

She sees a tall young woman, standing by herself, looking around with curiosity and a touch of apprehension.

She's older than I'd thought, Frances thinks to herself, but that could be an advantage. Nicely dressed, I'd say, and it looks to be well-sewn, too. It would be useful to have someone who could do something in the sewing line.

Frances flaps the reins on Prince's back, and he takes a few steps forward.

Christine Berger? Frances calls out to the girl.

Miss Berger turns. Frances gazes at Christine, notices a face that is serious, and handsome rather than pretty. Good cheekbones, a strong jaw, a straight nose. Her eyes are an unusual feature: so light a color of blue. Under a broad brow, softened only a very little by the curled fringe of her hair, her eyes look out, with directness, toward the voice she has heard.

Ja, Yes, ma'am, she responds, smiling with nervousness at her lapse into Swedish; she walks toward the buggy.

Mrs. Carpenter, alights, walks toward Christine with her hand outstretched:

How do you do, Christine, she says, and shakes her hand. I am Mrs. Carpenter.

* * * * *

No, not so long ago, Christine thinks, not so much time, but all the difference in the world. The new friends she has made, and John, and living here in this house, learning the nice ways of a fine city household. It is like she is back home, as a young girl with Johanna in the old yellow house in Sweden, a house that is beautiful, a house that is a joy to keep clean. She's felt the same way about the Carpenter house, she likes it to be shining, she is proud of it, her work has made it almost seem as if it were a house of her own. She never has been tempted to do her housework in a slip-shod way, to slight details. When she sweeps, she sweeps clean; when she polishes, windows shine.

And it is a grand house. When it was a new home for her, she tried once to describe it to her mother.

Dakota State Bank
Sioux Falls, South Dakota
November 4, 1891

Dear Mama,

Now I send my greetings to you in answer to your letter. I think this letter came very fast and I hope now my letter to you also will travel quickly. I have news about my new job. You see my address is up above. That is the bank where Mr. Carpenter works. They say that letters from Sweden should be sent to me there so I will for certain get them.

I wrote you about maybe I would get this job and I did. I came to Sioux Falls and talked to Mrs. Carpenter, and she showed me the kitchen and where things were and then said if I wanted I could make them supper and she would show me how to serve it to them. I said I had never served at a meal before since I came to America and she said she would show me and that it would be all right. So I put down my bag and I put on an apron she had one all ready for me and then I started to get ready for supper. She said I should make what I know, and I said can you show me what you have. She said potatoes and lettuce and a chicken. So I looked at the stove and it is very nice and big and I got it going and I took the chicken and put it in a pan to roast, and then I started to get potatoes ready. In the kitchen there is a big icebox and inside when I saw the eggs and milk, I asked her if we should have a pie, and she said yes and showed me where the flour is and the fat. She has water too right in the house. So she gave me a pie pan and I made a custard pie to put in with the chicken. So when it was time to eat she would say, now Christine bring in this and put it here, now Christine, here is how you pass the food. There were three people only to eat, her and Mr.

Carpenter and their son nearly a grown man. I think it is good to have such nice ways as they do, and now I can learn them too.

Now I must send a few words in this long letter about the house. It is very big, three storys. Two storys with rooms and the top floor an attic. My room is on the second story. Also it is on a high hill. The hill comes up from the town, it is very steep going up to the street we are on, very hard for horses, even to walk carrying things. We are on Duluth Avenue. It is a fine street with many houses that are also very nice. But I think our house is the best. It is not wood like the Gustafsson's house. It looks more fancy too. The bottom is brick, and then there are slates that the roof is made from that come down too over the second story. This makes the house cool in the summer time. There are two porches one in the front on Duluth Avenue the other a side porch here is where the family mostly comes in and goes out. The kitchen is in the back, with its own door to the outside. The iceman and the milkman come to this door and other people who bring things. It is the door I can come in and go out of too. The kitchen has a nice window that is to the back of the house. I have an icebox and running water, they make things easier, and there is also gas lights downstairs. It is a big change from where I was before. There is a little stairway by the kitchen I can go up to my room from there. I have to answer the door when the bell rings and I serve at the table but otherwise I do not have to meet their friends very much. I feel good being in the kitchen. But Mrs. Carpenter is very nice, she comes and works with me sometimes in the kitchen and she is a fine cook. She shows me how to do things I do not know. Someday she says I should show her how Swedes cook. I could show her things we used to make. I also clean and do the washing and ironing. I am glad you showed me how to iron nice things and I learned to do that at the Gustafssons. Mr. Carpenter has nice shirts and he says he likes how I do them. They have a son, too Mr. Gale Carpenter, and he has a young lady, Miss Flora Daniels, and I think before long they might get married.

Mama, you would be surprized at the inside of this house, and I was too and I still think it is the most beautiful house I have seen. Downstairs is a big music room and living room with doors you can open to make one big room and there are fireplaces in each room. The dining room is big, too, with a special closet for all the dishes. In the front of the house next to the front door is a big staircase upstairs. The bedrooms are there but there is a room

135

of books too, and a little sewing room where Mrs. Carpenter likes to sit, and from there she has a window that looks down to the town.

> *I still hear from friends in Dell Rapids and the Olsons but I think I will make new friends here too. Not far from the Carpenters house is the Swedish Church and I can go there on Sundays. It is good to hear the old language and the church service. There are some people I have met, Mr. and Mrs. Carlson who live nearby and invited me to come over and visit.*

> *And now I close this long letter with every good wish from your daughter, Christina*

* * * * *

Mrs. Carpenter thought she had found a treasure in Christine. She had endured the flighty ways of her previous hired girl but had finally decided that half-help was worse than no help: carelessly dusted rooms, indifferent cooking, and serving at table that could only be described as casual. And Charley was always muttering about not having the laundering done to his expectations. So, when he came home one day from a bank directors' meeting—he must have been muttering at the meeting too—with the name of a country girl Gust Uline from Dell Rapids knew, someone he thought was looking for a new position, she had decided to take a chance on her, though the girl had never worked for a town family before and had only been in the country a few years. And the decision had proved to be right. Christine cleaned the house as if it were her own, she learned quickly how to serve at table, and she was developing into a first-rate cook. A light hand with the pastry, and a delicacy in the way she presented anything she made. It was a pleasant change to receive compliments on Christine's rolls and Christine's sauces, rather than to feel like she should apologize for Nora's lumpy gravy. And best of all, she was a person in whom you could confide without her taking advantage or assuming an inappropriate familiarity. Christine, undoubtedly, knew her place. As quiet as she was, and shy, she'd never presume to begin conversation, or to speak to guests! But, on those not-infrequent times when she worked alongside Christine in the kitchen, it was pleasant to be able to talk about the worries she had, or the annoyances, or the pleasures, knowing anything she passed on would go no further. Christine was quiet, she never put herself forward and Mrs. Carpenter was comfortable with her, believing that Christine felt a loyalty to the family as if she were one of them.

In fact, Frances Carpenter believed she could read Christine pretty well, and that she would succeed in managing her with very little difficulty.

Christine wasn't truly a girl anymore; she was, let's see—about 25, Frances thought, she wasn't foolish like a girl, but still she seemed young, inexperienced. I don't suppose she's ever been in love. Too serious for that! Too quiet, probably to attract a man. Of course, what with having traveled in steerage across the Atlantic, and then living chock-a-block together in that farmhouse out in the county, she must have seen a lot. But it hasn't seemed to affect her; she still seems unworldly, naive maybe. Looking at her she seems as clear as a pool of water. And so susceptible to a little praise! My goodness, when Charley praised the way she did his shirts she looked like someone had given her a prize! Of course she may feel lonely, being here with none of her family around. I wonder if she doesn't like the feeling of taking care of us; perhaps we put her in mind of them. One thing is certain, I've never had a girl who could work like her. It's good for us she's so eager to please. I think a little praise, doled out now and then, is going to be all the management she'll need.

And so life went on, for the Carpenters and their hired girl, Christine.

* * * * *

Christine, Mr. Carpenter and I have decided to take a trip back East. It's been a hard year, and I think a change of scenery might do him good. Might be good for us both.

Ja, he looks better, though, don't you think?

Yes, I do. In fact, if he didn't seem as if he felt better I would be nervous about making such a long trip. Of course it is always a worry with diabetes, keeping it under control is hard, but I do think lately he has had a good long stretch of feeling well. Really, he has seemed much better to me recently. I'm glad you think so too.

His color is better, I know that.

Well, we've made our plans, and we're taking a train to Albion next week. We'll be at my sister's place there. When we go why don't you take a little vacation yourself?

Is Mr. Gale going too?

Oh no, he'll be at the Bank, that's one reason Mr. Carpenter thinks it is all right to go, Gale will be here tending to business. But he can be on his own, in fact he'll probably be having all his meals with Flora over at her mother's house going over wedding plans. Why don't you take a few days and go visit your friends in out in the county, I know you were talking about that little girl, what's her name—Agnes was it?—who wanted you to come visit. While we're gone why don't you just plan a visit to them?

* * * * *

Christine was back at the Olsons' when the two letters arrived from Sioux Falls. Ole had picked both letters up at the post office and had already read the one addressed to him by the time he handed Christine her letter.

It's bad news, Christine, he said as he handed her the envelope.

Christine took it and read the letter inside.

I have to go, she said, at once, as soon as I can. He got sick out there in New York, Mr. Carpenter, maybe he'll die, and they're coming home. Mr. Gale went out there too. Isn't there a train this afternoon? I'm sorry to have to go so soon, but they need me to open the house, and what if he does die?

138

They'll need somebody there to get ready for the funeral, there will be a lot to do for that, all those people who will come.

Her bag was packed, good-byes were said, and before the day ended, she was back at the house. By then the word had come that Mr. Carpenter had died.

* * * * *

From The Sioux Falls *Argus Leader*, May 21, 1895:

Never did Sioux Falls pay more respect to the memory of a departed citizen than was paid today to the late Charles C. Carpenter, whose funeral services took place at 10 a.m. from the family residence at the corner of Ninth street and Duluth avenue. Before the hour for the services Duluth avenue and the adjoining streets were filled with carriages. The house was for the most part reserved for ladies, and the yard and streets were filled with men. All the business houses and offices were closed during funeral hours. . . The procession which moved to Mt. Pleasant cemetery was about three-quarters of a mile in length.

* * * * *

Everyone had finally left, the events of the day had concluded. People had started arriving long before 10:00, to get a good seat, Frances supposed. The house was packed. Heaven only knew who had been outside, but that she would learn when she looked at the book of condolences. The funeral—nice that the Bishop came, even though she and Charley weren't Episcopalians. But of course, he'd been a part of that whole dreadful business with Helen. All that music. Well, she supposed, some people like that, and it would have hardly been possible to say no. And then that long procession out to Mt. Pleasant. It took forever for everyone to get there, and meanwhile they just had to sit there, by the grave, waiting, with the coffin in front of them. That had been hard.

Seeing his grave, right next to where Helen had finally been buried, it brought back the shock of that terrible time.

It's hard to believe, she thought, that it's been eight years since their daughter died. It seems like it just happened.

Then so many people who had to be invited back to the house. We could never have gotten through this without Christine. Thank God Gale had the sense to let her know before he came East that we would be needing her at home.

Gale and his mother were sitting in the parlor. Not saying anything, both too tired from the day and from their grief to make an effort. He looked over at her, sitting there by the table. It was really time for the lamps to be lit. Sitting here in the gloom was no way to end the day. She was leaning her head on her hand, just gazing vacantly out at the carpet.

Well, it's over, he said.

What?

The day, it's over. The funeral. I knew it would be big, but I never guessed there would be that many people.

It's nice isn't it, knowing that many people would turn out to show respect for your father. Exhausting, though.

There's a nice write up in this evening's *Argus Leader*.

Oh, I'll look at it tomorrow. I'm too tired tonight. Do you want supper?

Not really, I don't feel too much like eating. That was a fine spread we had, though, for people who came by.

Wasn't it nice. I couldn't believe Christine was able to put that together in such a short time. Gale, I tell you the truth, when we all got back here, I think I would have just broken down to see a cold empty house, no lights in the windows, all shut up and dusty. It's a blessing you thought to get her back. I never will forget it, there she was at the side porch door, just so calm and sweet, and had coffee ready for us, and a clean house and fresh beds to get into. She was a comfort, she truly was. It was almost like having a daughter at home.

I'll bet she's tired too, after today.

Gale got up and went to the kitchen. Christine had been putting dishes away, having just now finished all the washing and cleaning up.

Hello Christine, he said.

Hello Mr. Gale. Can I bring you something? Would you and Mrs. Carpenter like some supper?

No, no thank you Christine. Why don't you leave putting those dishes away, come into the dining room with us, Mother and me, and we'll all have a cup of coffee. It's been a long day for us all. Here, I'll pour us all a cup.

And he placed three cups of coffee, a pitcher of cream and bowl of sugar on a little tray.

Now, you open the door for me, he said and carried it into the dining room. Hesitantly, she followed. Untying the apron and dropping it on a chair as she left the kitchen, smoothing her hair with her other hand, she entered the dining room and stood there, beside the door.

Mother, come and have some coffee with Christine and me.

Oh Gale, thank you.

Mrs. Carpenter rose to her feet and came into the dining room. She took her usual place at the foot of the table. The afternoon had darkened into a spring evening, but Gale had lit the gas lamp, and its light formed a hazy circle of yellow on the dark walnut table where he placed the tray. As she lowered herself into her chair, she reached out her hand, gesturing to Christine who still stood by the doorway, hands folded in front of her, and said,

Yes, my dear, you must join us, yes, sit down right here. We all could use a little time together after this day. Christine, I was just telling Gale how much we have depended on you these last few days. What a comfort to have the house ready for us, and then all you did for today, it was spotless for all those people, they filled up the whole downstairs, didn't they, it's a mercy you had everything dusted and polished up so nicely, I don't know how you got it all done. And all the cooking and baking as well. I never thought so many would be here to eat, but thank goodness you had made enough, even with some of those people coming back more than twice. You truly thought of everything, and you knew just how we would like things to be. You couldn't have been more thoughtful if you were one of the family.

* * * * *

Christine feels sleep stealing on her. Like a comforting refrain, she hears again the voice of Mrs. Carpenter: "and you knew just how we would like things to be." As she drifts into her dreams, the voice becomes Johanna's saying,

Ja, my little Christina, that is a good job you've done. I am so proud of you! You are growing up to be a fine woman!

THE CARLSON HOUSE

One house, important in Christine's story, is not a place she lived or worked in, but a house she visited.

The Carlsons, Louis and Kjerstin, lived at 618 North Summit Avenue, in Sioux Falls. Their house, like the Carpenter house, was located on the steep hill that rises from the flat land by the Sioux River and the business streets of Sioux Falls. In fact, the house was not far from the Carpenter house on Duluth Avenue; Summit is the next avenue to the west and 618 is located only six blocks to the north. However, the intervening six cross streets marked a change from "Nob Hill" to workingmen's cottages. The small tidy bungalows that still face the six hundred block of Summit are modest. 618 no longer stands, but looking at its neighbors, we can suppose it to have been a frame house, probably white, with a small front porch, a story and a half. Not a far walk from the Carpenters, and not a far walk from the Swedish Lutheran Church, located on Spring Avenue, just a few blocks west of Summit.

Kjerstin was related to a number of the young Swedes in Sioux Falls, and in the Sioux Falls area, and Louis helped a number of men, newly arrived, find work. Their house was a center, a gathering place, for a variety of reasons: because, for some, the Carlsons were relatives, a link with the family left behind; for others, because it was a place to go where you could enjoy the comfort of using your own language; for others, a place where familiar customs were continued, and holidays celebrated in the old Swedish ways; and for others, a place to make friends in this busy, bustling city. It is likely here that Christine meets Kjerstin's nephew, John Benson.

One of Christine's correspondents was Sofy Benson, sister to John Benson, Christine's husband-to-be. Like Christine, Sophy worked as a hired girl in Sioux Falls, but then moved to Portland, Oregon and settled there. In one letter she refers to the Carlson house as a place which was a center of holiday—and probably other—celebrations.

Yes last year at this time I had new year among you and had real Christmas days, that time when ... I ... was with the Carlsons. ... We have had such beautiful weather this Christmas. It was freezing so on Christmas morning the sidewalks were white with hoarfrost. Last Sunday night it was snowing a little also. But it is probably not as cold as with you. I do remember how cold it was to walk to Carlsons. So you were many at Carlsons on Christmas Eve.

One of photographs kept by Christine shows Mrs. Carlson entertaining a small group of ladies, the sort of young ladies who probably made up Christine's circle of friends. On the back of the photograph's matte, we find names: from left to right we see Sophy Benson, then an unidentified lady, then Mrs. Carlson, the hostess, standing in the middle, then we have a Mrs. Lindblad, and at the right, Elise Benson who was married to Mrs. Carlson's nephew, Lewis Benson.

At first glance, it looks as if this coffee party is taking place in Mrs. Carlson's sitting room. The table is laid with a fringed cloth, as indeed it would be at any coffee party. A cloth-draped cake plate is placed in the center of the table, with a few cookies arranged on it. A coffee set appears to be a Rose Chintz pattern; additional cups are stacked beside the cake plate.

But if the scene is examined more carefully, it appears that the coffee party is staged, that the ladies are arranged on a set in the photographer's studio, and that the "action" scene is contrived. Mrs. Carlson, standing, is pouring coffee, presumably into one of her guests' cup; but, not giving a glance to cup or spout, she stares fixedly straight ahead into the camera. The scene is one of posed elegance, impressive and comic at the same time; and we wonder, looking at these ladies, if they would themselves have seen any humor in the staged party, and laughed to see their poses.

These years of Christine's life in Sioux Falls combine a variety of experiences. There is to be sure the Christine who is the hired girl at the Carpenter house, but also there is her life with her friends, and especially with friends like these pictured in the photograph, proper young women, under the tutelage of Mrs. Carlson, who models for her young relatives and acquaintances behaviors and manners appropriate to American social life, whether she is entertaining on a set in a photographer's studio, or in her own house on Summit Avenue.

* * * * *

It is Christmas, 1893. Kjerstin Carlson is preparing for a party.

It is a late hour for her to be making dinner, but it is Christmas Eve. Some of the guests will be coming in from the country, from farms where they will have had to finish their chores, then clean up and get dressed in their best clothes before hitching up the horses for the buggy ride into Sioux Falls. Two of her guests are hired girls; they will probably have had to cook and serve a

145

meal themselves before coming. But having a late dinner on this night suits them all, for after dinner they will stay together until the 5:00 a.m. Julotta Service. Some may find a quiet corner for a little sleep, but most will keep company together until it's time to put on their wraps and walk over to Spring Street to the Swedish Lutheran Church.

It will be a big crowd for their little house, she thinks. Her brother Charley and Anna, his wife, and their little girl Jenny coming in from Corson will be here all night. That's three. Her sister Christina and her husband John Anderson, they'll be at their own house, celebrating with their girls at home. Still, she counts to herself, there's her and Louis, and their own children, and now Sofy is staying with her too, that will be another person. And now Lewis is married so there's him and Elise. Well, if the boys want to sleep, they will just have make do with whatever space on the floor was left over. The boys, her nephews—John, Olander, and probably Siegfrid and Edwin too—yes, they're sure to be here. They always turn up when there's going to be a good meal. But it's nice to see the cousins together, and nice for Sofy to be with her brothers. She hadn't been able to see them much when she'd been working for the Boyce's.

Well, all the baking is done, and most of the cold food is ready. Sofy was a big help with the baking, and also her friend, that girl who works over at the Carpenter house. Between them they had made all the cookies: the buttery, pale yellow spritz, shaped into tiny wreathes; the krum kakor, the sweet batter fried in hot deep fat turning wafer-thin, speckly-golden, then the hot cakes rolled quickly on the rod into a crispy delicate cylinders; and, her favorite: the smörbullar—the little butter balls, coated with white powdered sugar, sweet and melting in your mouth with their buttery taste and crunch of nuts. Hidden away from her own children in tins, they are ready to be laid out on plates. Kjerstin herself baked the bread, and she has some nice strawberry preserves and watermelon pickles and beet pickles she's saved from last summer. The potato sausage has been made, the brown beans are baking. The potatoes are

146

peeled. In its big pan, the slab of lutefisk is soaking. She has ground the beef and the pork for the meatballs, and now Kjerstin stands by the table, hands working the breadcrumbs into the meat, squeezing and mixing. She hears the door open.

Aunt Kjerstin?

Ja, Sofy, come in. Oh, shut that door, I can feel the cold wind all the way in here!

Sofy comes in, unwrapping a shawl she'd draped over her head and around her neck. Little clumps of snow had adhered to the wool; she gives the shawl a quick shake, scattering tiny white pebbles onto the shining linoleum floor where they melt into droplets. She carefully unpins her hat, which, protected by the shawl, has not yielded one feather of its cockade to the December wind.

Sofy! Don't make puddles! Don't you know we don't have time to mop again?

Oh, don't worry, I'll get those up, they're just drops, and anyway I don't think you want me opening the door again to shake it outside, do you?

No, that's for sure. I got to make sure the cookstove stays going good. Soon as you get your things hung up, come here and I can give you a job.

Sofy unbuttons her coat and hangs it carefully on one of the hooks on the kitchen wall by the back door. She finds a clean apron in a kitchen drawer, loops it over her head and ties it behind her waist.

Aunt Kjerstin, this apron is so nice, shouldn't I wear something a little bit used?

Why? You don't have to cook like a pig, do you? If you can't make a meal without making a mess, then I say you're not much of a cook. Now, get me some eggs, then you can get the fat melting so we can brown these meatballs.

While Kjerstin works the eggs into the bread and meat mixture, and the other ingredients, salt, pepper, just a pinch of nutmeg, Sofy brings the big iron

147

skillet to the cookstove and puts some butter on to melt. Then she and Kjerstin start forming the meatballs, rolling teaspoonsful of the mixture into dozens of tiny balls.

So, who's coming tonight? Will the boys be here?

Ja, they're coming. They got to come in from Corson, you know, but they should be here before too long. Probably they'll have Edwin and Siegfrid with them. I hope they're not too late, so we can eat when things are ready. And Lewis and Elise, I expect them. And your Uncle Charley and Aunt Anna, they'll be here with their little girl.   The boys won't come together though, there's not room in Charley's buggy. They'll have to come on their own.

What about Aunt Christina and Uncle John?

Not this year. You know what I think? I think it's because we'll go to the Lutheran Church here. You know they like that Covenant church out there, I think that's why they're staying out to the farm. Well, that's their business, I guess. I say there's nothing wrong with the Lutheran church, but they think they're more holy I guess out there with the Covenant church.

I hope it doesn't keep getting colder. We'll freeze walking over to the church. At least I hope the wind goes down.

Another knock at the door. This time, the newcomer waits to be admitted. Sofy wipes her hands, and goes to the front of the house, peers through the curtain stretched over the pane in the door, and called out to Kjerstin:

It's Christine!

Well, tell her to come in and don't stand there and let all the heat out!

Come in, come in. God Jul! I'll help you with your things, what's all these little parcels? Don't mind Aunt Kjerstin, you know how she likes to fuss.

Christine, who had unwound and shaken her shawl while on the front porch, takes off her hat and coat, giving them to Sofy. She walks through the kitchen, puts an arm around Kjerstin's waist and gives her a squeeze. Tiny Kjerstin, she comes only to Christine's shoulder.

148

I know Mrs. Carlson, all right. God Jul, Mrs. Carlson. It smells so good in here, and it's so nice and warm. Oh Sofy, don't you worry about them packages. Here, give them to me, I know what to do with them!

Christine leaves the room for a minute, taking several small packages, each wrapped in bright tissue paper, into the front room.

Now, she says to Kjerstin, what job do you have for me?

Sofy had asked two of her friends to join in the party at the Carlson house. Bergitta had wanted to come but couldn't get off. Christine was lucky; the Carpenters were going to be with Mrs. Carpenter's sister for Christmas Eve, and then go to Mr. Artemus Gale's house for Christmas Day. Mrs. Carpenter had told Christine they would just have a family breakfast on Christmas Day, what with the big dinner ahead of them, and after that she could visit her friends until the evening. Sofy was glad Christine could be with them, she didn't have any family in town, or even in America. Bergitta at least had family out in the country near Sioux Falls. And she herself was lucky, with her brothers and with three sets of aunts and uncles and her cousins all nearby. Still, Sofy wanted to try another location. She hadn't told anyone yet, only Christine, but she was planning to go west, to Oregon. She'd written to her uncle Louis, her mother's brother, to ask him if he could help her find a place. As soon as she hears from him, she'll make her plans to leave.

She looks around the table, at the remains of the festive meal, at all the guests, flushed from the warmth of the room, and tingles with the excitement of her secret.

They don't know what's in store for me, she thinks. Next year they'll all be here, same as always, and I'll be in another part of America!

She catches Christine's eye, and they smile at each other.

I guess she knows what on my mind, Sofy thinks. I'm glad I told her. I know she'll keep it to herself. I hate it when people go around talking about,

"I'm going to do this and I'm going to do that" and then don't do anything. It'll be time enough to talk about it when I'm know I'm really going.

But in the meantime, it has been a pleasure to confide in Christine, to have someone to share her excitement with, to help debate the good side and the bad side of going. She knows what Aunt Kjerstin would have said:

What? All the way out there? What's the matter, not enough excitement for you here? You mark my words, my girl, there's more to getting along in life than excitement. You know John and Lewis went out to the west coast, and they didn't think it was so fine, did they? Back they came in no time, ready to settle down and get serious. It won't be long before you find out the same. I don't know what's wrong with Louis, why he didn't settle here with the rest of us. But it's your business. Go, if you want, but if you want my opinion, you'd be better off just to stay put right here.

Yes, Sofy knows what she is going to hear from Aunt Kjerstin.

Now Kjerstin has stood up and begins to clear off the plates. Aunt Anna gets up too, and Christine. Sofy picks up her own plate and stacks it with those beside her.

Let's clear up, Kjerstin says, then we'll have some rice pudding and coffee before the Jul Tomte comes.

While they had been eating, the tea kettle had been heating up. Kjerstin pours the steaming water into a big metal dishpan and starts carrying it to the dry sink under the window. Christine takes the pan from her hands, puts it down in the sink, and from the hand pump splashes some water into the pan, cooling the boiling temperature just enough to be able to stand its heat on her hands.

I'll wash, she says. You know where to put things away, and Sofy can just keep bringing me dishes.

Thanks, Christine. It's nice you know the business end of a dish rag.

Well, that's one thing I do know, I guess.

150

As Sofy scrapes and stacks and carries, Christine washes, Anna wipes dishes and stacks them on the kitchen table for Kjerstin to put in the cupboards. The feast had disappeared: the lutefisk, the mashed potatoes and cream gravy, the meatballs, the pickled herring, the brown beans, the fried parsnips. Now, Kjerstin has cleared some working space on the table, and is ready to bring the rice pudding out from the oven where it had been staying warm. The hot milk, poured over top just at it had finished baking, had formed a delicate skin, the lightest of golden brown. The yellow color of the crockery dish it was baked in anticipates the rich creaminess of the pudding within.

Lifting it with the sides of her apron, Kjerstin carries it into the long table in the front room.

Bring in the bowls, Sofy. Anna, bring the coffee. You, Christine, you bring the cups and saucers. We'll serve it in here.

Standing at the end of the table, Kjerstin ladles out the pudding, a big spoonful into each dish. Before passing them around, a quick pour of thick cream and little cinnamon shaken on. She passes one dish to her left, one to her right. They go down the length of the table till everyone has a serving. Anna has been pouring coffee, Christine has handed the cups around. Sofy brings in the cream pitcher for coffee, and the sugar. They are circulating around the table.

Having served them all, Kjerstin sits down, and picks up her own spoon.

Var så god! she says, God Jul.

Tack så mycket! they respond, and to you too, a God Jul.

They all begin to eat, the buzz of conversation resumes. Suddenly,

Oh! Christine is holding her hand to her cheek. Her mouth is full of rice pudding. She is smiling, but dares not open her mouth to talk. But Sofy knows what has happened:

It's the almond, she says, Christine has got the almond!

Christine! they exclaim. Who's the lucky man? Anyone we know? — Sofy, when are you ever going to get the almond? —Well, all I can say is (Uncle

Charley is heard laughing), I'm glad Anna didn't get it. I think one husband is enough for her!

The hours after dinner pass quickly, surprisingly quickly. On this night of the year no one seems to think of bed, although the littlest children have had a few hours of sleep. Before long, it will be time to go to church. But before they go, they must pick up the clutter of tissue paper and colored string and cardboard boxes, the left-over evidence of the visit of the Jul Tomte to the little ones. And put the furniture back where it belongs. They'd pushed it all up against the walls when they decided to dance. It had been Olander's idea, to join in the old dances they all remembered from Christmases back home. It had been years since Kjerstin had swayed around the ring, to the lilting tune of "Räven Rasker Över Isen." Nobody had a fiddle, but they all remembered the words, and they were all pretty good singers. It was a pleasure to see everyone's faces: eyes flashing bright, smiles to right and left as the patterns of the couples moved through the dance, and to feel Louis's arm around her as they glided, circling around the floor. It was crowded, but it was jolly.

Too bad we didn't have more girls, she thinks, while carefully folding up the paper to be used again next year. The boys had to dance together! If Christina and John had come, they'd have brought Alma and Nellie. But maybe they wouldn't have danced anyway, being so proper and holy. Well, before too long those boys'll probably find their own partners. Now Lewis has taken his own wife, his childhood sweetheart Elise from their home village, Våxtorp. And Olander is still young, and Edwin and Siegfrid. John, he's probably about ready to think about a wife.

Having tidied up their own corner, Sofy and Christine sit head-to-head.

Christine, you were too good. So many presents. You had one for everyone! And so generous to me, what a sweet little box this is. Just what I can use to put my brooches in. You were a real Jul Tomte all by yourself!

I just wanted to do it, Sofy. It's such a nice Christmas, so nice of you and your aunt to have me come to your family party. It made me happy to bring the little presents, they were just small things.

They were just small things: a box of handkerchiefs for Kjerstin, a fountain pen for Louis. For Anna and Elise, a sachet each; for Charley, a box of candy, little toys for the children. For each of the boys—Lewis, Edwin, Siegfrid, John, Olander—a scarf she had knitted. Each person was surprized when, after the Jul Tomte had distributed the presents to the children, more packages were still stacked under the tree, and a present was discovered with his or her name attached. When the tag was read, "from Christine," some were touched by her shyness. She blushed when she was thanked, and only smiled and nodded. Kjerstin was moved to give her a quick hug, and say, for no one else's ears as she leaned toward her:

You're a good girl, Christine, and always welcome here!

Bundle up! It's cold out there!

Suddenly, the night has slipped away so quickly, they see they are nearly going to be late to church, for Julotta.

Everyone is bunched at the door, pulling on gloves, pinning on hats, wrapping shawls over heads and shoulder.

At least the boys will be warm, says Louis, they've got nice new scarves! How are you doing Charley? What've you got?

Oh, just this old thing. Anna, you'd better get busy or my nephews will make me look bad.

Oh, be quiet and get ready. Here, let me button the top of your overcoat. That scarf will do for a long time yet, make no mistake. Stand aside, let those young people go, they don't take so long to get ready as the old folks do.

The night is still and very, very cold. Overhead the stars are points of thin white light in the blue-black sky. Standing with her head bent back, gazing at the night's sky, Christine sees thousands, millions and millions, of tiny stars, going off further than her eyes can see. It is a moment of quiet, and she can nearly hear the silvery tinkle, the sounds she always imagines the stars to make as they dangle and turn, up there in the night sky. Sofy links arms with her,

Come on, it's too cold to stand there stargazing!

Christine laughs and leaves the moment behind. Always, on Christmas Eve, she feels a sadness as she remembers the ones she still misses so much. But it's no good letting other people know, they have memories too, she supposes, and nobody wants to be the one to make other people sad. So she swallows the sorrow away, and squeezes Sofy's arm as they walk down the icy street.

Here, let's skate!

Olander seizes her left arm. Come on Christine! Let go of her, Sofy; me and Christine are going to skate to church.

Ssh! Sofy tries to quiet him. She lets go of Christine's arm, and laughs at her brother, but realizes that in the quiet dark houses on either side of the street sleep people whose Christmas festivities are over, or have not yet begun, and who would not welcome their boisterous noise.

You're going to both break your necks! she says, but softly.

Olander and Christine, holding hands, take a running swoop and slide straightaway down Summit Avenue, their arms flying out for balance.

Hoh! John exclaims. Watch me!

And with a powerful push off, he slides past them. Lewis and Elise, the young married couple, continue to walk sedately, but for Sofy, Christine, Edwin, Siegfrid, Olander, John, now it is every person for himself or herself, and they run and skate and slide, making use of every level stretch, until they reach the little white frame church. They are flushed, and even in this cold night, warm from laughter and exertion. Sofy and Christine pat their hair back into place while the older persons, and the younger, catch up with them at the church door. Kjerstin purses her lips and shakes her head, but Charley is laughing at his niece and nephews, and Sofy's pretty friend.

No need to tell them to settle down as they enter the church. The solemnity of the night flows out from the yellow panes, through which they see a number of friends and neighbors already gathered. Entering in a sedate line, Kjerstin first, followed by Anna, then their young children, then the husbands, then Elise and Lewis, then Sofy and Christine together, then the boys—they all make their way to the pews where the Louis Carlson family always sits. They take their places on the hard straight pews, lean their heads forward toward the back of the pew in front of them, and shut their eyes. Christine's prayer is pictures: she sees Johanna, she sees Anders, and Charlotta. She imagines their new baby, her own nephew Harald about whom Anders has written so proudly; she thinks of little Anna and Agnes Olson, their mother Selma, and the other children celebrating Christmas, or perhaps not celebrating it, on the farm.

Julotta begins, as always, with the old hymn "När Juldagsmorgon Glimmar." The hymn's melody and familiar words fill the little frame church.

> When Christmas morn is dawning,
>
> In faith I would repair
>
> Unto the lowly stable,
>
> My Savior lieth there.

As they sing, the words take them back, each of them, to childhoods that seem, now, long ago, and to places far away. The night is dark outside, and cold. Beyond the church, beyond the city streets, the prairie stretches away, like their hopes and dreams, unfathomable, unknown, full of possibilities, and perhaps, dangers. But within, the brightness of a gentle light, a comfort of a gentle song. They are soothed and quieted as if stroked by a beloved hand, by the words that remind them of home, by the tender melody that rises and lilts in its old familiar cadence. The service ends, they sing: "Var Hälsad Sköna Morgonstund":

> All hail to thee, O blessed morn,
>
> To tidings long by prophets borne
>
> Hast thou fulfillment given;
>
> O sacred and immortal day,

When unto earth, in glorious ray,

Descends the gift of heaven!

Again, Christmas has come.

It's time to go home. They are subdued, sleepy. It is still very, very dark. They walk down Seventh Street. From Spring Avenue, where the church is located, to Prairie Avenue, then to Summit. No sliding now, no noisy laughter for Sofy to hush. She and Christine are again arm in arm, her brothers and cousins walking silently on either side of them. At Summit they pause, it's four blocks to the left for them to reach home, Christine will go to the right, over to Ninth Street, then down one block to Duluth, back to the Carpenter house.

Good night, good night. Come over as soon as you can tomorrow, God Jul, and thanks, thanks again for the presents, thanks for all your help. Thanks for having me, God Jul—everyone is shaking hands, giving a last Christmas greeting until tomorrow.

I'll walk with Christine, John says. It's too late for her to go alone.

THE WEDDING

In the last of her letters to Christine, Selma writes:

And my eyes got real big when I read your letter. I want to wish you much happiness in your intended union. You are now so wise that you well know what you are doing. And I want to wish that you will be really happy.

The "intended union" Selma mentions is the marriage of Christine to John Benson, an event that occurred July 1, 1896.

The wedding invitation is a stiff white folded sheet, deckle-edged, its front side decorated by two wedding bands, printed in gold, and the names of the couple in elegant script. Inside is printed:

Your presence is requested at the

marriage of

John Benson

to

Christina Borga

Wednesday morning, July 1, 1896,

11:00 o'clock

618 North Summit Avenue

Sioux Falls, S. D.

As the invitation indicates, Christine and John were married at the Carlson house. One of John's attendants was his brother Olander, the other his cousin, Edwin Nelson. Christine's attendants were also John's cousins: Alma and Nellie Anderson. One wonders whether the Olsons from Dell Rapids were there; if there were guests at the wedding who knew Christine best, who wondered, not what sort of wife she would make John, but what sort of husband he would make her. One wonders whether Christine felt that Kjerstin Carlson stood in place of a mother for her that day, or represented only her new husband's aunt.

* * * * *

Christine's wedding day dawns clear and sunny. It is going to be warm. For a week now, after having given her notice to Mrs. Carpenter, Christine has been staying at the Carlson house, where the wedding is to take place.

As the time came for Christine to give her notice, to say good-by to Mrs. Carpenter, she was struck with unexpected emotions. She had not anticipated any sadness from this change. She was finding such pleasure in thinking about living in a house of her own, something she had not done since her childhood days in Sweden. She could hardly imagine a whole house to walk around in, not just one little room for her own space. She loved to think about scrubbing her own kitchen floors, of making meals on her own stove for her own family; she imagined the pleasure of choosing for each meal whatever she wanted, whether a chicken or maybe a ham, whether to boil the potatoes or fry them: whatever she did, her choice. All of these pictures filled her with happy anticipation.

Still, that day, early in June when she stood in front of Mrs. Carpenter, there in the parlor, then it was not so easy as she had thought.

Come in Christine, did you say you have something to talk over?

Yes ma'am, I do. I just must let you know I am going to be leaving. I am going to soon be getting married.

Well, I have to say, I'm not surprised. I suppose it's that nice-looking young man I've seen walking home with you? John, isn't it?

Yes ma'am, John Benson. He is farming now, and has a good place out by Corson.

So that's where you'll be. Does he own?

158

No, not yet, but we're saving up, and we hope it will be soon he can buy something.

Well, if he is half as sensible as you are you should do fine. You're both right to keep your mind on getting property. You'll never get anywhere if you have to keep renting, that's a lesson to keep in mind. But I'm sure you know that too. When is it going to be?

The first of July.

The first of July. Well, I do thank you for giving me a good notice so I can look around for another girl. We'll miss you, of course. You've been a real good girl, Christine. Are you getting married back in Dell Rapids?

No. You know those people, the Carlsons where I go sometimes?

Over on Summit Avenue?

Ja, they're the ones. She, Mrs. Carlson, she's John's aunt. His mother's sister. With his parents being in Sweden, she's sort of looked out for the boys. Anyway, that's where it will be, and she said I could stay there before the wedding.

I'm sure you wish your own mother could be here. But it's nice you have some family. Well, Christine, I give you my best wishes, and tell John when you see him that I said he is getting a mighty fine young woman. I do wish you every happiness, and I know you will make a nice home on that farm.

The weeks elapsed, June was nearly at an end, tomorrow Christine would be packing her belongings, and taking them with her to the Carlsons' house. She was finishing serving dinner to Mrs. Carpenter, her son and his wife, and their guests: Mrs. Carpenter's brother—Mr. Artemus Gale—and her sister—Mrs. McKennen. She brought in the coffee pot and the coffee cups, and placed them in front of Mrs. Carpenter, seated as usual at the end of the long dining room table. As she was leaving, Mrs. Carpenter said:

Oh, Christine, when you've finished the dishes, come into the sitting room. We have a little something for you.

Christine felt anticipation, and pleasure at the idea of a surprize. But as always, her shyness made her timid. Over the years she had served at many, many meals with Mr. Artemus Gale and Mrs. McKennen present, but still she felt for them a respectful awe. He was one of the most important persons in Sioux Falls, one of the founders; and Mrs. McKennen was one of the wealthiest women in town. All three of them, brother and sisters, had big dark eyes, and thick black brows. Mr. Gale had a big black mustache and a booming voice. She wouldn't want to make a mistake in front of him! Or Mrs. McKennen either. Mrs. Carpenter, now she could be pretty particular, but Christine felt good around her; she knew Mrs. Carpenter liked her work, and liked her too.

When she came into the sitting room, the young couple had already left for a meeting of a Whist club. Mrs. Carpenter was sitting in a low chair by a table, Mr. Artemus Gale and Mrs. McKennen were on a sofa together, on the other side of the room. They had been looking at a photograph album that Mrs. McKennen was holding on her lap; Mr. Gale was pointing at one of the photographs. Beside Mrs. Carpenter, on the table, was a little package, wrapped in white tissue paper.

Sit down, Christine, said Mrs. Carpenter, pointing to a chair on the other side of the table by which she sat. And so Christine did, smoothing out her dress, and folding her hands in her lap.

Well Christine, Frances tells us you're getting married, said Mr. Gale.

Ja, said Christine, yes, that's right I am.

And soon, I believe.

This from Mrs. McKennen. She shut the album and put it on the sofa between herself and her brother.

Christine, continued Helen McKennen, you have certainly been a good help for Frances, and we've all appreciated so much what you have done for the family. I know you'll be missed. You've been here quite a while, now, let's see, about four years, isn't it? My goodness, it's been such a time we've had recently it seems longer. It's hardly possible, is it, that Charley's been dead only

160

a year. But Mr. Gale and I wanted you to have a little something to remember us by, and to show our thanks for everything. It's just a little something, use it for whatever you want.

She gave Christine a small white envelope, on the outside was written "For Christine With the good wishes of Mrs. McKennen and Mr. Gale." Inside was a cheque.

Oh thank you, thank you very much.

Christine stood up and walked to the two seated figures. She shook their hands.

And I do know what I want, she said. I am going to get an album, a nice album for pictures.

What a good idea, said Mrs. Carpenter. I will give you one of me!

Helen McKennen laughed.

Well, Frances, maybe that's not what Christine had in mind, to fill the album with picture of the Carpenters!

Christine blushed, but smiled, and said to Mrs. Carpenter,

No, I would like a picture of you. That would be very nice. I would like it a lot. And a picture of Mr. Gale, and his wife.

Well, we would be delighted to give you our pictures, I'm sure, as soon as we have some made. Now Christine, I have a little something for you too.

And Mrs. Carpenter handed Christine the little package. Christine undid the tissue paper, and there inside was a brooch. Open gold-work, on either side, ornately shaped, bordered a central gold-worked decoration. It was very beautiful, it was very fine. The metal glowed richly, red-gold in the gas light.

Christine held it in her hands. She could hardly think of the words she wanted to say.

Tack så mycket, tack så mycket, she said, to her own surprise and her embarrassment.

Mrs. Carpenter smiled and leaned over to pat Christine's arm.

161

Wear it in good health, my dear. It has always been a favorite brooch of mine, and it is pleasure to give it to you. I hope it will remind you of us, and some happy days here in this house, though we've had some sad ones too, haven't we.

Mrs. Carpenter, this is so kind of you. The brooch is so beautiful, I will keep it always. You have been so kind, all of you, and I will remember how nice you have been to me.

When Christine went up to her room that night, she looked at her trunk, standing there in the middle of the floor, its lid open. Only a few more things to pack tomorrow morning and she would be ready to leave. She opened the tissue paper to once again look at the brooch. She held it up to the lamp, admiring the way the light turned and glistened on the curves and the indentations of the metal. She held it up to her throat, admiring how fine it looked against the dark stuff of her dress. Then she smoothed the tissue paper flat on the bed, laid the brooch carefully, gently in the middle, and folded all the sides in securely to hold it safe. She tucked the little package down into the left corner of her trunk, right under her nightgowns. Leaving the trunk still open, she climbed into bed for her last night in this room.

The next morning, right after the breakfast dishes were washed and put away, Mr. Louis Carlson appeared at the back door. He had come with his wagon and team to carry Christine's trunk over to the Carlson house. Christine was dressed and ready, the trunk's latch was securely fastened. Mr. Carlson, who worked in the hauling trade, had brought one of his men to help with the trunk. They went up back stairs to her room, and together carried down the bulky grey box. It was not very heavy, but it was large, and Christine watched anxiously, fearing they would bump and scrape the walls. She was glad Mrs. Carpenter was occupied in another part of the house. But with a few shifts of handholds and a little jostling, and very muted mutterings, they succeeded in bringing the trunk down the narrow staircase with its awkward turns, out the door, down the back steps, and in few moments was loaded into the wagon.

We'll go on then, Christine, said Mr. Carlson. Do you want to ride with us or are you walking over?

I'll walk. I have just a little valise with a few things, and I need to say good-by to Mrs. Carpenter.

Then come over when you finish. I'll tell Kjerstin you're on your way.

Ja, I'll be there soon.

She watched the wagon roll down the street until it came to the corner. There at Duluth Avenue Mr. Carlson turned left and away they rattled, over the pink paving bricks, headed toward Sixth Street, where they would turn to go up the hill again, one more block to Summit Avenue. As she watched, she saw the trunk bump around a bit, but Mr. Carlson's man kept an eye on it, and an arm over its top. It would be all right.

Now it was time, at last, for a real good-by. She went up to her room, smoothed the quilt on her bed, closed up her valise. She looked around at the room, the iron bed, the washstand with its bowl and pitcher, the small chest of drawers. The chair by the window. She looked at herself in the mirror that hung over the chest of drawers, and smoothed her hair. She stood awhile, gazing at the reflection of her face.

This is the only room I have ever had to myself, she thought, I wonder if I will ever have my own room, a room to myself again.

She brought her valise down to the kitchen, then walked into the living room where Mrs. Carpenter was at her desk, writing a letter. Seeing Christine, she stood up and walked toward her.

Well then, this is good-by, isn't it. Oh, here, this is your last cheque. I've added a little something for a wedding present for you and John, you'll probably have to be getting some things. Bachelor farmers usually don't keep house the way a woman likes to keep house! And I know you, Christine, you are particular! I hope going back to the country won't be too hard for you. You tell John to give you some help now and then!

Christine took the cheque; she smiled, but surprisingly, her voice was gone, or at least untrustworthy. Embarrassed by her emotion, she put her hand to her mouth, and nodded. With an effort, with a breath, she smiled again, and found words,

You have been so good to me. My time here has been good. I wish I could have something I could give to you.

Just have a happy home, Christine. I want to think about you, being happy. And you stop by for a visit sometimes when John brings you town.

Yes, I'd like to come by to visit sometime. Well, good-by now. God bless you.

And you too, Christine, God bless you too. I'll be thinking about you on Wednesday, hoping you have a nice day.

Briefly, formally, the two women shook hands. Christine turned away, going back into the kitchen to pick up her valise, and to leave. Mrs. Carpenter followed, and stood at the back door, watching Christine walk down the steps, and down the sidewalk. When Christine turned back for a last look, she saw Mrs. Carpenter there, and each gave the other a little smile, and a little wave of the hand.

And so it was that Christine left the Carpenter house.

Now she is a in small bedroom at the Carlson's, in a room she has been sharing with their little daughter. She has been at the Carlson house several days, preparing herself for the wedding, and helping Mrs. Carlson prepare the smörgåsbord they will have ready for the wedding guests. The wedding is today.

Although Christine has been wide awake, long before the sun's rising, now, at dawn, she remains still in bed. Hanging near the open window is her wedding dress, every stitch completed.

It's going to be hot for that dress, she thinks. It looks fine, but it certainly will be hot.

John and Christine Benson

The little girl with whom she shares the bed, rolls over onto her stomach, and still in deep sleep, flings her left arm over Christine. Christine gazes at the arm draped over her own breast. She thinks of the years she spent in her own narrow bed at the Carpenter house. She thinks of the years ahead of her, a married woman.

Carefully, she removes the child's arm, and slides gently out of the bed, so gently that the child's sleeping is not disturbed. She exchanges her nightgown for an old housedress, one she can wear to help Kjerstin in the kitchen before it's time to get her dress on for the wedding. She folds the nightgown and puts it in the trunk. She takes the Bible which had been on the chest of drawers, the Bible she had received at her first communion, and she puts it also in the trunk. She closes the lid. The trunk will be ready for the men when they come to take it to John's wagon, after the wedding.

HER OWN HOUSE

1900. The hand-written census for Minnehaha County records that in this year, John Benson resided in Brandon Township. Included in the household were his wife, Christine, his son, Norton, and two hired men.

There is an old photograph of this farm, faded so much as to be nearly invisible, but it provides enough detail so that, along with the directions provided by our father who was born there in 1901, my sister and I, one summer's day nearly a century later, were able to locate this house just north of Corson, South Dakota.

Edna and I peer at the photograph and compare it with the present scene. We notice that not too much has changed. The farmhouse stood then, and stands now, on the west side of the road. The barn is west of the house, an out-building between them. Split Rock Creek runs just south of the farmyard; the road from Corson passes over the creek and in front of the house, and it continues north, running up the long sloping hillside on which the farmyard is situated.

This is John and Christine's first home. It is the place where their first two children, two sons, are born.

1903. Christine moves again. With John and her two sons, Norton and Elmer, she moves to her new home, the farm she and John have bought in Benton Township, Minnehaha County. A new address for the old gray trunk. Nearly its last move, and the place to which—at the end of the century—it will finally come home again.

* * * * *

It is a quiet September afternoon. Both boys are sleeping, Christine has finished the dishes from the noon meal and put them away. She sits at the kitchen table, a cup of coffee beside her, writing to Johanna in Sweden.

Hartford, South Dakota
September 18, 1903

Dear Mama,

Thank you for the birthday greetings you sent in Anders last letter which came here just a few days ago. It came in good time, so now I can write you to thank you for that greeting and to tell you that I am well on my birthday, and that we are settling well into our new home. I hope this too finds you well, and at home in comfort with Anders and Charlotta and their little ones. It would be good if you could see my little ones too and they could see their Marmor. Norton now is soon going to be four, in November, and Elmer is now two years old. They are both well, maybe Elmer is a little stronger than Norton sometimes Norton has a cough that makes me worry about the old illness of Papa.

Christine, through the years, had seen a number of births; in fact, she had helped deliver some babies. So, when it came time for her to give birth, for their first baby to be born, Christine knew what to expect. She knew there would be pain, and there would be blood, and there would be noises that no one would want

168

to hear. All of that occurred as expected, and the labor brought forth her and John's first child, a little boy. The year was 1899.

They named their son Norton Leonard. Norton was a fine sounding name, an American name, and Leonard was for John's cousin. He was baptized by the Swedish Lutheran pastor. And to be his godmother, Christine asked Agnes Olson, the little girl from Dell Rapids whom she had cared for when she first came from Sweden; a time that now seems so long ago, now Agnes is a grown-up young lady herself.

No, Christine knew what to expect, she knew that babies did not come easily into this world. What she did not know was how hard it was to keep a baby, once it was born, how to keep it well and safe. And somehow—she did not know how, but in the hard work of keeping the baby safe, she found herself losing something. A certain assurance, a belief and an expectation that the future would be her friend; and a certain confidence in herself, that her own hard work was sufficient security for her own well-being. No, she knew now, now that she was a mother, that you could never be completely sure, never be sure there wasn't an accident, a peculiar illness, to take everything away. She remembered Selma's words—May God help all of us with little ones—and she knew now what Selma felt. What was needed was vigilance, care, constant watchfulness.

John, do you hear that?

Christine's voice is low, but urgent. John mumbles and rolls over.

John, listen!

What? What did you say?

The baby, don't you hear him? Listen to how he's breathing. It sounds bad.

John mutters again, and rolls over again, turning his back to her.

What did you say? Christine asks.

Christine, he sounds just fine.

Listen! she says again. I think his croup is back.

John sits up in bed.

Christine, he sounds just fine to me. Look, go see him if you want to, but I'm going back to sleep. I have to work tomorrow, and I can't take care of a baby all night and work all day.

John's voice has gotten louder as he speaks. Now the baby is awake, and howls. And his howls are broken by a dry, rasping cough.

Listen to him! Christine jumps out bed. He is sick again, just like I thought. Now look at what you've gone and done.

She walks a few steps to Norton's cot, and picks him up, cradling him against her shoulder, rubbing his back. She walks out of the bedroom, crooning to the baby, and paces slowly up and down. While she walks, the baby quietens, and nestles, when she stops to sit in a chair, his back stiffens, and he turns red, coughing and shaking. She walks through the night, alternating between the restful moments when he is nearly lulled to sleep, and the moments of near-panic when, to her eyes, he seems to be struggling for breath. When the sun rises, the baby's fitful sleep becomes deep slumber, and Christine lies on the bed, Norton beside her, as John rouses and gets up.

I'll get breakfast in just a minute, she whispers, just wait a few minutes.

No, he says, you better stay there for now. I guess I can take care of myself this morning.

But here we all are now in our new home, and it is a very happy birthday for me. We are going to make the house bigger, but now it is good enough until we can make the changes. We have three big rooms downstairs a kitchen a sitting room and a bedroom and then washroom off the kitchen and a nice pantry and then a porch, and upstairs two bedrooms. So you see already we have a nice big house, room for us all. It is a white house, and across from the house a big red barn. I have chickens and a few geese, and a cow, so now I have my own eggs, and can make my own pillows, and we have lots of milk and butter and cream. This year we have had a good garden. Now the potatoes are ready to dig, and I have made pickles. Next year I will make more. There is a cellar too, under the house, there I can put my pickle crock, and we can store the potatoes there during the winter.

She pauses, now, and looks out the east window. Down the hill, below the house, she sees a corn field stretching away toward the pasture. The stalks have turned a pale yellow, they rustle in the warm fall breeze. She can just make out the leaves' movements. Beyond the field, which slopes down beyond her sight to Skunk Creek, rises the broad expanse of the hillside that marks the eastern boundary of their farm. Its grass too is a yellowish brown. She pictures in her mind's eye their cows, clustering in the shade of the few trees that edge the creek. The cows, the corn-picking soon to come, the granary still to be finished—So much, she thinks, so much for John, or Papa, as she now calls him, to do. She is thankful their children are boys, boys who before too very long will be able to help their Papa with the farm. To have this place, to have her own house: it's more than she had wanted to let herself hope for. Now, having it, she feels a constant gratitude to God; and gratitude to John for bringing her here to this place; and she feels wonder, wonder that it can be truly theirs. When she looks at her clean, orderly rooms—how spacious, how solid—she feels satisfaction in her own achievements too. But alongside her happiness and contentment is, to her surprise, an unexpected disquiet. Sometimes she feels an anxiety she had never before experienced—what if this security—achieved with such hard work by John and by her—were to be lost? What would she do then? And it's not just herself she has to take care of now, but her boys. It's John and owning the farm, their own land, that makes them safe. But before now, people had thought they were safe and secure—think of her own mother, when her father was alive, and herself as a little girl. That didn't last, did it? How can you ever be sure you are safe? The only answer Christine knows is to work, work, hard and save what you can, whenever you have extra.

But now, she thinks, now there's Elmer too. Elmer, who slept through the night early on, only waking to eat, and then returned to sleep. Elmer, who cries only when there was something to cry about. On this September afternoon, she thinks about Elmer with gratitude, with relief. It is as if the anxiety that Norton brought is calmed by Elmer with his placid ways, and his good health. Oddly, she feels that God has sent her this second boy to give her the courage and strength to keep up her battle for her first-born. We all have to help Norton, she thinks, he is not strong. Now I have to be so careful with him. By and by, when he gets older Papa has to not expect him to work so hard, Elmer can take up for him when the time comes.

These are her thoughts, as she muses about the grandchildren her mother has not seen. She continues writing:

We had a picture made of Elmer and I am sending it to Anders for you all to see. He has a sweet smile, and he is a very good boy. This picture was when he was baptized, now he is bigger, over two years old, and getting tall.

Christine has finished her letter, she folds it and finds an envelope. She addresses it to her brother, Anders Gustaf Bergius, in Emilsdahl, Värmland, Sweden. Tomorrow Papa can take it to the post office when he goes in to

Hartford. Still the boys are sleeping, so she takes her little wooden mending box into the sitting room, and makes herself comfortable in a chair by the window.

These are good times for us, she thinks. All of us well, good crops this year. The note paid off. Land of their own, land for the boys someday, so they will not have to work so hard, and so they will not ever have to work for somebody else. If only they can keep it all together, the farm for the boys!

Christine remembers when she first looked at the land where she now lives, and realized it would her home.

* * * * *

Come on, Christine, aren't you ready yet?

John has hitched the horses to the buggy and is impatient. They are taking a day or two away from the farm, driving west of Sioux Falls to where John's brother Lewis lives with his wife Elise and their three children on a farm he has recently bought. It is a fine, sunny day in late October, the first October in the new century, 1900. The hay is in, the corn not yet ready to be picked, and there are a few days to spare. It is fully a twenty-mile drive, and so they've decided to spend the night with Lewis and Elise and have a good visit. Lewis and Elise have three children now, Arthur, Walter, and Esther, who is just over a year old, just about Norton's age. Christine thinks she is pregnant again, but she feels good, and she looks forward to having a little time with her sister-in-law.

I'm nearly ready. I have to get the basket with the Norton's blankets. Here, put this in. I just want to pack up some jam I made to give Elise. I wish you had told me before yesterday about this trip so I could have done some baking.

Christine is walking and talking and climbing into the buggy. She has a little basket in which Norton can sleep when she is not holding him in her arms.

It is a warm day for October, the sky is a brilliant blue, and John does not hasten the horses' pace. The gravel road crossing the rolling land east of Sioux Falls carries them up a number of steep hills, hills that force the horses to pull hard in their harness, turning their glossy hides black with sweat. They drive near Sioux Falls, but they do not stop, they continue west out of the city, on the road that leads toward Hartford, a bustling little town about fifteen miles west of Sioux Falls. They head toward the town, but they will not need to go that far, since Lewis's farm is located several miles this side of Hartford. The road goes west, then they turn north for a few miles, then, at the top of a range of hills they turn again west. Having traveled this journey before, Christine knows that soon the hills will slope down steeply into the broad bottom land of the creek, before rising again in another line of hills a mile or two to the west.

They reach the top of the hill, just where the road starts running down in a long stretch to the iron bridge which spans Skunk Creek.

John pulls up the horses, stops the buggy, climbs out.

Come on, climb down, I want to show you something here.

He takes Norton from Christine's arms while she bunches up her skirts, trying to hold them out of the dust, and climbs out of the buggy. John leads the horses over to a fence, and ties them there.

Holding Norton, he turns and walks up the little incline that borders the road, Christine hurries to catch up, and together they walk through the long grass that catches at their clothes, climbing to the peak of the hill that rises up to the south of the road. A few dozen yards, and they are there. To their left, running off to the south, the hill on which they stand continues in an undulating line; in front of them, looking to the west, the land slopes down and further down. There at the bottom of the hill, lies the creek, coiling around on itself like a sleepy brown snake, with the water, flowing in front of them from north to south, sparkling here and there in the sun. In some stretches the creek is bordered by steep banks which it has cut in the earth, the banks blackish-brown slices through the turf; in some stretches the stream broadens out, and yellow

174

sand lines the water. In some low muddy places, rushes and cattails grow. Near the place where the creek flows out from under the bridge it sparkles and ripples as it breaks over rocks visible to them just under the water's surface. Beyond the creek stretch the fields of a farm, and beyond them, nearly a mile from where John and Christine stand, are the trees of a farmstead's windbreak and, only glimpsed through the trees, the farm buildings. Beyond that farm, she can see the farmstead of Lewis and Elise.

Do you see that farm, Christine? Just this side of Lewis's? It's the one across the road from them.

Yes, I can see it. I've seen it before, when we've been at their house.

But you've never seen it from here. Look at how nice it looks from here, with the trees there and the creek and the pasture, that's part of that same farm. It's pretty isn't it.

It is, it is. It makes a pretty sight, on a day like this. Look over there—and Christine points to her left, to the south, where one hill in the range rises to a higher prominence—Look over at that hill, and the trees there. You don't see trees like them very much. They're so bright, the leaves, they're so bright. That's a nice sight too.

I wanted you to see this. All the way from the road that's between this farm and Lewis, all the way to the top of those hills right up here, and from about half a mile from here where we are on over to the section line, that farm's for sale. Lewis told me about it last time I was with him, and I think we could buy it. We can't move on to it yet, the house needs some work, and anyway we have the lease at Corson, but I think we can buy it now, if you think it's a good idea too.

Christine does not answer right away. She and John have been renting the farm they moved to on their wedding day. It is a good farm, and close to John's relatives. She has gotten used to life on that farm, used to the house, she has a garden, and chickens, even flowers. But every time John sells the crops, it's two-fifths for the owner. Whenever she thinks about doing

175

something to the house, she remembers: in fact, it is not her house. It is more her house than any she has had before, and she will always remember it as the house she came to as a bride, the house where her first baby was born. And, before very long, where her second baby will be born too. But they do not own it. It is not her house, not John's land.

She gazes at the land stretching away before her, the pastures, the square patches of the fields: whispering stalks of corn, never still in the prairie wind, golden stubble where wheat had been harvested, a grey-green plot where hay had grown. She sees the cottonwood trees clustering to the north and the east of the farmstead, some leaves still on the branches, brilliant yellow in the October afternoon. She imagines how they will stand against the bitter winds of December, and how they will murmur in the summer's sultry evening breeze. She thinks how nestled the house must be, how safe and protected she would feel inside. As she stands there, the wind catches her hair, pulls it out of the combs which bind it. She reaches up to tuck the strands back into place and sees John looking at her. He looks puzzled, even anxious. She realizes she has not answered him. Do you think it's a good idea, he has said. She moves to face him.

Yes, she says.

Then, turning back toward the valley, she takes John's arm; they stand side by side, looking out over the prospect.

Yes, she says, I think this is a good place for a home.

* * * * *

And so, early in the spring of 1903, in March when rental leases on farms expire, while there is time to settle into a new place before crops must be planted, Christine moves again. John has been farming the land, getting help from his brother across the road when needed, while still keeping up the Corson farm. They have paid off the note early. The land is theirs, and the house. It is moving day.

Mr. Carlson helps them again, and Lewis and Olander, with their wagons move the furniture from the Corson farm to the new home place. Christine stands at the door, telling them where to put the furniture as they carry it in. Soon things will be in place, and everyone can go across the road to Lewis's house where Elise has a nice hot dinner waiting. In comes the bed, with its high oak headboard, carved with small flowers. In this bed two children were conceived and born. Any maybe more, Christine thinks.

Take it in there, she motions to her right, to the small north room.

In comes the square oak table.

That's for the front room, she says.

It's the front room now, but soon she will be able to call it a dining room. John has told her about his plans to build a new front room, and a porch. Mrs. Carpenter has already given her furniture for it, a settee and rocker she was replacing with something more modern. For now, they will store the furniture, but soon she will have a front room, and a dining room too.

The tall oak cabinet is next.

That's for the front room too, she says, but be careful with that. We don't want that glass to break.

This had been the one purchase they had made for their new house: a beautiful cabinet, it was a bookcase and a desk too. On the left, a glass front with shelves inside; on the right, drawers and a slant-top that lowers to a desk; across the top, a mirror. In her packing for the move, she had taken the books that had come with her and John on their journeys: her Bible, the New Testament John had been given at his first communion, her Swedish Psalmbook, and most precious, the little *Pilgrim's Progress* Johanna had given her, long ago—taken them and packed them safely in her trunk. Tonight she'll put them on the shelves of the new cabinet, situated nicely in the front room.

In comes the round oak table, and chairs.

That's right here, in the kitchen, she says. That chest? That goes into the pantry under the shelves across from the cellar door.

Quickly, with so many people to help, things go into place. Boxes and cartons of dishes are stacked in the pantry. What a pleasure it will be, to put her things on those shelves she has scrubbed shining clean, to put her knives and forks and spoons, her kitchen towels and carefully folded aprons into that pine chest in the pantry.

Where should this trunk go?

Oh, just put it in the front room for now, she says. I'll unpack it when we come back from dinner, then you can help John take it upstairs. It's too big for our bedroom. It can stay in the attic, I guess, I'm not moving any more.

John

LEAVING HOME

For John, perhaps unlike Christine, it was not a question of whether he would go to America, but rather when he would go. And unlike Christine, his emigration occurred in a context of relatives already located, and brothers and sisters to accompany him or to join him in the new land.

By the time John had grown up into a young man, and was ready to think about going to America, several sisters of his mother, Pernilla, and three of her brothers had already emigrated to America and had established businesses or farms. Her sister Christina, married to John Anderson, had settled on a farm near Garretson, South Dakota, just east of Sioux Falls. Very near-by was Pernilla's brother Charley, married to Anna, who farmed near Corson. Also farming near Corson, at least for a while, until they returned to Sweden, were Pernilla's sister Anna Stina and her husband Sven Peter Nelson. A brother Pål and his wife Neta were in Iowa. Kjerstin, Pernilla's youngest sister, was married to Louis Carlson and, as we know, lived on Summit Avenue in Sioux Falls. And Louis, a second brother, had gone the farthest; when he emigrated to America, he went all the way to the West Coast, to Portland, Oregon.

And John had a brother who emigrated with him, and one who was to come later: Ludwig, now Lewis, and Olander. Lewis and Olander, like John, came to farm. To work on a farm, to save money, to buy their own places. All three were successful in accomplishing their aims: Lewis was the first to own property, buying in Hartford township; John followed, buying his farm right across the road from Lewis's, and Olander bought a farm close to the eastern edge of Sioux Falls. And sisters came too, Sofy, as we have seen, first to Sioux Falls, then moving to Portland, Oregon. She visited her old home, but returned again to America, to Oregon, where she married and made her home. A younger sister, Albertina, also emigrated, and two sisters—Elfrida and Annie, though they eventually returned to Sweden, also spent time in America.

181

John's emigration, the emigration of his brothers and his sisters seemed to have been a success. As the young father and landowner who is pictured in the 1909 photograph looked back to that date in 1889 when he left Sweden, he may well have thought:

Ja, coming here was the right thing to do, that change made things possible that could never have happened in Sweden. Look at me now: I own my own farm, and a big farm too, not just a few rocky acres. I have a house, a big house for my family.

And yet John would have known that not every immigrant's story was a success. Now, having achieved at least some of his goals, he must have felt pride in his accomplishment, and he might have attributed his success to his own hard work, nobody's handouts. But, in 1889, as a young man of 21, crossing the Atlantic to a new country, a new life, his success would have been a hope, but not at all assured. Even as a confidant young man, he would have had not only ambitious dreams, but also—surely—doubts and uncertainties.

* * * * *

In brief notes, John recorded the facts of his trip from his home in Sweden to what was to be his new home in Dakota Territory:

From Copenhagen the 4th April, 1889 and from Liverpool the 9th April, 1889 and we came to New York the 17 April and boat over North Sea was called Brave Hull and I came to Sioux Falls the 24 April, 1889. Bothnia was the name of the boat over the Atlantic.

He tells us the names of the ships, the dates of the journey. Of what he felt about the journey, the sights he saw, we know only a very few fragments.

I asked my father once: Did Grandpa ever talk about what it was like, crossing the ocean coming over here?

He pointed across the barnyard, and said: *See that silo out there? He used to say the waves were so huge they were as tall as that silo. Imagine a little ship going up and down on waves like that. And another story he used to tell: one day the waves washed a little fish up on the deck. Dad picked it up and threw it back in the ocean. He said: You can grow up. When I travel back to Sweden you'll be a great big fish, worth keeping.*

The fish may have grown, may have been harvested by the North Atlantic fishermen, but John did not make the return voyage.

* * * * *

John Benson, born Johan Bengtsson, was the third child of Bengt Peter Svensson and his wife Pernilla. His older brother Ludwig—whose name was anglicized to Lewis when he emigrated—was born in 1866; Sofy was next in 1867, then Johan was born in 1868. He was followed by Augusta, two years later, then Elfreda, Emilia, Olander, Albertina, and Annie.

Bengt Peter Svensson was a farmer and lived near the village of Våxtorp, in the province of Halland, in the southern part of Sweden. A visitor coming to Våxtorp will be shown the parish church. Here is where Johan received his first communion, as is noted from the inscription in the New Testament presented to him on that day, June 9, 1883. It is a white church, built of stone and plaster; the oldest section, the old tower, was built in the 12th century.

Surrounding the church is the burial ground where the tombs of Bengt and Pernilla, lie adjacent to the walkway to the church, "Lantbrukären," meaning "farmer" inscribed on Bengt Peter's tombstone.

The farm where Johan was born was located near a smaller village than Våxtorp, a little place called Killhult. There, even now, one can find the location of that farm where Johan and his brothers and sisters were born. But to picture it as he would have seen it, one can look at the painting that Johan's sister Elfrida sent him in America: a charming red house and barn, nestled behind the protection of a grey stone wall. A road slopes down from the farmstead into the foreground of the picture. The grass is green, the buildings are richly warm in color, the whole enclosure bespeaks security and comfort.

This place, however, is not the home where Johan grew up. When Johan was a year and a half, he had two older siblings; another child was on the way. Perhaps Bengt Peter could not support his rapidly growing family. Perhaps Pernilla—understandably—was overwhelmed by the prospect of caring for four children under the age of four. For these, or other reasons, Johan was taken to stay at his grandfather's home, his father's father, Sven Bengtsson.

* * * * *

Pernilla Svensson is seated at her kitchen table. It is a small room, with one window that looks out towards the woods behind the house. It is afternoon, a winter afternoon, and darkness has fallen. Daylight hours are short in a Swedish winter, but today the daylight has seemed even more than usually tenuous; it has been a gloomy day, not cold, but there had been all day a foggy, grey dampness that reduced the sunshine into a wan, pale light.

It is chilly in the room, the fire in the kitchen stove had burned very low while she and Bengt and the children had been gone. Now Bengt is out in the barn, seeing to the horses and the cow, and children will soon have to be fed. They had had a meal at Farmor's and Farfar's, but Pernilla wants them to have some warm mush before they are put to bed. For the moment she has laid the baby, Emilia, in her cradle. Emilia is still nursing, and Pernilla will need to feed her soon, but the baby is sleeping now. The journey home had lulled her to sleep.

It will be hard for Pernilla to sleep tonight, and hard for Bengt, too.

They had been looking forward to this day for a long time. And now, they come back, just the same as before, without him.

Times had been so hard a few years ago. Pernilla remembers how sick she had been after Johan was born. Three babies in three years. Ludwig was a naughty two-year-old, always needing her to watch him. Sofy was a little sickly, it was hard to get any rest when she was always crying at night with first an earache and then a bad cold or maybe just to cry because her mother was with Ludwig. And for some reason, though her other births not been easy, giving birth to Johan was more painful and difficult than either of the other two. The woman who came to help with the birthing had looked scared when she took

185

her first check of Pernilla's progress, and looked worse as the afternoon and evening wore on, and still no baby. It was something about how he was situated. And after he was born, Pernilla was too weak to do anything for him. Thank goodness Bengt's mother came to stay with her for a little while, and her own mother Charlotta was able to help. But after they went back to their own houses, and she was alone, she just felt so listless.

Before, when Ludwig was a baby, she had had energy enough for two mothers, people said. She hated for the day to end, there were always so many things she wanted to do, and she could hardly wait for the sun to bring another day, she was so eager to be at her housekeeping and baby tending, and so happy to be sweeping and baking and nursing. Even when Sofy came, she had good strength. But with Johan it was different. She tried to pick up with her work, but things did not get done. The house wasn't clean anymore. Sometimes when Bengt came in from his work in the fields, he would find her in bed, babies crying, the stove cold, and no meal ready for him. She could hardly blame him when he would leave the house and not come home until he could be sure everyone was asleep. And when he would finally come home, he'd sometimes be drunk or near to it. She knew he wondered the same things she did: how would they manage? A baby every year, and times so hard. How would he be able to take care of these children who just kept coming and coming?

Somehow—and Pernilla even now, sitting here in the dark afternoon, even now she can't understand it—somehow it came to be in her mind that all these troubles were Johan's fault. When he cried, and he didn't cry too much, but when he did, it made her angry. It made her feel like he knew just how little patience she had and that he was going to use it right up. Sometimes she just stood and let him cry, and was glad to see how upset he was, his red face, his flailing fists. Then she was so frightened by that, by her cold anger, she'd pick him up and hug him too hard. Sometimes when he looked at her with those big dark eyes, not crying, but quiet and still, some of those times it frightened her to think he had figured out she didn't love him.

But she did love him! She loved him just like she loved Ludwig and Sofy. What kind of woman doesn't love her own child? It was just that there was too much for her, and she didn't know how things were ever going to be better.

Then, at the last, when she knew she was pregnant again, then both she and Bengt knew something had to be done. Pregnant again, four babies now. When she had told him, Bengt just shook his head and left the house. The crops weren't good. Everybody was talking about going to America, her own sisters and brothers were talking about it, but what good was a dream like that to a man with more children around his table than he had bowls on the shelf?

And so Bengt talked to his father, and one day Sven came and took Johan away with him, to his own house. She had packed his little clothes, and she and Bengt stood in the doorway of the house, watching Sven drive off in the wagon with their son. She felt like she should weep, but there were Ludwig and Sofy to think of. They cried when Johan left, cried because they wanted to go along with him to Farfar's house. Her crying too wouldn't have helped matters.

Johan had cried when he left. He hung onto her neck when Sven reached over to take the child in his arms. Pernilla did not weep that day, but today, sitting and remembering, the tears come.

It had seemed the right thing to do. She did not know what else they could have done then, at that time.

The years had passed. Not too many, but enough to make a difference. Augusta was born, a sunny happy baby, and, thank God, an easy birth. Then Elfrida. Still more and more children it seemed, but she was stronger, not worn out like she had been. And the farm was doing better, the crops were good, and they were getting along.

At regular intervals, they would say:

Now, soon, we'll go get Johan. He's been there long enough. Things are better now. We don't want him to forget where his home is.

187

And then they would say:

Just a little bit longer. Let's wait till we've sold the rye. Let's see if the cow has a calf we can sell. Let's wait till the other children get over the measles. Let's wait till the baby stops nursing.

But at last the day had come. And that day was today. Bengt had written his father, had said he and Pernilla were coming with the children for a visit, and would take Johan, now nearly five, home with them at last. Bengt's parents lived not far away, but too far for easy traveling back and forth, and Pernilla had seen her son only occasionally, at Jul or at the Våxtorp church, when they happened to be there on the same Sundays. She could tell, when she saw Johan with his Farmor that the old woman had grown attached to her little grandson, and he to her. Seeing that was a reproach, and at the same time a relief. Johan had been better off, she thought to herself. It was better for him to be there rather than stay with us. And he'll soon be back home again.

So today they had all traveled to Farfar's house. A farmhouse, like theirs, but with more comforts. The old man still farmed a little, but Farmor had all her time for the house and Johan. The old couple knew why Bengt and Pernilla were coming. They had brought together Johan's things, but they couldn't bring themselves to tell the child what was going to happen that day. In fact, his grandmother had tried, but each time she began to tell him he was going to be returning to his parents' home, her own sorrow at his leaving stopped the words in her throat.

When Bengt and Pernilla arrived, and came inside the house, there was a good meal set out on the table for them. Beans and pork roast and bread and herring and a thick parsnip soup. First they ate, and they all kept the conversation on the children and how well they played together. Johan looked healthy and strong, almost as big, though not as tall as Ludwig. He had bright dark eyes, and thick dark hair that fell at an angle over his broad forehead. While their parents and grandparents drank coffee, the children played hide-and-seek among the old painted chests and cabinets in Sven's house.

It was time to go. Pernilla sees the scene now in her mind's eye. She and Bengt put on their wraps. The daylight was nearly gone; they needed to leave as soon as they could get the children ready if they did not want to have to travel in the dark. She put on Sofy's coat, then Ludwig's, she wrapped up Augusta in a shawl, and Elfreda and Emilia in their blankets. Then she turned to Johan.

Johan, can you get your coat?

He stood there, looking at her with his big dark eyes, looking puzzled, saying nothing.

Here it is. His grandmother handed the coat to Pernilla.

Pernilla began slipping his arms into his coat sleeves; she felt his body stiffen.

Here, now, Johan, show me what a big boy you can be, she said coaxingly, as he put his small strength against hers, as she tried to put his other arm inside the sleeve.

Here, I'll do it, said Bengt, and he brought his stronger arms to bear.

But Johan's silence was over.

No! he screamed, putting his arms out in front of them, to keep her and Bengt away. No, no! Farfar! I want to stay with Farfar!

Tears streaked his face and he turned away, clinging to his grandfather's leg. Sven said nothing. Bengt looked at his son. Johan's shoulders were shaking, he was wracked with sobs.

I suppose he's afraid of us, Bengt said, more to himself than anyone else.

He stood there, his arms at his side. Then, when the child's crying had quieted, he placed a hand on Johan's shoulder.

There, there boy. I don't want to scare you. If you are at home here, I won't make you come. Home's not a place you should have to go to if you don't want it.

Sven loosened the child's grip, and picked him up.

189

You know he is always welcome here, Bengt. But he's your boy. You do what you have to do.

No, Papa. He can stay for now. When he's older, not so little, he won't mind so much. And we thank you for the good care you and Mama have had for him. So, now, Pernilla, we'll go, and say good-by to you Johan. Johan, say good-by to your brothers and sisters. We'll go home today, and you can come to us another time.

So they rode home again. No more in number than they had been on the trip over. Bengt and Pernilla rode silently through the damp gloomy afternoon, each in his or her own thoughts.

Pernilla stirs herself, as she hears Emilia crying. Time to put some wood on the fire, time to put some coffee on. She wipes her face with her kerchief, she wipes her hands on her apron.

Another time, she thinks. Another time, a little bit later, I will have my boy back, and I can show him that I want to be a good mother to him. I will make up for these years. He will be my own little boy again.

In the meantime, there is supper to make, children to put to bed, a baby to nurse. She hears Bengt, coming in from the barn, with Ludwig, now old enough to help with chores.

The coffee is hot, she says. I'll pour you some.

* * * * *

In the 1920's John's brothers Lewis and Olander, both successful farmers, planned a trip back to Sweden to visit their parents and see their old home. By this time, nearly forty years since the three had left Sweden, the grandparents had died. Lewis and Olander asked John if he were going to travel with them.

No, he said. There's nothing there for me now.

190

* * * * * *

Among John's things was a little black metal strong box. It contained a number of interesting items, among them two letters from his father. One is written in 1904, and begins in such a way as to make us wonder about the relationship between Bengt and his son.

Killhult the 24th of March, 1904

Dear Son Johan,

After a long silence between us, I will write a few lines and let you know that we are in good health here at home and all is about as before, we are doing quite well, and we hope that these lines will find you in good health and comfortable for when health and love are in the home so is success also.

Now I must tell you that we had a good crop this last year, namely rye and barley but the potatoes were poor and we have 6 sheep and we have sold one cow since Christmas and we have two horses and we have 16 hogs, 10 small and 6 large. We shall butcher 3 in about 14 days. We butchered 3 before Christmas.

Now I must tell you that we have a very nice winter now not very cold and not any snow and it has almost been unusually nice all winter.

I can even greet you from your sisters that they are well and Frida and Emeli have it good but Augusta has it quite hard because they have many children and small income.

And I can tell that we had a funeral for August Pers on Sunday. He died of a stroke. He was Lars brother-in-law. He moved to Karl's home in Killhult earlier for then it was sold because Barden was dead but Karl he lives with his old temper, drinks brandy like a rascal. And Engvar he died last fall.

I can even greet you from Johannes Ottes and Johannes Svens. Johannes Ottes has two boys and two girls and Johannes Svens 5 girls and one boy. And Johannes Petterson in Pershult is now as before and not married, neither is Nita. Now it is soon time for Sven

191

Petersa to begin to get ready to leave America. We have heard it said that they are going to return to Sweden soon and it will undoubtedly be as we have heard that the oldest boys will not come along. He said otherwise that he did not want his boys to marry any American girls, but one is already married, but what she is we do not know [Sven Petersa is Bengt's brother-in-law, John's uncle. He had lived a number of years in America, farming near Corson, SD. Several of his children remain in America, and several more later emigrate. They are John's cousins.].

Now I must stop for I do not know of anything more to write about this time except to greet you heartily from us to you. Greet Olander so much and when you write give Olander's address. Greet your wife and acquaintances so warmly. But first and last are you greeted from us.

Friendly

Father and Mother

B. P. Svenson

Mother Svenson

The letter refers to the "long silence" between Bengt Peter and his son John, but as the letter progresses other references—or omitted references—prompt curiosity about Bengt's relationships with other sons as well. Bengt Peter mentions Olander, but not Lewis, no greeting is sent to his eldest son. And even though Bengt Peter sends greetings to Olander, he lacks Olander's address; perhaps there has there also been a "long silence" between those two also.

The second letter is dated 1915, written when Bengt Peter is 73 years old. It is, perhaps, the last letter John received from his father, and it tells of the changes in his life, of family news, and family worries.

Hörsabeck the 9th of Dec. 1915

Dear Son John,

I must quickly write a few words to tell you how we are these days. We have good health and have lived well up to the time of this writing and we hope that you are well and also have a merry Christmas. Now I must tell you that we sold Kilhult recently to Anton Gustafson from Knapparp. We got 7900 kr. and we bought here in Hörsabeck last fall. It is only a small place, not more than 9 acres of land to it and trees on half of it. It isn't so one can feed a cow, but there shall surely be enough fodder when we have had it a while. We do have 1 cow and 1 hog and a number of chickens so now when it is winter I do not have much to do. We bought from Schoolteacher Larson Stauhus and they had built it so there is a good living house and a little outhouse. . . .

Now I must tell you that here we had a fairly good crop this fall, but everything is very costly. Those who have only a little place have sold and sold for much money. Milk is doubled in price. We got 15 ore for a liter last month. And that is because of that terrible war. For those who have to buy everything, it is difficult. Augusta [one of John's younger sisters] *has great hardship. She has 4 children and herself to feed and no one to earn anything because he is dead. I wrote in Ludwig's letter that from what we hear you have it very good so it would be pleasant and welcome if you could send her some money. We have given her a little at Christmas. I can tell you that Petersa in Pershult are dead. Stena died last summer and Peter recently. He was not sick more than 3 or 4 days. He was 94 years old. Bengt Oteson lives but lays in bed all the time. He hasn't been able to get out of bed for a couple years. This winter Lars Andreyas was in a hospital a while and had something taken off his toes but now he can walk but is lame. And Sven Peter in Haslof lays and has pain in one leg. Otherwise all is well. This year they have made alot of money but Arvid has been away for military training all summer and will be there until Jan. 10.*

I can greet you heartily from Alfred and Annie [Annie is John's youngest sister. She spent a few years in America, but returned to Sweden to stay, marrying Alfred and raising a family there]. *They are well and have it good and their two children are big and good for their age.*

Now at last we wish you a merry Christmas and good wishes for the new year. Now I must close with many dear greetings from us to you.

Sincerely
Father and Mother Swenson
B. P. Svenson

A litany of events that are the everyday experiences as we age: illness, death, high prices—and a reference to "that terrible war" that was raging in Europe, from which at this moment America still stood protected by its ocean boundary. It is a picture of the "dear old native land" that does not entice one to return home again. As John reads this, perhaps he congratulates himself. Perhaps he says, Yes, I was right to leave. There is nothing there but sadness and trouble. This place is the place for me.

AMERICA

April 24, 1889. Sioux Falls is a busy place. In a few months, South Dakota will become a state, and Sioux Falls is its biggest city. It has a number of well-established industries: the Cascade flour mill, a brewery on North Main that flourished despite the Temperance societies in the town, a pork packing plant, an Iron Foundry and Machine Shop run by the five Pankow brothers. It has several railroads that transport Dakota crops to grain markets like St. Paul and Chicago. It has numerous churches. Construction began in 1888 on the Episcopal Cathedral. Financed by a donation from John Jacob Astor in memory of his wife Augusta, when completed it will boast windows by Louis Comfort Tiffany. Many other churches are also established, representing nearly all other denominations, both Roman Catholic and Protestant. There are a number of Lutheran churches: one for Swedes and several for Norwegians and Germans. It has literary societies, and Masonic orders. It has several brothels outside the city limits across the river, including a particularly popular site, the Willowdale Mansion.

Sioux Falls is expanding in all directions from the little village that was established in the 1870's. Up on the ridge of the hill just west of the shopping and business district, the houses of the wealthy are going up. Downtown, on Main Avenue, construction is beginning on the Minnehaha County Courthouse, a structure designed by the locally famous architect Wallace LeRoy Dow. The courthouse is being built of pink quartzite, a native stone of exceptional hardness that is quarried in East Sioux Falls. The building, as it grows, is slightly reminiscent of the Town Hall in Renaissance Florence, a square, fortress-like shape that is surmounted by a single tall tower.

This quartzite is seen in many of the new structures, in public buildings as well as private houses. It is the stone chosen by Bishop Hare for the construction of the building of All Saints School; Hattie Phillips, the widow of the founder of Sioux Falls, Dr. Josiah Phillips, has her mansion constructed of quartzite. When, through the political connections of Richard F. Pettigrew, Sioux Falls is chosen as the site for the State Penitentiary, he specifies quartzite as the building material, and it is quarried by the convicts. Even some streets are paved with these mauve-colored stone blocks.

Outside the city, the rolling hills of the prairie are quickly coming under the discipline of agriculture. By 1889, no longer are there open tracts which homesteaders can make their own, simply by setting up tree claims. But property is still fluid here, land changes hands often, as it is bought and then sold by speculators who want to make a quick profit, who make that profit and move on to other ventures; or as it is sold by homesteaders who find life on the Dakota prairies a lonely substitute for the dreams of success and profit they have held within their mind. But for the new immigrants, those dreams are still new and enticing. All that's needed to get some land yourself is to work and save, to get some capital, and then to keep your eye out for something you can buy. And once you have your land, farm it well, and buy more when you get a chance. In Sweden, if a family had a farm, it would get smaller through every passing generation, divided among the sons. Here in America, a man can get a farm, and you can get more land after that, so in the next generation, each son can start with property, on his own farm, with as much land as his father had had, maybe more. That's the difference between Sweden and America.

* * * * *

Louis Carlson has pulled his wagon as close as he can to the depot. He sits there, watching the passengers get off the train from Chicago. He's been sent to the station to bring home Kjerstin's two nephews, Ludwig and Johan, whom they expect to be arriving today at the end of their long trip from Våxtorp, Sweden. Kjerstin has been up since dawn, cleaning and cooking. For her to have her nephews here, Pernilla's boys, makes her feel like she is connected once more with her own Swedish family.

Louis and Kjerstin have done pretty well in America, so far. They have a cozy little house on Summit Avenue. Not so big, but big enough for them. Kjerstin's brother and her brothers-in-law have all gone into farming, but Louis thinks he'll do better staying in Sioux Falls. He'd had enough of farming in Sweden to last a lifetime. No, Sioux Falls, is the place for him. He had never lacked work in his hauling business, and now, with the quarries in East Sioux Falls, and the new building going on everywhere, he expects to do pretty good. And Kjerstin agrees. She likes city life, not being out on some farm, with nobody to talk to.

He remembers the two boys from the days when they were young teenagers, and so when he catches sight of them, stepping off the train, he recognizes them right away. Both are dark, like Kjerstin and their mother Pernilla, dark hair and dark eyes. Johan's face is a bit broader than his brother's, his mouth more full-lipped. Handsome boys, he thinks, alert and confidant. They ought to do all right.

Over here, he calls, Johan, Ludwig, here I am.

He climbs out of the wagon, shakes hands with the boys, claps Ludwig on his shoulder. Close up, they don't look so confidant, he thinks. Close up they do still look like boys, though Johan is 21, and Ludwig 23.

Your Aunt Kjerstin is at home, but she's sure eager to see you two. She's going to have a lot of questions about her mama and papa, and your mama.

Johan and Ludwig climb into wagon, being as careful as they can. Although their clothes are travel stained and dusty and show the signs of having been slept in for days, still they are the best clothes each of them has. Louis flaps the reins, and the horses lean into their collars. Jolting over the ruts, the wagon rolls out of the depot yard.

How was the trip? Louis makes conversation over the rattling noise of the wagon on the paving stones. Did you get sea-sick?

197

Johan did, Ludwig says. He spent most of the voyage leaning over the rail.

You spent most of it hanging onto the bunk and praying.

Well, I guess it's good somebody prayed, we made it. It was good to get off the boat, and it's good to get off that train. There were so many people getting on that train in Chicago we couldn't get a seat. We had to stand between cars for a long way.

That's a pretty trip, though, Johan says. Iowa, is that the name of the province we went through? I've never seen such open country in my life. You could plow all day on one of those farms and never get to the end of the field. It is like that here too?

Not such good farms as in Iowa. Your uncle Pål settled down there. No, the land isn't as good here, but it's easier to get. If you want to farm, you've got a pretty good chance here. After you get some money, of course.

How is Aunt Kjerstin? Ludwig asks.

She's feeling pretty good. You know we just had a baby last winter, so now we have three little ones. Hauling business has been good, though, and we're getting along pretty good.

When they pull up to the little frame house, the boys jump down out of the wagon, and Louis helps lower each of their trunks to the ground. He drives the horse and wagon around back to the little barn behind the house. Ludwig and Johan carry their trunks up to the porch, just as Kjerstin, who has been watching for the wagon, and had heard it pull up in front of the house, opens the door to greet them.

Kjerstin is small, like their mother, and her nephews tower over her. She shakes hands, first with Ludwig, then with Johan. In their faces, she sees the remembered features of her sister Pernilla.

Welcome, Ludwig, and you too Johan. Come in, come in. Leave those trunks there, we'll bring them in later.

Entering the small front room, the three stand awkwardly for a few moments, uncertainly, not yet at ease after the long years of being apart. Kjerstin, like Louis, remembers the two as boys, two of the many children in Pernilla's over-full and hectic household. Now, here they are in her living room. What was she going to do with them? Coffee, she thinks. We can all talk better sitting around the table.

Kjerstin remembers her own journey to America, the days and days with no chance to wash her face, to change her clothes. The best thing about arriving was getting rid of the clothes that smelled of travel and sweat. But she sees that her nephews had wanted to look their best when traveling. They look like immigrants to be sure, no one would mistake that, but they don't look like they're refugees. They don't look like some immigrants she's seen arriving, Poles or Jews, or whatever they are, who looked like they only got out with just the rags they wrapped around themselves and called clothes. No, her nephews look like immigrants who expect to get along all right, dressed in those nice-looking suits. They wouldn't be throwing those clothes away; no, she'd have to see what she could do about getting them cleaned up and pressed, then they'd be ready to wear to church, just as nice as anyone's good suit.

Ludwig, you sit down here. Johan, here's a chair for you.

Louis comes in through the back door and takes a chair at the corner of the table.

Aunt Kjerstin, that's not my name anymore. And we're not "Bengtsson" either. They changed our names at Castle Garden. Ludwig, he's Lewis now.

They changed my name from "Ludwig" too, says Louis. They changed it to Louis too. L-o-u-i-s.

Well, I don't know why, but they spelled his different from yours on the papers—L-e-w-i-s—but said it just the same way. And I'm John, not Johan. John Benson.

Yes, they do that a lot, change a person's name. I don't know why they didn't change mine. "Kjerstin." Maybe they didn't know what to change it to.

I like it, Johan says. My new name. It sounds more like an American name.

Well, don't expect me to call you John Benson. Maybe I'll get used to it, but you were Johan when I left home, and he was Ludwig, and those old Swedish names are good enough for me. How is your Mama and Papa, and brothers and sisters?

They're about the same, Ludwig said. I guess they will be glad for some room in the house. And you know Sofy is coming to American too. She and Olander will be coming together in a year or two. He is still a little young to come.

I know your Mama is missing you, and probably wonders right now where you are. You'll have to write them a letter.

Yes, we'll do that, Ludwig says.

I guess Ludwig is thinking about someone else missing him, Johan says.

What's that?

Kjerstin's interest makes Louis smile. She won't be happy, he thinks, until these two boys were married off. Well, she's probably right. They do need a woman to help them settle into life and keep house for them.

Oh Johan, he likes to talk.

Come on, Ludwig, you know you want to talk about her.

Who is "her"?

Do you remember Per Svensson? He had two children by his first wife, Alfred and Elise, then she died, and he remarried and had a whole other family? They went to the church in Våxtorp.

Ja, John adds. Alfred and I were confirmed together.

Ja, I remember them, Kjerstin knits her brows, and brings their images into her mind's eye. Who is Ludwig interested in? she asks John.

Elise.

Well, Kjerstin says, I say, Good for you Ludwig. I hope it works out for her to come, and soon. Are you bringing anyone over, Johan?

No me. If I find a wife, it will have to be someone in America.

If he finds a wife, Ludwig says, that will be a surprize. He hasn't talked to a girl in his whole life, as far as I know.

Well, Kjerstin says, maybe he just hasn't seen a girl he wants to talk to. When he sees the right one, he'll probably think of something to say. If not, we'll have to help him out. Now it's time to get you two cleaned up. There's space in the back bedroom for you to sleep tonight, put the trunks in there for now. After supper we can have a talk about what's next.

* * * * *

What was next for John was work: work in Sioux fall, hauling the quartzite from the quarries. Carrying the pink slabs that grew into the courthouse. Working on farms outside of Sioux Falls, for his uncles, perhaps. Being their hired man. Saving his money.

His notebook— "Daily book of Johan Bengtsson"—includes not only brief references about his voyage to America, but also bookkeeping memoranda he kept after his arrival, written on one page. There are columns drawn in pencil, one for listing the item purchased, the others the expense: the dollar amount and the cents.

Blenket	1	75	
Skor		2	
Nunnerna		2	
Madus		1	
Sop			5
Tabako			50
Skjint		50	

Kundet			20
Fix skor	1		
Visinkit		30	
Post stump			10

In another listing, some of the same purchases are included: again, a blanket, this time more expensive ($2.75), more soap ($.10) and less tobacco ($.25). At the bottom of this list, he tallies his expenses:

7 d. 10 c. for the month of November

and below another sum is added: 9, 1.70, .75 for a total of 11.45. Does that total sum up the money he earned?

Was his income for that month the difference in the two totals? $4.35?

* * * * *

By whatever careful calculations, by whatever minute economies, little by little the profit grew. By 1896, perhaps before, he was renting on his own. No longer a day laborer, no longer someone else's hired man, he was his own boss on a farm. Not his own land, but his own business.

At some point he met Christine Berger, perhaps at his aunt Kjerstin's house. It may be that Sophy Benson brought her friend to the Carlson house to meet her bachelor brother. Perhaps they met each other at church. But whatever the beginnings of their acquaintance, it developed into a relationship that led to marriage.

The only letter, written by John, is one found in Christine's box of letters, a letter he wrote a few months before their wedding.

Dear friend Christina,

Since I promised you I would send you some words and tell you that I am healthy and feel well and I hope you have the same which is the very best even though time seems long. I don't have much news to tell you this time but I have sowed 80 acres of wheat now and I've got half a dozen hens from Jan Anders. I think I will be coming next week but I can't tell you which day. I wish I would have gone to see you tonight but I can't. I did not go home last Sunday evening from the Carlsons. They scared me [probably the concern was about weather conditions] *so I stayed there till Monday morning so I came home at 4 in the morning. I told you I would write on Sunday but then I thought the train doesn't leave until 6 o'clock and it could have been delayed so you wouldn't get the letter until Monday. And I had meant for you to go to the Post Office but I didn't want that because I thought that you would be disappointed.*

So now I have to finish my few words for this time and now a friendly farewell, signed in friendship by your friend of friends. Excuse my sloppiness. Write soon, J. Benson

I WILL COME AS SOON AS I CAN

In July 1896, he married Christine, and she joined him on the farm he was renting near Corson. Three years later, Norton, his first child, was born. Norton's name appears in the 1900 census record, along with Christine and the names of two hired men. John had indeed prospered. As the new century began, the twentieth century, John had made the immigrant's hoped for transition. No longer a worker dependent on an employer's decisions for his livelihood, he was now himself an employer. Instead of being someone else's hired man, he now had two of his own. And as the century moved into its first year, 1901, John achieved his goal: buying his own farm.

February 2, 1901. A mortgage, witnessed by Albion Thome, Notary Public of Minnehaha County and Wallace Le Dow, the noted Sioux Falls architect. Signed by John Benson, and his wife, Christine, the mortgage is for the purchase from Nis Byg of 160 acres in Minnehaha County, the location of which is described in terms of the Government Survey. Attached to this document is a Promissory Note in the amount of $1400.00, due "on or before: February 2, 1904." Written across the note: "Paid, Feb. 1, 1902, Nis Byg"

John and his wife, landowners.

THE FARM

The land to which John and Christine moved in the spring of 1903 was a quarter section of land on the western boundary of Benton Township.

Just as Christine and John had experienced their transitions—from life in Sweden, through immigration, to settling into American life—the land itself had undergone a series of changes, being transferred, in almost this same period of time, from owner to owner.

The first portion of the land to be owned was Lot 1, the eastern half of what was to be their farm. This portion was ceded by the United States—Ulysses S. Grant, President—to a man named John Alguire. The year was 1877. John Alguire did not own the land long; in 1878 he sold it for $400.00 to John Scott, a good investment for the buyer, as it turned out, since about four years later Scott doubled his money, selling the lot for $901.00. The new owner, however, sold it again in the very same year, again for a profit, though small. It was bought by David P. Russell for $1040.00, and resold the next year, 1883, to Frank L. Boyce, who in turn sold to his brother Jesse Boyce in 1883. There was also a second lot, just to the west of the first, with its own—though shorter—history. In 1886, the United States—Grover Cleveland, President—ceded this property to Henry H. Moore, from whom in 1887 it was bought by Jesse Boyce. Thus the two sections, the land that eventually John and Christine bought, were formed into one tract of land.

The first owners may have established their right of possession merely by planting trees on the property rather than by residence. Perhaps none of these early owners lived on this land, certainly not the Boyces, well-known lawyers in Sioux Falls with their own established residences. With the next owners, things were different. In 1888, Jesse Boyce sold the entire 160 acres to August and Sophie Guemmer, who lived there until 1891. The farm was home to them, and to the children who were born to them during this time. The next owners, again a pair of brothers, were John and Henry Schaetzel. The Schaetzel brothers maintained ownership of the land for eight years. In 1899, John sold his portion to brother Henry, and in 1900, Henry Schaetzel sold the property to Nis Byg, of Hartford.

Nis Byg, like John and Christine, was an immigrant from Scandinavia. In fact, he was a person they would have known, since they all attended the same Lutheran church. Nis came to America from Denmark a generation earlier than John and Christine, when land was nearly free for the having. He established a large farm of 600 acres in Hartford Township, and, most likely, bought this particular farm as a speculation. And in 1901, on February 2, he had a buyer: John Benson, and his wife, Christine.

With this transfer, the farm became a home, a home to John and Christine, to their children, and to their children's children.

* * * * *

John is plowing in the field southwest of the house. He is turning the earth over, cutting through the stubble of last year's crop, making long black furrows through the yellow brown stalks. He has corn planned for this field, this season. It is a big field, one of the farm's best. Forty acres! That's a whole farm in Sweden. There are some rocks in the field, just like at his father's farm back home, but compared to that, only a few. He's picked some, and there are more to pick. That's a job you can only do little by little. You have to be on the lookout, plowing, not to hit one of those big ones. You could do damage to your plowshare that way. Hauling rocks is a hard job, but there's use for them, too. John is stacking them carefully, down where he plans to build the foundations for his granary and corncrib.

The early spring twilight is fading. Not too much daylight left, but he wants to make the most of it. He has to finish this furrow at the end of the field, then he'll turn around and plow another furrow before going in to supper.

He's made the turn around, the horse pulls into its collar, and John holds the plow steady into the ground, his own strength keeping the shiny blades on course, his own strength forcing the slicing edge into the earth, turning over the soil which will soon be worked and softened and smoothed to receive the seeds of corn. The line of black, shiny in the last light of the sunset, extends behind him. The gulls circle and wheel over the newly opened furrow, swooping down on worms and insects turned up by the plow.

Gazing over the rump of his bay horse, over the prongs of the horse collar, he sees to the end of the field. There comes Christine, carrying Elmer. Norton is sitting up by the fence line. They've come to walk home with him. He pauses the horse for an instant, waves to let her see he's noticed them, and resumes his concentration on the plow.

But Norton has seen his wave, and he runs forward to meet his father, to travel the last yards of the furrow with him.

Papa! Carry me!

No, no, I can't, look I have to put both hands on the plow or it won't cut right. Wait, I'll put you up on Prince's back.

And John hoists the little boy up on the big work horse. The horse's back is so broad Norton's legs spread out in a nearly horizontal line, but he doesn't mind. He grins down at his papa and hangs on to the straps that lay over the horse's wet shiny back.

John clucks to the horse, and they go on, finishing the furrow just where Christine is standing.

John, is that safe? I think he's too little to be up on that big horse.

Oh he's fine. Prince isn't going to run away. Look, he liked it.

And Norton does look as if he had liked it. He is raising his arms as if he'd won a victory, then beats his fists on the chest. His childish shouts are one with cries of the gulls.

Elmer reaches his arms out to his papa, straining away from Christine's grasp.

206

Me too! he says.

No, no, Elmer, not you too. You're too small, you just wait.

John lifts Norton down from his perch in order to unhitch the horse from the plow. Then he puts the child back on his seat, takes Elmer from Christine, and the family walks toward the house, Norton above them all, riding home in lordly splendor, as the sun's setting streaks the western sky beyond the hills in Lewis' pasture, creating broad bands of crimson, lemon-yellow, and mauve.

February, 1905. It's been one of those bright, almost warm winter days, one of those days that makes the winter-weary anticipate the softness of spring, but at the same time, seduces them back into loving winter, with its blue-brilliant sky and white, white snow, piled in soft, transforming drifts.

It's a day that provides a welcome change for the Bensons and for their neighbors as well. During the four previous days, winter had been the enemy. The storm began with a grey sky, and a bitter wind from the north, driving the snow from the plains of Canada, snow that fell thickly, so heavily that for a day you couldn't see across the barnyard. The wind brought the snow, and when the clouds were emptied, the wind continued to blow. The temperature fell: down, down, 30, even 40 degrees below zero. Even when the wind stopped, the bitter cold it had brought kept all the neighborhood locked in a frozen prison.

They were able to keep warm enough in the farmhouse. They kept the stove going with cobs John had piled in the cellar. With the cellar trap door in the pantry, they never had to go outside for fuel. And they kept the boys with them, sleeping all together in the downstairs bed. Upstairs the windows were frosted over, and it was so cold you could see your breath. After the snow stopped, John was able to get out to the barn. The path he shoveled was nearly a tunnel, but he was able to feed and water the horses, and the cows he had managed to get into the barn before the storm hit.

But now, this morning, the bad weather has broken, and a mid-winter thaw has started. It's too much to hope that it will be the last storm of the winter, but it might be the last bad one. March can be freakish, but bad weather won't last too long, not in March.

Christine has felt her spirits rising all through the day, and when John comes in for supper, she says,

Can we get out tonight? I feel like it's been a long time since we got out. Maybe we could get up to Lewis and Elise's? I feel like it's time for a visit. What do you think?

I think we could do it. It's been warm enough today to shrink some of those snowdrifts. There are still some pretty big piles though, that we'd sink through walking. I guess I'll walk Prince up and down a couple times, that will break a path. Then you and the boys should be able to make it all right.

John looks over at Christine. She's pregnant again, their third child. The baby is due in May, but tall as Christine is she's still not showing very much. It's been four years since the last baby. Thank goodness they're not having a family the way his own mother and father did, with one baby and then another right away, over and over again. Christine didn't want that either. She'd seen too much of a life like that when she worked for the Olsons. He wonders, though, if she's up to this winter's evening walk.

You want to go for sure? he asks. It's not too much?

I want to get some fresh air, get some outside air. I'm tired of being cooped up like this. I'm not so sure about Norton, if the night air won't be bad for him, but if we bundle him up good and tight, he'll probably be all right. They're getting cross too, sitting around the house with just each other and me all day long. I could carry him if it's too hard for him.

If anybody has to carry him, it will be me. But for goodness sake, a little walk like that should be all right for him. He's five years old, after all.

Well, we'll see. Sit down now, Papa, have supper, and then we can get ready to go.

John was right, the walk is not too much for Norton. He and Elmer run and throw themselves in the wet, soft snow. Christine worries about the dampness soaking through the layers of wool. When she gets to Elise's she'll put the wraps by the cookstove so they'll be nice and dry for the walk home. The lane is long, but Prince's huge feet have pressed down the snow into trails that she and John and the boys can walk along easily. The snow is too wet to be icy, and though Christine walks cautiously, she does not fear a sudden slip and fall. John walks at the head of the line, Norton and Elmer circle round him, and she brings up the rear. At the end of the lane, they walk up the short rise that connects their own driveway to the township road. When they reach the road, they can see that bobsleds have traveled over it during the day, making broad tracks for easy walking. Once they're up on the road it is only a few dozen yards to the short driveway leading to Lewis' and Elise's house.

John, still in the lead, climbs up the steps to their front porch, opens the door, and pushes his head inside.

Hallo! you've got company, he calls.

Lewis comes into the kitchen, walking in his stocking feet.

Well, what are you doing here? Did you get frozen out down there and need some nice warm place to come into? Christine, come in. Hello boys. Here Christine, I'll take your things. Elise, come on out here, we've got company.

Elise, a short little woman with a round face and bright, alert eyes, comes into the kitchen with a gaggle of children tumbling in after her: Arthur, Walter, Esther, and Ruth.

I'm glad you've come up, it's good to see a different face. We've been just sitting here doing nothing, and now we can have a visit. I know the children will be glad for a change. They're tired of each other after being cooped up all during the storm. Here, Christine, you sit down. Are you going to be warm enough? My goodness, you are brave, coming out in all this snow. I hope you haven't caught a chill. Wasn't it slippery?

209

While Elise bustles from one spot in the kitchen to another—putting on the coffee pot, settling Christine at a chair at the kitchen table, shooing the children into another room, swatting Walter's bottom when he starts to tease Esther—Lewis and John move into the sitting room. The stove glows and crackles, and the room feels nice and warm after the chill of the evening air. John had taken off his boots at the door, and he and Lewis, both now in their stocking feet, sit in easy chairs, at a comfortable distance from the stove. John takes out a tin of snuff, and passes it over to his brother, who helps himself to a generous pinch and hands it back. John takes some himself, and settles in for a winter's evening.

Elise will make us a little coffee, by and by, Lewis says.

We just ate before we walked up here, John says. No need to rush. I imagine they'll want to talk over this and that out there in the kitchen. Christine had the idea of walking over. You know how it is with the women. Sometimes they get an idea and then that's that, they've got to do it. For me, I could have just sat home. But no, she said she was tired of being cooped up. So we bundled up and came along.

Wasn't the snow too soft to walk in?

Well, I drove Prince up and down a couple times, and got a path packed down. It wasn't too bad, we walked single file.

I'm a little surprised Christine would want to come out, you know, with everything. But I know when Elise was in the family way, sometimes she'd get notions about this or that and then, you're right, you'd just better do it.

The brothers are silent, listening to the soft chatter they hear in the kitchen, the animated voices of their children who had withdrawn into Lewis' and Elise's bedroom, just off the sitting room. The two fathers hear a few shrieks of laughter, hear some suspicious thumps and bumps, but give no sign of noticing. If any child tending is needed, the women can come and see to it.

Ja, with weather like today, it makes a man think about spring planting, Lewis says. I guess I'll put in more oats this year. The oats I had last year made a good crop, better than wheat ever did. If the price can stay up like it was last year, we'll do all right. This storm wasn't so good, but we needed some moisture. It was pretty dry last fall. Did you have any problems with your stock during the storm?

No, it wasn't too bad. I got nearly all the cows in, and I've seen the others down in the trees, so I guess they made it all right. I had a hard time of it, getting to the barn on that first day, but I made it. Once the snow stopped it wasn't too bad. Ja, I'm thinking about putting in more oats too. But I'm thinking about doing some building before I can get in the fields. You know I've been thinking about adding to the granary.

You still have that on your mind? I thought you'd given that idea up.

Well, it's not so much that I've given the idea up, it's more like I'm not sure yet what the idea is. I guess when I think about it, I probably won't get it built this spring, I'll probably end up just with a patch here and there, but one of these days, as soon as I can get ahead a little bit, I'm going to do something with that granary. I've been thinking, what if the granary stayed where it was, and I built the new corn crib behind it?

What? Down that slope? One thing, John, you've got a good farm, but I always wondered how you'd fix the farmyard buildings with that slope you've got to the east and behind the barn to the west and south. You don't have much level ground you can build on. Even behind the house, to the north and east you've got that slope, of course that doesn't matter since that's where you got the trees planted.

Well, what I say is, why not take advantage of the land you've got, use your brains so that you can get something out of the slope. Now, for instance, that slope behind the granary, that would be the place for a pig house. All that pig slop and smell, keep it away from the house, no runoff, no pig yard to look at. And another thing, with the corn crib right beside it, it's an easy job to get the feed to the pigs. Just open the chute and fill up the feed basket and you're right there.

Lewis nods, but John can tell his older brother is not impressed. John keeps his enthusiasm to himself, but as they sit there, soaking in the warmth and friendly sounds of the house, John continues his plans in his mind. He sees them taking shape. He doesn't need to tell anyone, he doesn't depend on his brother's advice. It's his idea, he'll see it through.

What if, he says to himself, I do build that corn crib down the slope. It will be twice as big as if it were level with the granary. The front I'll use for oats and grain, the back part for corn. And the pig house right across from it. Then someday, when I start getting cattle for fattening, I'll build a feed house for them down that slope too. And a steer yard. A good place for the steer yard will be that grove of cottonwood trees east of the house. Cool and shady in the summer.

But about that granary. . . And his winter thoughts and plans grow into sturdy buildings, painted red, filled to bursting with crops.

The evening draws to an end. The younger children are getting sleepy. Christine and Elise have talked of women things. Elise has shown Christine some little girl clothes she can use, things of Esther's and Ruth's in case the new baby is a girl. Time for a girl, Elise says to Christine, and laughs.

The grownups sit around the kitchen table. Elise pours them coffee, and cuts into a pie she had made with dried apples. The children have had cookies. They don't complain when it's time to bundle up, but put on coats and scarves and mittens and boots. John and Christine put their wraps back on too, toasty warm from being by the stove.

Good night, good night! —Thanks for walking up! Don't fall on those steps; John, you take hold of Christine. —Come down to see us. Thanks for the pie! —Good-night, good night!

They walk home in silence. Above them, high above the eastern pasture hills, the moon is whitely radiant, the banks of snow reflect the quiet light, revealing the dips and curves of the distant hillside. The snow on either side of the path is brightened by the moon's gleaming and also is crossed with marks of mysterious blue-black shadow. The silence is deep. Christine walks in her thoughts, John in his. He looks down the lane, and as his children scamper through the snow in front of him, he sees his granary, broad and red and sturdy. He sees a new barn where the present barn now stands, a big barn, with stanchions for milk cattle, two long rows, and big wooden stalls for his horses; he sees the big brown horses standing there, two by two, snuffling their oats. He pauses in his walk, as the sight takes shape before him. Christine, walking with her eyes to the ground, bumps into his back.

My goodness, John. What are you doing? Stargazing?

I guess I am, he says, and laughs. Well, it's a nice night for it. Don't you think so too?

September, 1907. The first day of school is right around the corner.

This year Elmer starts school, starts the first grade. Norton is two years ahead of him, and has told Elmer what he can expect.

First, you've got to stay away from the big boys. They're mighty tough, and they'd just as soon knock you down as look at you. They probably won't notice you, though. Nobody cares anything about first graders.

Elmer is silent, wide-eyed.

And you've got to eat everything in your lunch pail. Whether you like it or not. And you've got to be careful not to get the teacher mad. That teacher we had last year, she really liked to use the switch. By the end of the day sometimes everybody would be crying.

Christine walks into the room and hears the end of this conversation.

Norton! You be quiet. You're making all that up. Elmer, it's not so bad as Norton says. You wait and see. You'll like school. It's time you learned more English, you've got to know that even if we speak Swedish here. And you'll have Norton to look out for you, and you'll be there with Arthur and Walter too, and Esther. You'll be just fine.

Elmer is not too sure, but says nothing. He knows there is no escape, and that tomorrow he will be going with Norton to the Wilder School, just a half mile from their house, down the road to the north.

On the morning of the first day, Christine has packed sandwiches for each boy in a little pail with a lid. She's dressed them up in good clothes, too. Elmer has a pair of pants, and a little jacket to match. Christine has made both of the boys' outfits, and has made each a little cloth hat that matches. They grumble as a little as they put their feet into the stiff shoes. All summer long they've run in their bare feet throughout the farm, and now how tight and uncomfortable the shoes feel.

John walks into the kitchen from the washroom, and hears them muttering, as, red-faced, they lean over to lace up the shoes.

You just be quiet about that, now, he says. You just be glad you've got shoes to put on. Nobody is going to say John Benson's boys go to school barefoot. Now I'll take you today because it's the teacher's first day too, and I want to give her a ride. Tomorrow she'll do her own driving.

214

The teacher this year is new. Jenny Johnson is her name, and John and Christine know her from the Swedish Lutheran church they go to. Her mother is a Norwegian and had gone to the Nidaros church before she married, but now she's gotten used to the Swedes, and Jennie's family all go the Swedish church.

Jenny is pretty young for a teacher. John wonders if she'll be able to keep control, especially with some of those big boys. Well, they won't be in school for a while yet, not until the corn is picked. By then she'll probably know what's what.

It was Christine's idea to have the teacher board with them. Later in the school term she'd probably go off to another family. But for now she was with them. They were one of the closest places, so she wouldn't have far to travel. Christine liked the idea of Jenny Johnson being with them because Christine always was interested in things that had to do with school and learning, maybe she thought it would be good for them all to have a schoolteacher in the house. What John thought too was that Christine liked having another woman around, a woman with nice ways and an education. Now that Emma was born, a little girl after all, he figured Christine would start to get all sorts of ideas about what a girl should have. Well, he had two boys anyway, two boys to help with farm work, two boys who can take over the farm someday, maybe another farm too.

And another thing, he thinks as he hitches up the horse to the buggy for the short ride to the school, Christine is always looking out for Norton. With the teacher living here she can give the boys a ride to school. Though he wonders if they wouldn't rather walk; they wouldn't want to be called teacher's pet. Maybe children don't tease each other in schools here like they did back home. One thing is for sure, the boys will get their English good in school. That's one thing they'll need.

Jenny Johnson has finished breakfast. She thanks Christine, tells her good-bye and goes out to the waiting buggy. The little boys are already in place. That Norton, she can tell he'll be a handful. A smart little boy, and he knows

215

it too. Elmer looks shy. And he looks scared. He probably won't have much to say. Sometimes that's what a teacher needs, a child who keeps quiet.

She's pretty scared herself. It's her first year of teaching, and her first day. When the big boys get to school later in the fall, they will all be taller than she is, and some of them will be older. She will just have to remember what her mama said: Jenny, it's not size, it's brains. Use your head, and you'll be all right.

And that's what she intends to do.

When the day comes to an end, she walks out of the schoolhouse, down the wooden steps. She sees John Benson approaching in the little buggy. In groups of two's and three's the children walk home. There are a few other buggies that have pulled up on the road beside the schoolhouse, a few other father or mothers that are giving their children the special treatment of a ride home on the first day of school. There is Lewis Benson in his buggy, his children are clambering in, full of things to say, and giving each other a few shoves.

Norton and Elmer are beside her now, and they all climb into the buggy.

Well, how was it? John asks, as he clucks to Prince and they start to drive away.

Jenny waits to let the boys answer. For herself, if she were to answer she would say, mighty tough, but I can do it. But she wants to hear what they will say.

I think I'm going to know everything in my grade this year, Norton says. I sure know a lot more than Esther, but she thinks she knows more. But I could read all the words in the story in our reading book and I had to help her with five. And guess what? This year at recess the big boys wanted me to play baseball with them.

What about you, Elmer? How did you like your first day of school?

Elmer looks at Miss Johnson.

216

I liked it, he said. You're nice, Teacher. But I like to be home too. Do you think Mama missed me? She's only got Emma now to be with her.

I bet she did, John says. You'll have to tell her all about it when you get home.

Breakfast is over, and John is ready to get the horses hitched up and get into the fields. It is August, 1909.

It's time to get out into the oats field. He's cut the oats, he's setting it up into shocks now, getting ready for next week when the threshers are coming with the big machine. It's time, it's past time. The sun's been up already over an hour. But he lingers in the barn, uneasy in his mind. Outside he sees Elmer, dressed to work in the field with him, playing a solitary game of hopscotch traced out in the gravel of the barnyard. He hears the shanty door open, and sees Christine carry out the dishwater from the breakfast dishes. She flings it out, down the hill on the ash heap, and goes back inside. It's quiet again inside the house.

John takes a seat on the wooden steps going up the haymow. He just needs to clear his mind a little before getting to work.

It's not like Christine to fuss. Usually if there is something she doesn't like, she's just quiet, and when he figures out what's the problem they get back to normal. Usually whatever he wants, she wants. So they get along just fine. At least that's what he's thought all along.

But this morning was different.

Well, it didn't start out different. It started out just the same. He woke up, like he always did, pulled on his overalls, and went out to milk the cow and feed the horses. While he was working in the barn, Christine would get up and get some bacon frying, and get the boys up. They'd roll out of their beds, sleepy-eyed and come on down to the breakfast table. Norton might have to be called more than once, but when he got back in the house, there they'd all be at the table. They'd all eat breakfast, and then the boys would follow him out. Whatever he was working on, he'd find something they could do too.

It's the only way, he thinks. How else can they learn how to farm, if they don't do it?

Now today, today he'd have to agree that the work they had to do would not be any fun. Working in the oats, it's hot and it's dusty, and it looks to be a day hotter even than yesterday. He knew that sometimes Norton had some trouble with oats dust, maybe he had a little asthma. But it was no more than that. Lots of times he had a cough himself, after working with grain, but what if he did? The grain's got to be harvested, you can't let a cough keep you inside. And he knew that Norton had been pretty quiet last night, just went up to bed without saying much.

But this morning, when he came into the house from chores, there was only Elmer at the table.

Where's Norton? he'd said. He should be up by now. Do I have to go up there and wake him up?

He's awake. I woke him up. But he's not going out to the field today.

What do you mean, he's not going out to the field? I need him. We've got a lot of oats to make into shocks before next week.

You heard me. He's not going out. It was too much for him yesterday, he's coughing bad this morning. He can take a day off, it won't hurt anything.

What about the work that has to be done? What do you mean, it won't hurt anything?

Well, you've got Elmer, don't you?

John looked at Elmer, sitting there at the table, the plate of bacon and eggs in front of him, untouched. He looked wide-eyed, listening to his mama and papa, as their words became quicker and louder.

You go on outside, Elmer, John said. I'll come out when Mama and I have finished.

But he hasn't eaten anything, Christine said, as Elmer slid out of his chair, picked up his hat and left the kitchen.

It's better he should have an empty stomach this morning than to listen to what's going on in here. Mama, are you aiming to make a baby out of Norton? He's nine years old, nearly ten. And he's big for his age. He's old enough to help out.

"Help out." I don't call what he has to do, what you expect him to do, "helping out." You expect him to work like a man, and he's just a little boy. And don't tell me what you had to do at his age, and don't tell me how your papa expected you to do this and do that. I don't care what you had to do, if Norton is not so strong as you, he shouldn't have to do as much. You don't know what it's like when someone gets the lung disease. I do, and I won't have it here in my own house with my own boy.

John stood there, not saying anything. It was like once she got started, Christine didn't know when to stop. He didn't know what to say. He turned to go outside, he picked up his hat and he headed for the door.

Elmer, John said, Elmer's only eight. What about him?

I know you've got to have some help, Christine said, her back turned to him. She stood there, staring out the east windows.

Elmer's stronger, she said, still not looking at him. He likes farm work. Norton's different. I don't know if he's cut out to be a farmer.

She had nothing more to say. Neither did he. He walked out of the kitchen.

Now, sitting on the steps, as the conversation plays itself back again inside his head: Not cut out to be a farmer. Not cut out to be a farmer? Then what? And what was the use of everything he was doing if his son wasn't cut out to be a farmer? Now that's something you'd never say about Lewis's boys. Arthur and Walter, they were farmers through and through. What could be better than being a farmer? Own your own land, people respect you. And with land, it's always there. Businesses, they come and go. A man could run a

219

grocery store, hard times come and you're out on the street. Hard times come and it's not easy being a farmer, but you always have the land, it's always there. If he's not cut out to be a farmer, what is he cut out for? Well, of course Norton's smart, he's always been smart. Maybe Mama has something in mind she's not talking about yet. Maybe she thinks he'll be a schoolteacher or something. She's right about one thing, Norton doesn't like farming. Never has. Not like Elmer. And sometimes I wonder, when he's around me and Lewis, or Olander, and we're talking farming, sometimes he just sits there and looks, and I have to wonder if we sound like dumb Swede farmers to him. He's quick, that's for sure. I can't always get all the things he talks about, things from school. Maybe that's where Mama's headed. One thing she said, though, I'd forgotten, about her brother and father. Maybe she thinks Norton has their weakness. Well, one day at home isn't going to make any difference. She's right, I've got Elmer. He's big help for a boy his age.

John walks back into the kitchen, where Christine has started her morning's work, baking bread. She looks up from the dough tray as he comes in.

Tell Norton to stay in today, he can try it again tomorrow. Pack up a little something for Elmer to eat when he gets hungry. We'll go out now.

Christine nods, with a softened look in her eyes. She wipes her floury hands on her apron, and turns to make up a little packet for John to take out into the field.

Thank you, she says, as she puts it together, wrapped in white paper with a little string tied around.

Elmer, she calls, here's a little something for you, for later.

She gives it to the boy, and places her hand on his cheek, as he smiles up at her.

Now, work hard, like a big boy, and help Papa.

220

Part IV: Changes

John and Christine continue to live on the farm to which they had moved with their two sons. Emma, born in 1905, completes the family. The three children are confirmed at Benton Evangelical Lutheran Church, the Swedish church about five miles away, which takes its name from the township in which it is located.

All three attend Wilder School for grades one through eight. Their report cards, kept by John in his little black strongbox, show the parents' signatures for each report card period. The report cards reveal that while Norton and Elmer were moderately good students, Emma's marks were very good indeed. One by one the three children graduate from Wilder School. Now the differences among them begin. Norton graduates and goes on to high school, when Emma graduates, she does the same. But one boy is needed to help on the farm, and that boy is Elmer. Perhaps—he was a shy boy—the choice was his own preference.

Norton finishes high school at a preparatory school in St. Peter, Minnesota, and then enrolls at the college with which it is affiliated, Gustavus Adolphus College. He majors in history. He plays on the Gustavus football team. Emma attends Augustana College, in Sioux Falls. It is nearby, and it is good to have a girl close to home. She majors in English.

After he finishes college, Norton teaches high school. Emma teaches also, in several small towns, not too far from her family. Eventually Norton goes to law school, at the University of South Dakota, and sets up practice in Hartford.

What about Elmer? In the early 1930's a young woman, Nellie Pearson, comes from Illinois along with her sister, Freeda, to visit her cousins: Arthur, Walter, Esther and Ruth Benson. Their mother, Elise, is a sister of Alfred Pearson, the father of Nellie and Freeda. They are Elmer's cousins also, because their father Lewis is John Benson's brother, and their home is the farm just across the road from the John Benson farm. During this reunion of cousins, Nellie and Elmer meet, a courtship develops, and on June 19, 1934, they marry. After the wedding in Illinois and a honeymoon at French Lick, Indiana, Elmer brings his new wife to his South Dakota home.

At first, they live together with John and Christine, but before long, the older couple, now in their mid-60's, move off of the farm, leaving it to the younger generation. John's farming years have been successful. He owns not only what they call the Home Place, but also another farm called the North Place, and land west of Hartford as well. But now John is ready to turn the work of the farm over to his son, and so John and Christine make their last transition; they move three miles away into Hartford.

They buy a substantial, handsome house, just a block from downtown. They settle into town life; John twice serves as mayor of Hartford. When Norton begins to practice law, he lives with them until the 1950's. Eventually, when Emma marries, she and her husband make their home there too she that she can help care for Christine, who by this time has become ill.

In 1946, John and Christine celebrate the fiftieth anniversary of their wedding; we see them, pictured, on that day. They have a big family party at the house in Hartford, with many relatives; some of the attendants from the wedding fifty years ago are present. In their anniversary portrait they are still a handsome couple. John peers out, intently, sharply, as is his custom. Christine gazes more gently at the camera. Pinned at the neckline of Christine's good dark dress is the brooch given her so long ago by Mrs. Carpenter.

And there is another photograph as well—taken on the day of the celebration—one of the couple and their grown children: Norton, the lawyer, handsome in his double-breasted suit; Emma, in this picture just as in the 1909 photograph, between the two sons, Emma, herself a wife of only one year; Elmer, in shirt-sleeves, strong and substantial, a farmer and a father himself, a father of four young children.

It seems as if the dreams which brought John and Christine to America from Sweden have been realized: their own land, first one farm, then more. Healthy children, eventually grandchildren. Accomplishments of which they can be proud.   Respected citizens in their community and respected parishioners in their church.   All their hopes fulfilled.   Perhaps, perhaps not.

Just one year after their anniversary, in 1947, Christine dies. John is left, John and his three children, Norton, Emma, and Elmer. But there are the grandchildren by now, too, the four children of Elmer and Nellie, they and their parents still on the farm, on the Home Place.

Elmer and Nellie and their children, Edna Mary, Curtis, Marjorie, Mabel Ann.   The family has close ties with Grandpa, with Aunt Emma and Uncle Earl.   The spend holidays together, either in Hartford or on the farm. Nellie has coffee with Emma and Earl and Grandpa when she goes shopping in Hartford.   They all get together for Fourth of July picnics and fireworks.

Renting from his father, Elmer farms the Home Place, and also the North Place.   Eventually, in the early 1950's Elmer buys a farm of his own, called the South Place.   He seems on the same path as his father, farming well, accumulating land.   But it is just at about this time that the uneasy relationship between John and Christine's two sons comes to a head.

In 1952 Elmer receives a letter.   Norton, writing in his capacity as his father's lawyer, informs Elmer that the lease of the North Place will not be renewed, that a new tenant has been chosen.   The letter goes on to say that the decision about the Home Place is still pending.

As it happens, no changes were made in Elmer's tenancy on the Home Place.   But the damage was done; the hurt, the perceived unfairness was too great to be overcome.   Elmer cut off the relationship with his brother and his father.

The women were caught in the middle.   Nellie and the children continued to visit Emma, Earl, and John.   They visited Norton's wife Edna, when Norton married in the 1950's.   Emma and Earl were guests of the family at the farm for Christmas celebrations.   But there were no more dinners around the big dining room table in Hartford, and John and Norton were never again invited to the farm.

* * * * *

November, 1959.

Trinity Season—those long, seemingly uneventful years of childhood—is coming to an end. For a long while, for the girl who had been watching that time go past, nothing had changed. Now, it seems as if everything is about to. Edna and Curtis, having finished college, live in different states, Edna teaching school in Minnesota, Curtis in seminary in Illinois. They are seldom home, except for holidays. Marjorie no longer lives at home either, she is away at college. Only Mabel is still at home, and three more years after this one, and she'll probably be gone too. Elmer and Nellie see their children becoming adults, creating lives of their own. Leaving, one by one.

* * * * *

From where he lies in bed, John can see through the windows the tops of the trees in his yard and the neighbor's yard. Little by little the days are getting shorter, now the sky darkens into evening by a little after four. The thin black lines of the branches move back and forth, back and forth as the cold November wind gusts and then slackens. The lights have come on in the Fetters' house, across the driveway, and he can see that Emma has turned on the lights on in the kitchen. He hears her in there, moving around, starting to get supper ready. It's dark in his room. He could reach the cord to turn on his own lamp attached to the bed frame, or he could ring the bell beside the table and she'd come and turn on the overhead light, but he'll just wait. He'll just lie there until Dr. Petres comes, and then he'll have his supper and his shot, and then sleep.

I heard Mabel Ann come in tonight after school. I guess she's doing some schoolwork or something and then she'll come in and say hello. I guess she doesn't look forward to that, but I can't blame her. There's not much for her to say except for hello. She always was pretty

228

quiet even when she was little. That Curtis, though, he was always full of tricks. I remember when he was supposed to bring us a chicken from the farm, and he just opened the bag and let it loose in the kitchen. That made Mama jump up!—Papa, Papa! Come right away, come in here! And when I did there was that chicken, flapping away to beat the band. That sure was a sight. And that Edna Mary, she had a few tricks too. I remember Emma had to scold her more than once when she was little. Well they grow up fast. They're good children. Even when Nellie just came in by herself, she'd always bring them along when she came. I suppose to them it all seems like my fault or maybe it's Norton's fault, it's hard to say. But who would have thought that Elmer would take it the way he did. Maybe if Mama were still alive, he always listened to everything she said. Emma never did say too much, but I know she stuck up for Elmer most of the time. But it's only common sense that when you rent out you have to get a good rent. Otherwise what else do I have to live on? There's nobody going to take care of me now, if I don't take care of myself. He still had the home place, and that was plenty for me when I was his age, and he's got that south place, I never was so sure if he knew what he was doing, buying that, especially how could he take care of both of those places and the North Place too and still do a good job farming? That's what I want to know. He should have known I'd never want him to leave the home place. Where did he get that idea? I guess when I read the letter I never saw that part. I don't know what Norton had to put that in for, maybe it's what has to be done if you're a lawyer, you write it but you know nobody pays attention to it. Now Norton, he doesn't come all that much either now that he's married to Edna Nelson.

It could snow tonight, it's been that sort of grey looking day. I'll have to ask Emma if there's enough blankets on Mabel Ann's bed.

I wish it was time for Dr. Petres to be here. Sometimes I think he's the only one I can talk to. One thing for sure, he's somebody who knows what it's like being a foreigner. Now there's hardly anybody left who remembers what it was like in the Old Country, or even here when we were all just getting started. He's not old like I am, but he knows what it's like to live somewhere where everything is different from where you were born and raised. And it's not so different, him and me. He came from Hungary not Sweden, and for him there were all those Communists making things bad, but I had to leave home just the same, just as if

229

somebody made me. What would have happened to me, if I'd stayed there? One more mouth to feed, that's what my own papa would have thought. I guess no matter what Elmer thinks of me now, he'd have to admit he always had a good house to live in and good food to eat. And some day he's going to have a farm that's all his own. That's a lot more than my father ever did for me. What I did, I did on my own. Nowadays it's as if everybody thinks other people are going to do it for you. Well, they'll soon find out different. Maybe I should just leave it to somebody else, if that's the sort of father he thinks I am he can just see what it's like. But that's the farm Mama and I always intended for him to have, and then there's the children to think of. And the house, they're the ones who should be in the house, that's where we all got started. Someday he'll probably know I'd never have let them put him off the farm.

The light comes on suddenly, startling him. He hadn't heard anyone approaching the room.

Hello Grandpa.

He peers a moment at the girl standing by the railing of his bed, as if it takes him a while to see who she is. Then,

Oh, it's you. Hello.

How do you feel?

Oh. About the same.

Well, it was kind of a chilly day today, it feels like winter is just about here.

Ja, I suppose so.

Well, I guess Aunt Emma has supper just about ready for you. I'm going to eat early because I have to leave for the basketball game. So good-night, Grandpa, it's nice to see you.

Ja, good-night.

Good-night, good-night.

1961, the year everything changed.

On February 19, after a short illness, Norton died. When he was hospitalized and near death, the family gathered at his bedside. His wife, Edna, was there. John, who was bedridden was not there, but Emma and Earl were present. The night before he died was cold, and country roads were blocked after a recent snowstorm. At about 10 pm, Elmer, Nellie, and Mabel bundled up with boots and heavy coats and walked to down the lane to the road where Earl met them in his car and drove them all to the hospital. Mabel stayed in the waiting area, but Nellie and Elmer joined the others in the room, watching through the night until death came, at about 5:30 in the morning.

On Friday, April 14, John had a stroke, and was taken to the hospital. Emma stayed by his side during the next few days, and Elmer was there too. John died on Wednesday, April 19, two months after his son.

John was buried next to Christine in the cemetery of Benton Lutheran Church. Of the family pictured in the 1910 photograph only Elmer and Emma remain.

And there have been other changes too: since September, Curtis has been gone, not just in Seminary, but in Europe, studying at the University of Edinburgh. For the first time the family had not been together at Christmas, nor is he at home for the funerals of his uncle and his grandfather.

* * * * *

But now, in the fall of 1961, we come round to Thanksgiving, and everyone comes back home again. Everything—for these few days—seems just like it used to be, or nearly. We've had work done on the house: "modernizing it" is what the changes are called. We now have running water in the house; a bathroom has been installed where the pantry used to be, and to replace that we have cupboards built in the kitchen. Windows in the kitchen and dining room have been replaced.

We've all changed too: everyone is bigger, we take up more room around the table. Now Edna and Marjorie and I do more to help in the kitchen, which makes our mom even more nervous than her doing it by herself. Curtis and Dad keep arguing about politics, just like they used to, only more so. In the evening Edna and Curtis and Marjorie all go out, to movies or to see friends in Sioux Falls. I talk to friends on the telephone and watch TV. Tomorrow night all four of us are going to Sioux Falls and go bowling together. That's not something we would have done when we were kids. Things are changed, all right.

But on the cold winter night like this, when I look out at the white fields and feel the frosty air, and see the moon shining on the smooth pasture hills, it doesn't seem all that different to me from when I was just a little girl.

When I was a little girl, we still had two work horses, Dick and Queen. I remember the times—though they weren't very often—when it would be so cold that my father would bring them into the barn at night and put them in their regular stall. Their stall was the first on your right as you came into the horse barn. He would put them into the barn and throw down hay to them from the trap door just above their manger. Between the stalls were wooden dividers, just the right height and width for sitting on. Just right for me to sit on, to lean over and pat them. And then I would slide over and sit on Queen's back, so broad and smooth, and she never seemed to mind that I was there. Sometimes I would just stand in their stall and smell their horsey smell and feel the warmth of them, and listen to the quiet munching sounds they made. I knew it was bad outside, and I knew it was a bother for my father to have them in the barn, but for me it was nice.

So I would stay there, while my father was milking the cow. The barn cats would come and sit around him. Sometimes he would squirt a hot white stream right into their open pink mouths. Always he would pour a little warm milk from his pail into the cat pan. Then he would put up his stool and put his yellow mittens back on. Hearing that he was done, I would move away from the horses, and meet him in the passage where the cow barn and horse barn connected. We'd step outside, he'd pull the big barn door on its rollers shut behind him. We'd look up into the cold winter sky, with white stars shining, every one visible all the way to eternity. Just for a minute though. As we started to walk, I'd see our two big black shadows on the ground, preceding us. Then I'd glance over my shoulder to the left, to the dark slope leading behind the barn. What if there were wolves on this cold night, coming from the darkness I couldn't see into?

So I put my hand in his and we walk across the barnyard, our shadows moving ahead of us, through the back gate into the house yard, up the wooden steps into the back porch, and into the kitchen, and there we are, safe and warm inside.

Part V: Returnings

DISPOSITION OF EFFECTS

1993, and the rainiest spring anyone could remember. In Iowa, rivers flooded; Des Moines was a declared a disaster area. Grand Forks, North Dakota was threatened by the Red River, swollen by melting snow in addition to the unceasing rains. The image of the citizens of this small city captured a national audience, as we saw them on the evening news, working to shore up dikes all along the riverbank. We saw them working all through the day and the night, tirelessly, hoping to save their city, only to realize that despite their labor, the wall of sandbags would not withstand the force of the water. In South Dakota, fields stood unplanted, sheeted with flat glimmering expanses of water, fields too sodden to absorb another drop. Still the skies were gray, still the rains came, sometimes storms, sometimes drizzle.

On June 18, Edna, Curtis, Marjorie, and I—Emma's nieces and nephew—and some of our children were gathered together from our homes in North Dakota, Nebraska, and Wisconsin. The notice had been sent to the Hartford newspaper and also appeared in the Sioux Falls Argus-Leader:

ESTATE HOME & PERSONAL PROPERTY
AT AUCTION
Elegant 2 1/2 Story 4 Bedroom Home in Hartford, SD
Antiques & Collectibles, Furniture, Household Items

FRIDAY, JUNE 18, 1993

Personal Property: 1:00 P.M.

Real Estate: 6:00 P.M.

The Real Estate was the house where John and Christine, Emma and Earl had lived in Hartford, and the Personal Property was a combination of their furniture and personal belongings.

The ad featured a long column of what was offered for sale. As we read it, we tried to connect the item with its description: "Very Unique Oak Curved Glass China Closet Drop Front Secretary w/Carved Drop Front, Leaded Glass Rect. Cabinet, 2 Beveled Mirrors & Ornate Gallery Top w/3 18" Drawer--One of a Kind (Exc. cond.)."

I guess that's what used to be in Grandpa's room, someone said.

And listen to this one: "Walnut Loveseat & Matching Rocker w/Hounds Head Arms & Clawed Feet."—I remember sitting there in Aunt Emma's living room on that rocker, sticking my fingers in their mouths.

I did that too. I thought they were scary and that if I didn't pull my finger out just in time, they would bite it off. I think Aunt Emma said that Mrs. Carpenter gave those to Grandma after she got married.

And on and on, down the long column through the Antiques & Collector's Items, through the Stoneware, the Appliances, Furniture and Household Items.

Of course, during the months between our aunt's death and the sale, we had had plenty of time to choose which pieces of furniture, what silver, what china and glassware we wanted to keep, and how we wanted to divide the various household items. To Edna went the set of china Emma had hand-painted. Curtis chose the Lenox china, Marjorie the silver flatware. I took the crystal. The beds sets were parceled out. But there were so many things, things we knew we couldn't use in our own home, but nevertheless things that were hard to give up.

Weren't these mixing bowls Grandma's? I remember her baking cakes in them. That old cookstove in the basement, it's seen a lot of meals. Remember how there'd be pans covering the whole top when Aunt Emma and

Grandma were making Christmas dinner? —It seems a shame to let that lamp go, when you think of the time Aunt Emma spent painting it—and so on.

We all took some small items: a green Fiesta pitcher that had been used for lemonade, and the glasses the lemonade was served in. A set of Grandma's silver spoons, crocheted bedspreads, china dolls. A round wooden tray, decorated with painted flowers and the words: "Var så god" and a wooden plaque with the Lord's Prayer in Swedish painted on it. Finally we had made what we thought were acceptable choices, always keeping in mind that we ourselves could bid on any item as it came up for sale.

Early on the day of the sale, we all gathered at Aunt Emma's house in Hartford. We carried everything out of the house except the very largest pieces of furniture and the rugs, and we arranged all the desks and small tables, all the boxes of dishes, all the linens, the old suitcases, all the lamps and footstools on the lawn. The ground was spongy. The sky was overcast, as it had been every day for several weeks. But some days it remained cloudy with maybe a light misty drizzle at the worst. We hoped today would be that sort.

By 10:00 the misty drizzle arrived. John and Travis, Marjorie's son and my son, great nephews of Emma—were sent downtown to the Coast-to-Coast Hardware store to buy whatever they could in the line of plastic sheets, or failing that, garbage bags which we could cut open and tape together into sheets to protect the furniture sitting outside. When they got back to the house, we cut and taped, and tucked. A wind was rising, driving the mist under any flaps that were not securely fastened. The day became progressively cooler, instead of warming up, as we had hoped.

People poured in for the sale. Even on this cold, wet day. My aunt had been well known in the community, and some people just wanted to come and see her things and her house. Antique dealers were there, making their assessments before the sale began. The auctioneer had told us he had received inquiries from dealers from hundreds of miles away. Sometimes he would mention what a particular item was appraised at, and we would marvel and feel a little proud of the good things our grandparents and aunt had accumulated.

By 1:00 p.m. any hopes that the clouds would thin, and that the light rain would taper off into nothing had vanished. The rain was not a downpour, but the drizzle was steady, and the day became steadily darker and colder. The sale began.

Among the early lots were the stacks of cookbooks that my aunt had collected. We'd all taken a few, there were still dozens remaining. Also among these lots were mounds of handwork, some of the scores of doilies and dresser scarves she had made through the long years of her life, some probably the work of my grandmother. And Emma's craft materials: she had painted china, and there were boxes of old tubes of paint, some still good; there were bags of yarn, and canvas mesh where needlepoint pictures were in a state of semi-completion.

But every now and then, the auctioneer would pique interest by offering a substantial item for sale, a piece of furniture, or a "desirable" stoneware item. Before I knew it, the kitchen table was being auctioned off. I had never cared for that table. At some point, when antiquing furniture was a popular refinishing project, my aunt and uncle had turned the table into a sort of streaky mustard-yellow color which even as a child I had never thought was attractive. Even though the tabletop was usually covered by a cloth, the ornately carved base showed itself. It was not until the day of the sale, not until it was being sold, that I realized that it had been my grandparents' dining room table when they lived on the farm. Suddenly I was struck by the sense of how wrong it would be for that table to leave our family, and I was about to bid, but too late, it was sold. The buyer was a man I had gone to high school with, who now was an antiques dealer. I should have spoken to him at once, but delayed until the next day. By then it had been resold. Regret, and a feeling of loss, of an ending of things.

And that is how it came to feel as the afternoon progressed. The secretary, one of a kind, Sold. Marjorie cried when that was carried out. The dining room furniture, where we had gathered throughout our childhoods for holiday dinners, Sold. The hounds-head furniture, Sold. And so on.

By late afternoon, the rain had, if anything, worsened. Friends and cousins who had come earlier in the day, to help carry furniture and to set up for the sale were still there. David Melin was one. His mother Esther and Aunt Emma had been first cousins. For sale now were some of the many plates and bowls and vases which my aunt had painted. As the auctioneer moved from item to item, crying out the characteristics of each piece, David would hold it up high above his head so the few remaining buyers could see it. Rain dripped off his hat, running down his face, as he held up a vase that in the springtime used to hold peonies, a celadon-colored vase with a wreath of dark green ivy decorating its base. Sold, to the lady by the steps, a hand-painted vase, one of a kind.

Finally it was 6:00 and time for the house to be sold. At the appointed moment, we all moved inside. The rugs that had been sold were rolled up, so that they would not be soiled by our wet and muddy shoes. The few pieces of furniture that had remained inside were either marked as sold, or were being carried out by their happy new owners.

The auctioneer read the description of the house, and people walked through the first floor. The empty rooms echoed to their footsteps, and to their voices. The hardwood floors that had always been carefully tended were splotched with mud and wet grass, carried in on the shoes of the bidders and the curious viewers. They leaned up against her dining room walls, which I as a child had been cautioned not to touch. Now strangers leaned up against them leaving greasy smudges on the green wallpaper. I realized, as I had not realized before, my aunt Emma, and the past she had embodied, was gone.

After everything was over, my brother had to return home to Nebraska, but Edna, Marjorie and I decided we should go down to the nursing home. My mother would be asleep, and at any rate, she was not really aware that the sale was going on. But my father was, and would be wondering how the day had gone.

He was still awake when we arrived, but it was late for him, so we had only a short visit. We had tried to remember some particular sales that would interest him, things that had brought a price none of us would have expected.

Remember that little pitcher? Edna asked. It was a sort of speckled, and said Hartford Creamery on it. I think Grandma used to use it for syrup. It was just a little pitcher.

My father thought a minute.

Yes, he said, I think I remember that. How much did you get for it?

$300.00. Edna said. Can you believe it?

My father was silent for a few minutes. Then,

Did you say $300.00?

Yes, $300.00.

More silence. Then,

Can people be such fools.

MEMORY

Driving to my Aunt Emma's funeral, a September afternoon in 1992. Getting to the church was a complicated task. There were our own families to organize so that everyone knew whom he or she was riding with. We had to have one car available to go to Sioux Falls to pick up Mother and Dad at the nursing home, and we had to be sure that at least two of us would be riding with them, because neither was able to walk without help. As we arranged it, Edna and I went together to bring them to the church. My father had broken his hip that summer, and while he could navigate with a walker, we took his wheelchair also. My mother could walk, but needed support, and needed to be reminded how to bend and turn to get into a car. Edna and Dad were in the front seat, Mother and I in the back.

I wasn't sure, as we rode along, if my mother realized where we were going, if she realized her sister-in-law was dead. Just a few days before, when one of us mentioned that Curtis was pulling into the parking lot, she had said, Curtis? Wasn't there someone who worked for us named Curtis?

Well, I thought, she was right in a way. He had indeed, though the years, worked along with Dad, and so "for us." So,

Yes, I said, that's him.

Now, riding in the car, I search my memory for what might be fresh in hers. Even though it far from November, the colored leaves and the brilliantly blue sky make me think of Thanksgiving.

Mom, I say. Do you remember "Over the River and Through the Woods"?

Of course, she says. And she starts to sing.

And I join her. Driving to a funeral, over the river and through the woods, to Grandmother's house we go.

It was the hardest when her memory first started to fail. When she would stand by the kitchen sink, look out the window and say, sometimes in fear, sometimes in anger, I think I'm losing my mind.

It was hard to respond, because she was losing something, the strands that tied her experience to ours in a way we could understand.

I want to go home, she would say, again and again. And though we would respond, again and again, But Mom, you are home—she knew differently. What she knew is that she was not at ease, not comfortable, not feeling safe and secure like you feel when you are at home and everything is all right. She knew everything was not all right, and the metaphor that expressed that dis-ease was her plea to "go home."

Later, I think her uneasiness waned. There were times when she simply lived in the moment, and seemed to enjoy the reality that presented itself to her.

She always knew me when I came to visit, even if there had been the lapse of several months.

Well, look, if it's not Mabel! she would exclaim.

She remembered us all. We used to tease her about whether she remembered her husband.

Mom, do you know what today is?

No, what is it?

It's your anniversary, your wedding anniversary.

My wedding anniversary! How long have I been married?

A long time. Do you remember Elmer?

Sure, I remember him. How long has it been?

Fifty-eight years!

Fifty-eight!

That's right. What do you think of that?

Well, I think if it's been fifty-eight years, he must have liked it all right!

At the nursing home, Mother lived in a room with Tilda, and she and Tilda looked out for each other. They also went through each other's drawers regularly and shifted things as they chose. Sometimes we'd see Mother wearing an unfamiliar sweater, and realize it was Tilda's, and now and again Tilda would turn up wearing some of Nellie's clothes.

When we'd go to visit, each one of the two would take us aside—as best she could—to give a little confidential report on the other. Tilda would say, She's been real confused today. And Mother would report, She always thinks she has to go home before the corn pickers come. Now you know that's not right.

When there was a church service at the nursing home, Mother and Tilda would go together and sit side by side. They would sing earnestly and with seeming enjoyment the familiar hymns: "What a Friend We Have in Jesus," "Rock of Ages." Although the tune they sang was uncertain, it resembled the melody they heard in their memory, and the words flowed out with ease and assurance. When the service ended, neither would leave until the other was ready to go, then they would walk, hand in hand, down the hall, each believing she was looking out for the other.

When my mother died, it took a few days for us all to get collected and together. Edna and her husband had been traveling back to South Dakota from Texas when the death occurred, and some tracking down was required in order to notify them. In the meantime, Marjorie had come from North Dakota to open the farmhouse, which had been shut up for the winter months. Opening the house meant having the heat turned on and turning the water back on. When Curtis arrived from Iowa where he now lived, and I arrived from Wisconsin, she had bad news to tell us. The water pump wasn't working. The repairman had said he would come as soon as he could, maybe tomorrow, but in the meantime, we had to carry water over from the farm across the road. That meant a minimum of washing, and not flushing the toilet unless it was absolutely necessary.

We were sitting around the kitchen table as Marjorie told us the situation. For a moment we were quiet. Then we started to laugh. We laughed louder and louder. Marjorie leaned her head on her hands, laughing. I rocked back and forth on my chair, crossing my legs. Curtis shook his head to see us, but he was laughing too.

If Mother weren't already dead, I said, she'd die right now of a heart attack.

And dreadful as it was, we laughed and laughed.

The worst thing my Mother could ever imagine—and she anticipated it constantly—was running out of water. Whenever we came home, she would scold us for taking too many showers, or taking showers that lasted too long, for flushing the toilet when it wasn't necessary.

And don't think it's just me, she would say. Look at Laura, she even had city water, and she used to put up a sign on her toilet that said, Don't flush for just number one.

Mother, one of us would say, exasperated. We are not running out of water. If you think so, I will go over to the telephone right now and call up and order a tank of water to be delivered and pay for it myself. I just want to wash, is that so unthinkable?

It's easy for you to say, she'd respond. You're here and then you leave and then what if there's no water. And listen to that pump! It's running all the time. You know that can't be right. Let me tell you, some day I'm going to be here, and have a houseful of company, and then no water. And then what am I going to do? It's easy to use it up, but it's not so nice when it's gone!

And now, here we were, just where she expected we would be: a houseful of company—even if we were the company. And no water. Just what she had feared her whole life long, at least ever since she had had running water to worry about, had happened. She'd been right to worry, after all.

We laughed until we were worn out, and could laugh no more. Then, sitting silently around our kitchen table, still smiling, we were thankful she didn't live to see this day.

When we arrived at the church for Aunt Emma's funeral, two men who were renters on our farm, Layton and Duane Wehrkamp, helped my father get up the steep concrete steps that led into the church. We had thought he could be carried up in the wheelchair we had in the car, but he wanted to walk, and so he did.

What were his memories, I wondered, as he stood and looked at his sister in the coffin? He had known a person we would never know, shared memories of times we know nothing of. The way she looked as a child, things she may have said, times she made him mad. All of the bonds you share, brother to sister, sister to sister, brother to brother.

At the end of the funeral, the interment followed immediately in the burial ground next to the church. We had decided that Mother and Dad, and Esther, who was in her late 90's, would not go into the church yard for the burial, but would stay seated in the church until we returned in a few minutes. As the interment was ending someone came running from the church,

Come quickly, he said to us, something is wrong with your dad.

Although he was still seated, my father was slumped forward, unconscious. He was being held steady, and gently spoken to by Pauline, Esther's daughter, who was sitting in the pew behind him. Pauline, a nurse, lived in California, and told us later she had extended her visit to her mother because she knew how fragile elderly people became at funerals of friends and relatives, and she was worried about her mother. As it turned out, Esther was calm, but my father had fainted.

Someone called for an ambulance. My mother had already been taken down into the church basement, she was not really aware of what was going on. Two or three men helped lay my father down in the main aisle of the church and loosened his clothes. By the time the ambulance had arrived and the men had come in with the stretcher, he was beginning to return to awareness.

While he was lying there, I sat quietly in a pew with Marjorie. We said nothing to each other, but at the end of the day, when he was recovering in the hospital, and any threat of danger was over, we both admitted to having had the same thought: there are worse ways, and worse times to die.

* * * * *

It is Christmas. Hundreds of miles away from the farm where Elmer, Emma, and Norton were children, where Elmer and Nellie were first a young married couple, where I and my brother and sisters grew up, I am preparing for my own family's Christmas dinner. I'm making spritz cookies.

I almost never bake, but during this season, even I am enticed by the pleasures of reading old recipes, by the sense of bounty when all the ingredients are gathered, by the anticipation of the warm rich smells my effort will produce. After final examinations have been given at the college where I teach, and after final grades have been submitted, a few days still remain before December 24. I choose one of them and call it my baking day. I make spritz cookies because that is what my mother always made for Christmas. Little buttery cookies, in the shape of a wreath or a flower. It's a simple recipe: butter, sugar, eggs, flour, stirred together. I'm mixing the ingredients in a brown crockery bowl, with a wooden spoon, worn down on one side from years of creaming ingredients, from stirring sauces, from beating flour into a batter. The bowl itself is thick-sided crockery, earth-colored, with no decorations. It's the bowl my mother used when she mixed up a batch of cookies or a cake. Once upon a time, the bowl had been a gift from my mother to Christine, her mother-in-law, and when Christine died, the bowl was given back to my mother. It seems an odd present. I would not be likely to think of giving my mother-in-law a mixing bowl. I wonder, as I stand here, creaming the butter and sugar together, what did

Christine think, when her daughter-in-law Nellie presented her with that bowl? Did she think it was inappropriate, but no more than you would expect from someone from such an outlandish place as Illinois, and half German on top of that? Or did she think it was sensible, and a good choice: sturdy and solid, not a bowl that could be easily broken?

Pondering these two attitudes calls to mind another instance when I would have been curious to know my grandmother's reaction: what did Grandma think when Grandpa brought her a vacuum cleaner for a present? John had gone to a church convention in Minnesota, and, the story goes, he felt guilty for going away on this interesting trip, leaving Christine at home. So, to compensate, he bought her a Hoover and brought it home with him as her gift. The vacuum cleaner is still with us to this day, stored in what used to be the hired man's house on the farm. Was she touched by his thoughtfulness, his desire to spare her the hard work of carpet sweeping or beating them with a metal whisk? Or was she exasperated by his lack of imagination?

I've decided on a fruit salad for Christmas dinner: ambrosia. The fresh pineapple and fresh coconut and the oranges remind me of what used to be Christmas luxury and extravagance, the fresh fruit in mid-winter, fresh fruit that you would ordinarily have only when it was in season. My childhood was not so long ago that oranges were a luxury, but that idea was still a relic from previous generations, and when we would go into Hartford for the Saturday afternoon Christmas movies, after which Santa Claus would distribute little brown paper bags of treats to all the girls and boys, inside that bag, along with the hard ribbon candy and the Brazil nuts would always be included a nice big orange. And always I put an orange into the toe of my children's stockings, a nice big orange. They wonder why, I suppose, but simply put it aside while stacking up the other, more reasonable, gifts from Santa Claus.

The ingredients for ambrosia seem right for a festive Christmas dinner; and also, ambrosia is a part of the Christmas dinner tradition in my husband's Virginia family. But one reason why I make ambrosia, in addition to these, is that I have an opportunity to use my grandmother's cut-glass berry bowl and berry dishes. They usually stand at the top of my cupboard, unused from one year's end to the next, but now I climb up on a chair, and carefully lower the footed bowl to the counter, and then the two stacks of little round bowls. They are covered with a year's accumulation of dust, but when washed and polished, and set out on my kitchen table, they catch the winter's light, they sparkle and shine.

In some ways my grandma must have been terribly frugal, never overcoming the recollection of hard necessities of her childhood and first years in America. When my aunt died, and we had to sort through cupboards filled with old linens, we found dishtowels, kept from my grandma that were worn so thin you could see through them. When, I wonder, did necessity give way to comfort, to at least some degree of security, so that she would feel good about buying an extravagance like a cut-glass berry bowl? Or the silver spoons from Peacock's Jewelers in Chicago?

That sense of affluence is one my mother never did come to enjoy. The items that could be thought of as something beyond necessity were very few, and usually justified by some special event. When my parents had been married twenty-five years, my mother bought a set of silverplate flatware, service for eight. No person with the most costly sterling could have been prouder. And along with that, a set of china, with grey and pink flowers decorating the borders. My mother thought, and we all agreed, that when her dining room table was covered with an impeccably white cloth, stiff with starch and perfectly pressed, and set with this china and flatware, that no table could look finer.

Sometimes in the summer we would have fresh strawberries, sliced with sugar and served on top of scoops of vanilla ice cream. My mother would say, The Queen of England could not have a better dessert than this!

When we have our Christmas Eve meal, we will eat early, just as we did when I was a child, so that we can clear up before going to church. We will have Swedish meatballs and rice pudding and spritz cookies. Far away, my sister and her family will be sitting around the dining room table at the farm, set with my mother's china and silver, with the "Wheat Sheaf" stemware which my mother had, and also my aunt and grandma. Each piece collected by coupons from Englecke's store, so that among the three of them, they had a whole set of water goblets, small sherbets, and footed sherbets. Another family with its generations, keeping the holiday at home.

We had one last holiday spent together at the farm, Thanksgiving, 1992. Aunt Emma had died in September, and my parents were in the nursing home. Edna and Dick, her husband, were living on the farm. Their children came home, Marjorie and I and our husbands and children came home. Curtis came later in the day. We brought Mother and Dad from the nursing home to spend the holiday at the farm. The house was full, full of people, full of noise and talking and bustling. Edna roasted a turkey, Marjorie had brought pies, I made a sweet potato casserole from ingredients I bought in Hartford and brought out to the farm. The windows in the kitchen steamed up. We put all the leaves into the dining room table. We ate and ate. We took pictures: each family together, standing in front of the dining room window; and one of the whole family together, squeezed in and around Mother and Dad on the davenport. The photograph shows two frail, white-haired old people, surrounded by large grandsons and granddaughters, and by their own plump, greying children. It was the last time we were together, and the last meal where we were all around the table.

COMING HOME

Sometimes when I wake up here, I don't remember where I am. But even not knowing, it's pleasant, lying in bed, listening to the birds, birds singing so loudly they've actually wakened me up. "Cacophony" is a good word for their shrill sweetness and the energy of their singing, but their sound produces a more pleasant sensation than that word implies.

I listen, and let wakening and awareness come gradually. When I open my eyes, I see the thin white curtains moving slightly, blowing toward the bed, and I know where I am. I'm at home, in my old room.

I'm just here for a visit, it's my sister's home now, hers and her husband's. We wondered what would happen, years ago, when my parents went into the nursing home, and for several years things see-sawed back and forth: they came home and stayed with a caregiver, he quit; we hired another, he wasn't satisfactory either. My parents went back to the nursing home, but had to return at a different level of care, and had to stay in separate rooms. My sister's move back to the farm was like a rescue. When that happened, they moved back to the farmhouse, my mother and dad, and there they stayed, together and at home, thanks to the care of their daughter and son-in-law, until their health made staying there impossible.

But Edna is still here, she and Dick, and so I still come home.

Waking up can take a while. There's no rush. I'm on vacation. When the birds are convinced that they have succeeded in once again bringing the sun over the pasture hills, they quiet down. Now I start hearing sounds from downstairs. I hear Edna and Dick, walking from their bedroom to the bathroom, to the kitchen. I hear water running. I begin to smell coffee percolating.

I remember so many mornings as a child of waking up to these sounds. And I remember too the later years, times when—at home for a visit or to take a turn in caring for Mother and Dad—times when I could only cautiously sleep, waiting for the sounds of my mother getting up, times of wondering if she was just up for a trip to the bathroom, or if she was up and wandering, and wondering how long I should wait before going downstairs to see. It was the same as those nights when you would hear your infant cry and wonder if that sound was just an isolated whimper, or if meant he was really awake and needed feeding or a change. And I imagine my sister, one night, hearing my father get up out of bed, and hearing the thud, the heavy sound of someone falling, and coming down to see my father on the floor. The fall that meant she could no longer care for him and my mother at home.

Now I hear voices from the open bedroom window. Edna and Dick are walking down to the mailbox to get the newspaper. Still the Sioux Falls *Argus Leader*, but now brought by a delivery person. In the old days it came along with our regular mail.

I hear their feet crunch on the gravel, and their voices fade as they walk down the lane. In a few minutes they'll be back, but they won't mind if I'm not up.

Lying here, I can see the sky and to the south-west an open field, not yet planted. In the old days, when I woke up and looked out the window, there was a tree to keep me company. The tree that appears newly planted and fragile in the 1909 photograph grew and flourished for nearly sixty years. It is gone now, but it lived long enough to shade a child's room and to whisper its secrets in every season.

When I wake up again, I smell not only coffee, but bacon, and something else. What is it? I get up, pull on some jeans and a shirt, and go downstairs. Yes, it's bacon, and also a coffee cake. The table is already set. I sit down where, when we were all children together sitting around the table, Curtis would have sat. Now we don't need the extra leaf that made the table oval, now it's just a round circle.

After breakfast we'll walk down to the garden and see what's ready to be picked today, maybe some early lettuce, or radishes. Yesterday we walked through the gravel pit, the old gravel pit we used to walk through coming home from school. Our neighbor uses it for a pasture now, but the herd was grazing at distant end. Some spots looked familiar, but over the years the creek has cut new channels, and places we used to skate in the winter and swim in the summer are hard to detect.

There have been other changes too, not just in the route of the creek. The house is changed from the 1909 photograph; porches and windows have come and gone and changed shape. Old trees have died, new ones have been planted. In the farmyard, the buildings which were once red and sturdy have faded to a pinkish grey, some are sagging, some have been pulled down. Farming has changed, and barns are no longer needed to shelter cows and horses, nor do we need a haymow filled with hay to feed them.

Except for Edna, we all live in different places.

Some time while I'm here on this trip we will go to the cemetery, she and I, to put flowers on the graves of all our family members who are buried in the cemetery of Benton Lutheran Church. Grandpa and Grandma. Mother and Dad. Aunt Emma and Uncle Earl. Uncle Norton and Aunt Edna. Marjorie. While we are there, kneeling down, weeding, and digging and planting, we will see others, doing the same thing, decorating graves for Memorial Day. We will talk to them and talk about the persons whose graves they are tending, and they will talk about the persons on whose graves we are planting flowers; when they leave we will try to figure out where they fit into our own past: was she one of our Sunday School teachers? where did his parents live? were you in Confirmation class with his brother?

Then we will pack up our trowels and buckets and drive back home.

This is not my own home, now, but it is still my home, and at least for this time, it is the place to which I return. The circle is small, and also it is fragile. But for now, and as long as memory prevails, it is unbroken.

* * * * *

254

At the ending of *My Antonia*, Jim Burden, the main character, reaches a poignant and yet comforting realization. He has just spent several days together with his childhood friend, Antonia, with her and her husband and children who live in the same location—the Nebraska prairie—where he and Antonia had been children together. During these days he has renewed the old bonds of friendship between them, and the old bonds of connection with the land itself; he has realized that though these bonds may have changed through time, they have not broken, but are strong and vibrant still. Now it is time for him to leave.

Gazing at the tracks of the old road that ran from the town of Black Hawk to the farm where Antonia's family had settled, and to the farm where, as a child, he had lived with his grandparents, he reflects on that road's significance in his experience and in the experience of Antonia. This is the road they had traveled together the first night when they were each brought to their new homes, when they were both, as he recalls, "wondering children, being taken we knew not whither." This is the same road on which, leaving their childhoods behind, each of them traveled to his or her own destiny, into lives separated by education, by passion, by error. Now, years later, the road is abandoned, it is nearly invisible.

Yet, the speaker can track its faint lines, and as he opens himself to the mystery of recollection, he recognizes how this road has been the symbolic thread of his life, how it still pulls together the present and the past: . . . *the feelings of that night were so near that I could reach out and touch them with my hand. I had the sense of coming home to myself, and of having found out what a little circle man's experience is . . . . Whatever we had missed* [Antonia and himself], *we possessed together the precious, the incommunicable past.*

Notes

1. P. 3. "A Procession at Candlemas," in *The Faber Book of 20ᵗʰ Century Women's Poetry*, ed. Fleur Adcock (London: Faber & Faber, 1987), p. 158.

2. P. 13. H. Boone Porter, *Keeping the Church Year* (New York: The Seabury Press, 1977), p. 93.

3. P. 16. John Greenleaf Whittier, "Snowbound," in *American Poetry: The Nineteenth Century,* Vol. I (New York: The Library of America, 1993), p. 476.

4. P. 16. Ralph Waldo Emerson, "Fable," in *American Poetry: The Nineteenth Century*, Vol. I (New York: The Library of America, 1993) p. 282.

5. Pp. 99-100. Letter from A. G. Bergius to Christina Bergius, Dec. 30, 1894. Tr. Ebba Johnson.

6. Pp. 100-101. Letter from A. G. Bergius to Christina Bergius, Oct. 13, 1895. Tr. Ebba Johnson.

7. P. 102. Letter from Agnes Olson to Christina Bergius, Jan. 25, 1895.

8. P. 103. Letter from Augusta Olson to Christina Bergius, May 17, 1896.

9. Pp. 119-120. Letter from Selma (Olson?) to Christina Bergius, Nov. 19, 1895. Tr. Ebba Johnson.

10. Pp. 120-121. Letter from Selma (Olson?) to Christina Bergius, Feb. 14, 1896. Tr. Ebba Johnson.

11. Pp. 121-123. Letter from Selma (Olson?) to Christina Bergius, March 20, 1896. Tr. Ebba Johnson.

12. P. 123. Letter from Selma (Olson?) to Christina Bergius , May 17 1896. Tr. Ebba Johnson.

13. P. 125. "The Sioux Falls of Today, " in *Bee Hive Advertiser of Fun, Fashion, and Common Sense*, Vol. I, No. 1 (Sioux Falls, SD, 1892), p. 1.

14. P. 126. Quoted in Wayne Fanebust, *Where the Big Sioux River Bends: A Newspaper* Chronicle (Sioux Falls, SD: Minnehaha County Historical Society, 1985), p. 357.

15. P. 128. Letter from Ed. W. Dow to Christine Berger, May 16, 1895.

16. P. 130, P. 139. "He is Dead," Sioux Falls *Argus-Leader*, May 17, 1895; "Dust to Dust," Sioux Falls *Argus-Leader*, May 21, 1895.

17. P. 144. Letter from Sophy Benson to Christina Bergius, Jan. 1, 1895. Tr. Ebba Johnson.

18. P. 155. German Folksong, "When Christmas Morn is Dawning," tr. Claude William Foss, in *Service Book and Hymnal* (Rock Island, IL: Augustana Book Concern, 1958), #35.

19. Pp. 155-156. Johan Olof Wallin, "All Hail to Thee O Blessed Morn," tr. Ernst W. Olson, in *Service Book and Hymnal* (Rock Island, IL : Augustana Book Concern, 1958), #33.

20. P. 157. Letter from Selma (Olson?) to Christina Bergius, May 17, 1896. Tr. Ebba Johnson.

21. Pp. 191-192. Letter from B. P. Svensson to Johan Bengtsson, March 24, 1904. Tr. Emma Benson Spokely.

22. Pp. 193-194. Letter from B. P. Svensson to Johan Bengtsson, Dec. 9, 1915. Tr. Emma Benson Spokely.

23. Pp. 202-203. Letter from John Benson to Christina Bergius. Tr. Ebba Johnson.

24. Pp. 204-205. Information about the ownership of the farm based on research of Richard Haase.

25. P. 255. Willa Cather, *My Antonia*, p. 238.

Sources Consulted

Bailey, Dana R. *History of Minnehaha County, South Dakota. Sioux Falls, SD*: Brown and Saenger, 1899.

Olson, Gary D. and Erik L. *Sioux Falls, South Dakota: A Pictorial History.* Norfolk, VA: The Dunning Co., 1985.

The Oral History Project Collection. The Center for Western Studies, Augustana University, Sioux Falls, SD.

Richardson, Jeanne Schulte. *Here Lies Sioux Falls*. Freeman, SD: The Pine Hill Press, 1992.

Acknowledgements

A number of people have contributed information that has aided me in writing this book. First of all, I want to acknowledge my aunt, Emma Benson Spokely. Her careful collection and maintenance of family artifacts and her recording of family genealogies have enabled me and my sisters and brother, and our children, to have a sense of the particulars of our family history, and have also provided a legacy for future generations. A more modern family archivist who deserves recognition is my sister, Edna Benson Haase. Her home, our family farm, has in recent decades been the repository of clothing, letters, pictures, and documents that have helped construct and illustrate family events. I also want to recognize the help given me by the late Gale Carpenter McCallum, the great-granddaughter of Charles and Frances Carpenter. I was fortunate to be in correspondence with Mrs. McCallum for a number of years; through that correspondence she shared many interesting details about her family history and most notably, provided me with a sketch of the floor plan of the Carpenter house, which she remembered from her childhood.

Other help was provided by the translators of the letters Christine and John received. Some of these letters were translated by my aunt, and we found them attached to the original letters. The other translator was Ebba Johnson. I am thankful my aunt did those translations, and that she kept them along with the letters, and I am grateful to Ebba for her generous and careful work.

I also want to acknowledge the help of my own family. I thank Maria Ricotta, my daughter-in-law, and Benson DuPriest, my son, for their encouragement, and for helping provide the time needed for the last stages in putting the text together. Especially I want to thank my son, Travis DuPriest, for providing technical expertise and editing. It has been a family project, to be sure!